MW01687156

Rich Man
Dead Man

A John Standard Novel

Tom Towslee

Rich Man Dead Man is a work of fiction. Names, characters, and incidents either are the product of the author's imagination or are used fictitiously. Any resemblance to actual persons living or dead, or events, is entirely coincidental.

ISBN: 978-1-950613-75-5

Published by Taylor and Seale Publishing, LLC
Daytona Beach Shores, FL 32118

Cover design and layout by Chris Holmes

To Tim and Hanne

Prologue

The Oregon Coast

I threw the gun into the woods knowing no one would find it because no one would ever look.

This place would never be a crime scene. There would be no patrol cars or ambulances. No flashing lights, sirens, or yellow tape. No forensic technicians in white suits and booties. No gurneys or bodies under blood-stained sheets. No one would ever be questioned, accused, charged, or convicted of any crime.

Certainly, no news conferences by police about "persons of interest" or "on-going investigations." No 800 numbers or email addresses scrawled on white boards. No press releases with vague explanations of what had happened. There wouldn't be anything that qualifies as a cover up, only silence about the events at the house at the bottom of the hill, the house that overlooked a steel-gray ocean rising and falling like a giant beast breathing in and out.

I was the only one who knew the whole story—all of it, from beginning to end. Now it's over. I could walk away, confident no one would ever ask me how it all happened … or so I thought.

Four years later

Rich Man
Dead Man

1

Zihuatanejo, México

It took a while for John Standard to find out someone was looking for him.

All he had been doing was sitting on the beach and soaking up the sun while word filtered down in slow subtropical fashion through a sleepy but reliable network of bartenders, waiters, and taxi drivers. The news was eventually delivered in person by a beach vendor named Aurelio who sold homemade cheese out of a plastic bucket to skeptical tourists. In broken English, Aurelio, said he didn't know who the man was other than a *norteamericano* who had been walking around town wearing a baseball cap, long-sleeved white shirt, slacks, and dress shoes.

"Some say the man looks like an *el empresario*," Aurelio said. "He carries a *maletin.* You know? Briefcase."

"What kind of businessman?"

"*No se, Señor Juan*," Aurelio said. "*Seguro*, maybe?"

That made no sense, Standard thought. Why would some insurance salesman from the States be wandering the streets of a Mexican beach town looking to sell him home-and-auto or term-life coverage?

"Did he say why he wanted to find me?" Standard asked.

Aurelio shook his head. "He only says he will give money to anyone who tells him where you are. No one has, so far."

"How long has he been here?"

"Two days. I think. Soon someone will take his money and tell him where you are. What is it you Americans say? *El dinero habla*."

Standard sighed. "Yeah. I know. Money talks."

Since arriving in Zihuatanejo, eleven months earlier, Standard had tried to do little more than mind his own business by hanging out on the beach or in bars and restaurants. While there had been a couple of brief moments of panic and violence, he'd managed to navigate all of it without getting himself or his girlfriend, Emma Parrish, killed or hurt. He'd just come close a few times.

By mid-October the rainy season was over, the sun out and he was back to spending his days at his favorite beachfront hangout, an outdoor restaurant called The Tortuga. So far, the only people looking for him had been kids selling Chiclets, women hawking hand-painted plates and an old man selling bootleg mescal.

That an insurance salesman from the States was on his trail came as a surprise, assuming it was true. Chances were it wasn't. Rumors in Mexico had a tendency to take on a life of their own. Either way, there wasn't much he could do about it. After all, Zihuatanejo was populated by a revolving cast of tourists fueled by liquor, shrimp, and gossip. Best just to wait and see what happened.

He thanked Aurelio. "Let me know if you hear anything new."

With a polite, "*Gracias*," Aurelio headed off in search of any adventurous tourists willing to take a chance on hand-made cheese from a plastic bucket.

Standard pulled a chair into the shade and took in the ever-changing scenery. Playa la Ropa, the half-mile beach that stretched along the east side of Zihuatanejo Bay, was empty except for a few elderly couples out for a morning stroll. He knew that would soon change. The tourist season was just getting underway. Hotels and condos, shuttered since the previous spring, would soon begin filling up. Same with the restaurants and gift shops. The city he came to know the previous winter was returning after enduring a scorching spring and a soggy, monsoon-drenched summer and early fall.

His decision to stay in Mexico for the rainy season was more the result of inertia than a desire to endure two months of daily downpours. Emma thought he was nuts. In her fifteen years of living in Mexico, she had stayed for one rainy season with no intentions of living through another. After wishing him luck, she left in July to visit family in Montana. She was due back in another two weeks for her favorite Mexican holiday: *Dia de los Muertos*, the Day of the Dead.

Left alone, Standard did little but idle away the days and nights in the palapa house the two of them shared in the jungle above the beach. He watched the rain while reading a few dozen humidity-soaked paperbacks and reaching level 875 on Candy Crush. With most of the restaurants closed, he was left to fend for himself. He cooked a few meals but switched to frozen dinners purchased at the super mercado rather than cope with constantly cleaning the kitchen to keep the insects at bay.

Now, with the rain over and the skies clear, came rumors that an alleged insurance salesman was trying to find him. Maybe it didn't have to change things for the worse, he thought. Maybe the guy wasn't selling insurance. Maybe he wanted to deliver a check from a long-lost relative who'd died. Maybe it was the overdue and heavily litigated severance package from the newspaper back in Oregon that fired him five years earlier. No way could he be a cop. Standard hadn't committed any crimes in the States that he knew of and certainly none that justified sending a one-man search party to an obscure Mexican beach town.

Whatever it was, the more he thought about it the more it pissed him off. Who was this guy and where did he come from? What gives him or anyone else the right to track him down when all he wanted was to be left alone? He came to Mexico to hide out and put the past behind him. Was that too much to ask? Apparently, it was.

He could only sigh, order another beer and wait to see what happened.

~*~

Two days later nothing had changed. Standard was still hanging out at The Tortuga, looking out at the same bay with the same sailboats bobbing in the same anemic swells working their way in from a placid Pacific Ocean. He ate the same breakfast, drank the same bad coffee, and ate the same stale bread served by Pablo, the same long-suffering waiter. At least the beer was cold and the tequila passable.

He had ventured into town for a couple of hours to see how much of the sleepy city had come back to life. He went home after a few hours convinced that things were only a few days away from getting back to what he considered normal, which meant his favorite bars and restaurants would once again be open for business or close to it.

Back at The Tortuga, even the people walking the beach were starting to look familiar, there were just a few more of them, only now they included a man who looked totally out of place.

Even from fifty yards away, the gnomish figure with a doughy complexion and meaty midsection looked like he hadn't taken a taxi to Playa la Ropa so much as jogged along beside it. The sleeves of his dress shirt were rolled up above his elbows. Rings of sweat stained his armpits. He had a big, friendly face—the kind found in photos of past presidents of the local chamber of commerce. It was flanked by large ears and adorned with thick glasses on a narrow nose. Taken all together it gave Standard the impression of someone who had just parachuted behind enemy lines.

Insurance, Standard decided. Definitely insurance. Someone fun at the office Christmas party, but not much help in a bar fight.

The man was sticking close to the wet sand, skirting the weak waves making scallop marks as they worked their way up the beach. He wore a bright-blue Seattle Seahawks cap. His dark brown dress pants rolled up to his knees revealed legs that resembled the white out-of-bounds stakes at a local nine-hole muni. He was barefoot but holding a pair of sand-encrusted penny loafers in one hand. In the other, a well-worn leather briefcase.

When he reached the beach in front of The Tortuga, he dropped the briefcase, pulled out a handkerchief and ran it across his face as if trying to wipe away the weariness and frustration along with the sweat. When he took off his hat, he was bald except for a ring of thin, sweat-soaked graying hair that drooped over his ears and down the back of his neck. He ran the handkerchief across the top of his head and squinted into the sun as if looking for something or someone. Spotting the sign for The Tortuga, he picked up his briefcase and began slogging through the heavy sand above the water line. When he saw Standard sitting in the shade of one of the restaurant's thatch-roofed cabanas, a look of relief joined the beads of sweat running down his face.

"Are you John Standard?" he said when he reached the table.

"Guilty," Standard said.

"Thank goodness," the man said with a look of relief. "Mind if I sit down?"

Standard motioned to the chair on the other side of the plastic table.

"Thank you." He sat down so hard he almost fell over backward. He dropped his briefcase in the sand next to his chair and went back to wiping away a new layer of sweat. He took off his smeared glasses and cleaned them with the same handkerchief. It didn't seem to help. He put them back on and looked around.

"I don't suppose I could get a glass of water?"

"The waiter will be around soon," Standard said, "or maybe not."

"You're a hard man to find," the man said, stuffing the handkerchief in the pocket of his shorts.

"Apparently not hard enough."

"So you knew I was looking for you?"

"Jungle drums."

"At least you're not hiding out."

"Should I be?"

"No. No. Of course not," the man said. "Let me introduce myself. My name is Harrison Grimes. Most people call me Harry."

It was early-afternoon on Playa la Ropa. The late October sun high in the western sky, the temperature a sticky eighty-five degrees. The gentle breeze coming off the waters of Zihuatanejo Bay wasn't doing much in the way of cooling things off. Frigate birds circled overhead. Pelicans skimmed the surface of the water. Barefoot locals kicked around a soccer ball. Others sailed Frisbees back and forth. Little kids played in the surf. Further out, an elderly couple bobbed up and down in the bay's gentle swells. The oily smell of suntan lotion mixed with the sweet scent of bougainvillea and wood smoke. Even though the rainy season seemed pretty much over, ominous dark clouds still lingered on the mountain tops to the east, poised to invade the city at any moment.

"How many bartenders did you have to bribe to find me?" Standard asked.

Grimes looked surprised for a second, then smiled. "Not that many, actually. I met this nice man in a bar downtown. An American. He told me where I could find you. I gave him five-hundred pesos, although I'm sure how much that is in U.S. dollars. The bills down here look a lot like Monopoly money."

"This nice man have a name?" Standard asked.

"Yes. I have it right here." Grimes reached down to dig around in his briefcase then pulled out a beer-stained business card. "Here it is. Donlan. Richard Donlan. Says he's a vacation consultant and that you and he are a team. Something about having worked some cases together, although I'm not sure what that means."

Standard tried not to laugh. "You mean Itchy Donlan?" Grimes looked confused. "Short, a little pudgy, wears plaid shorts, a Hawaiian shirt, and a trilby hat. Probably asked you to buy him a beer."

"Yes. Yes. That's him, but he said his name was Richard."

Standard made a mental note to ask Itchy about the Richard thing, but only after learning why he ratted him out to a complete stranger for the U.S. equivalent of twenty-six dollars.

"Mr. Grimes," Standard said. "Itchy—or Richard, as you call him—and I are not a team and we haven't worked on any cases."

Grimes shrugged then pulled the handkerchief out of his pocket, went back to wiping his face while desperately looking around for a waiter with some water.

"People around here think you're an insurance salesman," Standard said.

Grimes shook his head. "Actually, I'm an attorney. I'm here because I need your help."

Standard had heard that before and it seldom turned out well. He never understood what there was about him that made other people think he could solve their problems. He'd spent most of his adult life as either a newspaper reporter or freelance writer, neither of which came with powers greater than the ability to ask questions, jot down the answers and write declarative sentences. The rest of his time he'd spent trying to do nothing but stay out of trouble. He had been pretty good at the first part. Not so good at the second. As a result at various times he'd been stabbed, kidnapped, chased, shot at, and beaten.

"I'll explain," Grimes said, "but that water would be nice."

When Standard raised his arm a second time, Pablo finally appeared. "*Sí*, Señor Juan?"

"*Una botella de agua, por favor*."

Pablo hustled off.

While waiting for the water, Grimes made small talk about the weather, how he and his wife were "Hawaii people," that this was his first trip to Mexico and he'd never heard of Zihuatanejo. "Although I did see *Shawshank Redemption,* if that counts."

"It doesn't," Standard said.

"Is it really as dangerous here as they say?" Grimes asked.

"Sometimes."

"But don't drink the water, right?" Grimes said.

"If you believe the beer distributors," Standard said, doing his best not to sound impatient. It wasn't working. "You've been here four days … Harry … wandering around town offering people money to tell you how to find me. Now you're here. So what do you want?"

Grimes smiled. "People here are very loyal to you, Mr. Standard."

"Except for Itchy Donlan. If it weren't for him, you'd still be looking."

"True," Grimes said. "So, I guess it's best to explain. I'm a partner in the law firm of Talbot, Grimes, and Abbott. We're headquartered in Seattle, but with offices in Portland and Boise. We represent a man named Nicolaus Adams, who goes by the nickname Nico. Interesting guy and sort of a character. He's flown helicopters in Afghanistan, bush planes in Alaska, weather choppers in San Francisco and corporate jets all over the world. He hasn't had the best of luck, though. It seems he's had to bail out of so many aircraft that he's earned a second nickname—Parachute Adams, which, I understand, is a popular fly fishing pattern."

When Pablo showed up with the water, Grimes thanked him then downed half of it, poured some in his handkerchief and used it to take another lap around his face.

"Anyway, earlier this year Mr. Adams was arrested by the DEA for smuggling drugs into the U.S. To be specific, he was caught using a helicopter to ferry cargo nets full of cocaine from a fishing boat off the Oregon coast to a remote beach near the City of Bandon."

"What's this got to do with me?" Standard asked, still vainly trying not to sound impatient.

Grimes held up a finger while he downed the rest of the water. "Four years ago, Mr. Adams was employed as the personal pilot for a wealthy businessman who died under somewhat … mysterious circumstances. Adams claims to have information about how this businessman died and is willing to divulge it in exchange for our help in getting him a reduced sentence. He told us that you can corroborate this information."

"This dead businessman have a name?"

"Scofield. Proctor Scofield."

Standard could only stare at Grimes in disbelief, thinking: Here it comes again. That things had settled down over the summer and early fall made him believe life was returning to what passed for normal. The kinds of troubles that always seemed to find him had given up the search. Fine with him. He'd paid his dues more than once. He was hoping it was time for fate to cut him some slack. Then some lawyer shows up out of the blue with a name that Standard would have given anything to forget.

"You a drinking man, Harry?"

Grimes looked at his watch. "It's only ten-thirty."

"Then we better get started."

Standard raised his hand again. When Pablo appeared he ordered two bottles of Corona and two shots of tequila.

Grimes gave a resigned laugh. "So, you knew Proctor Scofield?"

Standard chose his words carefully. "Everyone knew of him. Few actually knew him."

"Then you know that when he died he was the fifth richest man in the world. A self-made multi-billionaire and notorious recluse. Some considered him a visionary, a pioneer who saw the coming of the age of technology before anyone else. Computers. The Internet. Software. Smartphones. He built a world-wide corporation that makes and sells everything from mouse pads to mainframes. His business skills had earned him the nickname Prince of Snakes, an image Scofield apparently liked so much he incorporated it into his company logo. He was eighty-five when he died."

Not the Proctor Scofield he remembered, Standard thought, but kept it to himself. "You can find that on the Internet," he said instead.

"True," Grimes said, "But what I can't find on the Internet is exactly how he died. Our client, Mr. Adams, thinks you killed him."

"Thinks?"

"His evidence is thin and inconclusive. He saw you running away from Scofield's house the day he died." Grimes paused for a few seconds to check Standard's reaction. "That's his story. What's yours?"

"It was four years ago, Harry. Four long years, if you ask me. Not my favorite time of life. I'm not going to relive it to keep some drug smuggler out of jail. I don't care where he served or who he worked for or how many planes he's crashed. Proctor Scofield is old news. He's dead and buried and so is what happened to him. Best keep it that way. You've wasted your time coming down here."

When the drinks showed up, Grimes sipped the tequila like he thought it might be poisoned then eagerly downed some of the beer.

"We can make it worth your while," he said.

"You mean leave this beach, fly to Seattle and spend a few soul-sucking days in the rain?" Standard laughed. "You don't have that much money."

"As I said, we have an office in Portland. Since you're from there, perhaps you'd like …"

Standard shook his head.

Grimes looked around the beach then at the restaurant and the homes and condos dotting the hillside to the south. A smattering of people walked the beach, playing tag with the anemic waves. Hang gliders sailed over the bay. The first banana boat of the season skipped across the water behind a speedboat. The sun hung in a pale blue sky, the air heavy and muggy. More frigate birds skimmed the surface of the water. Children laughed. Dogs barked. A quarter mile away, on the south side of the bay, wisps of smoke from the kitchen fires of the palapa restaurants along Playa las Gatas rose above the palm trees.

"This seems like a nice place," Grimes said. "We could stay here while you tell me about Scofield. It's more important than anything I have going on back in Seattle."

Standard thought for a minute then shook his head. "I'm sorry, Harry, but you and your client are going to have to look elsewhere."

Grimes looked disappointed but made a few more lame attempts to change Standard's mind, each one quickly rejected. Finally, he reached down to pull a business card and a manila envelope from his briefcase. He slid both across the table.

"The envelope contains Adams' deposition detailing what he saw and heard the day Scofield died," Grimes said. "My cellphone number is on the business card. I'm staying just up the beach at the Casa Que Canta for the next few days. If you change your mind …"

"Unlikely," Standard said. "Enjoy the rest of your stay."

~*~

After a disappointed Harrison Grimes left to walk back up the beach, Standard spent the rest of the day nursing a beer and watching the sailboats on the bay. By mid-afternoon, a ketch and two trimarans arrived and anchored just off the beach, part of the annual in-migration of sailboats arriving for the winter. The pangas ferrying people across the bay from the city pier to Playa las Gatas and back again looked like targets in a shooting gallery. A passenger jet bringing more tourists to town flew low across the mouth of the bay, headed for the airport south of town.

Just after four p.m. Standard put Grimes's envelope and business card in his backpack, got an order of grilled shrimp and rice to go then walked home. The dirt track behind the beachfront restaurants was familiar territory after nearly a year of trekking back and forth between home and The Tortuga. Three of the four restaurants at the south end of the beach had just opened. Waiters, waitresses and bartenders, back for another season, waved as he walked by. He waved back, thinking that when Emma got back they would come down to one of the restaurants, have dinner and watch the sunset. The sooner the better, he thought.

The dusty turnaround with its waiting taxis and occasional bus from town was bustling with people leaving after a day at the beach. Others arrived for drinks and an early dinner. When he reached the path that led up the hill to the house, he thought about Emma again and counted the days until she returned—fourteen. The longer she was gone, the more he came to realize how much she meant to him, how desolate things were without her and how much he relied on her to keep his demons at bay.

Too bad she wasn't here now, he thought. The arrival of Harrison Grimes and the name Proctor Scofield had made it harder for him to fight those demons on his own.

When he got to the house he showered, put on clean shorts and a T-shirt and pulled a cold Corona out of the small refrigerator under the kitchen counter. He hit the hammock on the terrace. Five pages into a Philip Margolin novel, he nodded off. By the time he woke up, the sun was hanging on the horizon and sinking fast.

He climbed out of the hammock and wandered into the kitchen. The Styrofoam box with the shrimp and rice sat on the counter. He took it over to the table, grabbed a chair and started eating. Reluctantly, he pulled the deposition Grimes had given him out of his backpack. He had no appetite for reliving the events that led to the death of Proctor Scofield. That didn't mean he wasn't curious about what Grimes's client had to say about what happened that day. Standard remembered Adams but didn't know his name until now. Four years earlier he had been nothing more than a guy sitting in a helicopter warming up the engines. No way could he know who killed Scofield.

Standard kept reading, deciding that most of what was in the deposition was true, up to a point. While putting Standard at the scene, Adams didn't have any direct knowledge of what happened inside Scofield's cliff-side house. He didn't even name the other people who were there that day. Skimming through the rest of the deposition, Standard decided that Adams had heard very little and seen even less.

The best he could figure was that Adams needed him to fill in the gaps because he knew none of the others would.

With good reason, Standard thought, stuffing the deposition back in the envelope.

After putting the food away and wiping down the wooden counters, he fired up his laptop and searched for the law firm of Talbot, Grimes, and Abbot. It was started thirty years earlier by three graduates of Stanford University Law School and specialized in labor law with occasional forays into criminal defense. In addition to the three partners, there were at least a dozen associates, most of whom did business from a high rise overlooking Elliott Bay, Puget Sound and Seattle's bustling food-centric waterfront. He found a magazine article that said the firm hit it big representing national labor unions in lawsuits against right-to-work laws and public pension reform. The criminal work appeared to be pro bono and confined to cases that involved issues such as the me-too movement, black lives matter or freedom of speech.

None of what he read gave him any insight into why the firm had taken Nico Adams on as a client. Drug smuggling seemed a far cry from suing sexual predators, trigger-happy cops, and secretive government agencies. Standard could only guess that it had something to do with the connection to Proctor Scofield.

Even though he'd been dead for four years, how Scofield died had become a treasure trove for the conspiracy theorists and trolls who haunted the Internet. Speculation ranged from his being alive and living in Havana to being kidnapped by the Russians and held hostage while he taught them how capitalism was really supposed to work. When he searched Nicolaus Adams, he found a short Associated Press piece about a major drug bust on the southern Oregon coast that netted several million dollars in cocaine, three members of a Mexican drug cartel, two rented U-Haul vans, three crew men on a fishing boat and Adams, the helicopter pilot. He couldn't find any follow-up articles.

Standard shut down the computer, even more sure that he wanted nothing to do with Grimes or his client. He just needed to make one call to cover all his bases. He picked up his phone. The number he wanted was stored in his contacts. His call was answered on the third ring. He listened and talked for fifteen minutes.

"You're sure that's the way you want to go?" he said then listened again. "All right. I'll take care of it." He hung up.

The voice at the other end of the call echoed in his head for a few minutes. He'd made promises that, until now, didn't require him to do much more than keep his own counsel about what happened to Scofield. Not anymore. Now that he'd committed to taking care of it, he just needed to figure out how. One thing he knew for sure: Leaving Harrison Grimes on his own to muck blindly around in the past was not an option, certainly not after who he'd just talked to on the phone.

After an hour of staring into the jungle and downing a few shots of Patrón tequila, he called Grimes.

"Our Lady of Guadalupe," he said. "Ten a.m. tomorrow."

~*~

Our Lady of Guadalupe was a small, yellow-and-blue stucco Catholic Church on a street corner across from the artisan market and next to a raucous sports bar. Inside were rows of wooden pews and an ornate altar flanked by a statue of Christ on the cross and a painting of the Virgin Mary. At that time of day, the pews were empty except for a man praying over a handful of lottery tickets. Standard dropped ten pesos in the donation box near the front entrance then took a seat in the back and waited. Grimes showed up ten minutes later. He was sweaty and breathing hard.

"I decided to walk here," he said, wiping his face with what looked like a fresh handkerchief. "Is it always this hot here?"

"Pretty much. Kind of a tropical thing."

Grimes looked around the near-empty church. "Beautiful little church. You a religious man, John?"

"Not really. I just never saw the upside to being an atheist."

"I'm Episcopal myself. You know? Catholicism without the nuns or pedophiles." He wiped his face again. "Can I assume that you've changed your mind about helping us out?"

"I'll tell you under one condition: You have to listen to the whole story. It will take a while."

"Is it worth the wait?"

"Definitely."

"Fair enough."

"If I'm going to be my own Boswell," Standard said, "then we need to get out of here." He stood up and headed for the door, Grimes two steps behind him. "This is not a story fit for a church."

Three blocks away at the city square they found a seat in a shady corner of the bay-front basketball court. Behind them, old men sat around the open-air fish market guarding freshly caught Dorado, sailfish, snapper, and tuna that were laid out on the sand. Nearby, the fleet of pangas was pulled up on the beach, back from a night of fishing and ready for another. Across the sidewalk were restaurants, shops and the only place in town that served lattes. Standard left for a few minutes, returning with two Styrofoam cups of coffee and a bag of churros, donuts.

"I read your client's deposition," Standard said. "It was a little short on names and details. Other people were there the day Scofield died." Standard handed Grimes his coffee and a donut. "Why are you talking to me and not them?"

"Adams won't tell us their names. We're hoping you could help us with that. He seems to be afraid of them."

Thinking back to all the names that were connected to Scofield and his death, Standard decided Adams had good reason to be afraid.

"So?" Grimes asked, smelling the greasy donut before taking a tentative bite.

"It was August four years ago," Standard said, taking a sip of coffee. "It began with a dead guy in an outhouse."

2

Portland, Oregon

I've already told you, Harry, that the weeks leading up to the death of Proctor Scofield were not my favorite time of life. I wasn't kidding. I had no job, no income and, at one point, no place to live. What money I had was from selling my two-year-old Range Rover and buying a 12-year-old Honda Civic. In other words, my fall from grace, as it were, was worse than a head-first plunge into a bottomless abyss.

Before that, life was good. I'd had a great job at a decent daily newspaper, a beautiful home in a trendy Portland neighborhood, a lovely wife with a trust fund and covered parking for that Range Rover I once owned. There were occasional court-side seats for a Trail Blazers game, season tickets to University of Oregon football games, and the time and money to explore Portland's food scene.

Then it all fell apart. My wife left me. I ended up living in a run-down, two-room sparsely furnished apartment in a dumpy building where the stench of mildew mixed with the odor of hot grease and fried chicken from the dive bar around the corner. My landlord and only friend was a former circus midget turned website designer and part-time computer hacker. A stripper lived in the apartment across the airshaft from me. She practiced her new acts with the curtains open while I sat in the dark watching her and drinking cheap scotch. It was summer but felt dark all the time. I kept telling myself to suck it up. Move on. What happened happened. Get over it. Things can only get better. Except I knew they never would.

Then came the phone call that started everything.

Looking back on it, Harry, I wish I would have ignored it. If I had never answered the phone that morning, things would have turned out differently for me. Just not for others. People would still have died, but at least I wouldn't know who they were or feel responsible for what happened to them. That included Proctor Scofield.

But I didn't. Instead, I caught the phone in mid ring just to stop the noise, then mumbled "Hello." The first words I heard were: "Dead body. Portable toilet. State fairgrounds."

I grabbed a pen and a reporter's notebook. Cradling the phone against my shoulder, I flipped to the first blank page and sat poised to take notes. Then I realized where I was and how I got there. Damn was all I could say.

Get the picture, Harry? There I was sitting naked in front of an open window. It was early, but the apartment felt hot and stuffy. I looked down at my stomach and legs. Not even a goose bump, let alone a shiver. My beard felt harsh against hands that had done nothing more than write in a notebook and type on a laptop. The reality of what my life had become settled in

Anyway, back to the phone call. It was from Alfred Gitchell, a detective with the Oregon State Police. He apologized for waking me then explained that he'd run across something he thought I might be interested in. He described it as bizarre, but without additional details, suggesting instead that it might be fodder for one of the online tabloids I occasionally wrote for as part of my never-ending need to feel useful and earn some kind of living.

The clock on the wooden milk crate that served as an end table read 5:08 a.m. I threw the notebook and pen on the floor and asked Gitchell to give me the short version.

He repeated what he'd already said: Dead body. Portable toilet. State fairgrounds. When I agreed that it sounded like tabloid material, he laughed, called me "word man" and said he was just trying to help. "If you want any more details you need to get to Salem as soon as possible. The body isn't going to be here much longer."

Gitchell and I were friends, just not close ones. I hadn't seen him in the three months since the verdict—the one that found me innocent of vehicular homicide and leaving the scene of an accident. There may have been other charges, but those were the ones that counted. In other words, Harry, I walked. With no real friends in court that day, I had found myself looking toward the back of the room after the judge released me and dismissed the jury. The old detective was standing near the door. He approved the decision with a slight nod in my direction. After that he was swept into the hallway by a wave of reporters. Since then, we'd talked on the phone a few times, promising to get together for lunch, but never got around to it.

Before that, Gitchell had been a source for an article about a serial arsonist. While working on the story, Gitchell had provided free access to everything about the investigation. It didn't seem to matter to him that at the time I was free on bail and awaiting trial. Long hours in the car and over bottomless cups of bad coffee, Gitchell became an unlikely and some-time friend when I needed one the most. I figured his friendship was his way of saying thanks for giving him a prominent place in a story and credit for the eventual arrest. Now it looked like he was trying to do me another favor.

I remember leaning toward the window to get a better look at the sky. The city glow of downtown Portland illuminated the underside of a thin layer of clouds just visible above the air shaft. Clouds. Clouds meant rain. Rain meant relief from a week of ninety-degree temperatures, unseasonable for mid-July. An Oregonian praying for rain. I thought. Pretty bad. It was like a camel praying for sand.

When I put the phone back to my ear I heard Gitchell saying he'd fill me on what happened when I got to Salem then offered to buy breakfast afterwards. It was hard to say no to a shot at something that might earn a few bucks. A free breakfast was an added bonus. So, I promised him I'd be there in an hour then hung up and slumped back into the chair to stare up at the ceiling with its water stains and peeling paint. Money, Harry, that's what I needed. Money to get out of that place. There was a brief, but enjoyable period in my life when I didn't need to worry about money. Now, it was all I worried about.

If you haven't figured it out by now, Harry, this was all pretty depressing. There I was, thirty-five years old and living hand to mouth like a college kid again. Could things get any worse? Yeah, they could and probably would. Not that it mattered. By then I was immune to the pain of continual disappointment with the way life was going. A radio turned low in one of the apartments further down the air shaft played Creedence Clearwater Revival's "Born on the Bayou." The swamp-rock beat matched both weather and mood. I coaxed a cigarette from a pack on the arm of the chair, lighting it with a kitchen match scraped on the metal edge of the old milk crate. In the kitchen, I found a jelly glass in the clutter of dirty dishes in the sink. I poured ice water from a plastic pitcher and drank until the cold hurt my fillings. I propped my arms on the top of the refrigerator and let the cold air wrap around me. After that, I got dressed, found my car keys, and left.

At that time of morning, the drive from Portland to Salem took less than forty-five minutes. On the way, the clouds kept their promise. Huge rain drops beat down on the hood of my car until I pulled into a visitor's space near the main entrance to the state fairgrounds. Rummaging around in the back of the car, I rooted out a faded barn coat and a baseball cap then went off in search of Alfie Gitchell. A patrolman in a plastic slicker stopped me near the entrance to one of the exhibit halls. I gave him my name and explained the call from Gitchell. He checked my driver's license then pointed toward the far corner of the grounds. I nodded thanks and splashed my way through the puddles.

For what it's worth, Harry, the state fairgrounds is about two hundred acres of parking lots, exhibition halls and low-slung animal barns. It dominates the surrounding neighborhood of older homes and thriving canneries. Oddly enough, I'd been there two days earlier getting a close look at a gun show for an article I was doing for a Philadelphia magazine that wanted the wild-west view of the Second Amendment. I had negotiated a nice fee for a five-thousand-word article with photos by playing up the magazine editor's misguided beliefs that all Oregonians cling defiantly to their guns. The whole package had to be in by the start of the following week.

The gun show had been an eye opener. I'd spent several hours talking about NRA issues with those who bought, sold, and traded shotguns, deer rifles, semi-automatic weapons, and the occasional Uzi. There were plenty of quotes from high school dropouts about the evils of big government, how we would all be safer if everyone carried a gun and interesting theories about the true meaning of a well-armed militia. When one of them started rambling on about fake school shootings, crisis actors and homicidal immigrants I left, convinced that the Philadelphia magazine with its eastern, big-city readership was going to love it.

That I was back at the fairgrounds so soon, Harry, turned out to be a coincidence that would haunt me for a few weeks. But I'm getting ahead of myself.

Anyway, I found Alfie Gitchell standing with two uniformed officers and a woman wearing a blue plastic jacket with "Crime Lab" stenciled in yellow on the back. They were gathered around a portable outhouse parked on a narrow stretch of soggy, brown grass between two livestock barns. High-powered lights had been left on under the dark morning skies. The din of police radios mixed with the hum of generators. A second soaked patrolman barely turned his head as I ducked under the yellow crime scene tape and elbowed my way through a half-dozen people to the front of the outhouse.

Anything more than coffee for breakfast that morning and I would have lost it right there.

Have you ever seen a dead body, Harry? I don't mean at a mortuary or funeral with an open casket, but at a crime scene. Someone who's been murdered or died in some horrific way. I hadn't, at least not until then. I've seen plenty since. Too many. But this was my first time. No way will I ever forget it.

Try picturing this. Inside the port-a-potty, sitting on the toilet, was a man with his pants around his ankles, a piano wire noose around his neck and a tongue that looked like a tennis ball. His bulging eyes were a sickly yellow. His face was an indescribable color of red. All I could think of was a vulgar exhibit at a low-rent carnival or a scene out of a second-rate horror movie. If that wasn't bad enough, there was the smell. It was the putrid funk of death, shit, and Lysol. I backed away, sucking in mouthfuls of rain-soaked air.

When Alfie Gitchell moved in beside me, he asked if I was okay.

The only thing I could tell him was that he lived in a sick world to which he muttered something like "tell me about it." He turned around, asked everyone else to get back then grabbed my arm. He pulled me forward until we were standing side by side directly in front of the open outhouse door. Gitchell pulled a notepad out of his pocket and started reading. The dead guy's name was Ivan Krychek, a private security guard, who had apparently been sitting on this crapper for about forty-eight hours. That meant he was killed some time on Sunday, the last day of the gun show. Gitchell explained that even though the cause of death was obvious, there would still be an autopsy that wasn't going to tell him anything he didn't already know.

This isn't the last time Gitchell pops up in this story, Harry, so I guess I should describe him. Short, dumpy, and bald. Even a night standing in the rain couldn't wash away the smell of a lifetime addiction to cigarettes. His nose was dimpled like a golf-ball. His face round and cherubic. Dark blue blood vessels scattered across fat cheeks. Sad, brown eyes hidden under thick salt-and-pepper eyebrows had taken dead aim on a long-overdue retirement that was still a few years away. His raincoat was soaked from the night-long drizzle. His felt hat drooped on both sides so water ran off in a steady stream onto his stooped shoulders. He delivered the information about the dead man between drags on a soggy cigarette.

He handed me a surgical mask and motioned toward the back wall of the outhouse. Harsh lights shining through the thin walls and translucent roof made it look and feel like an aquarium. Flies buzzed around the body and beat against the Fiberglass walls. I forced myself to look closer at the dead body. He appeared to be in his mid-twenties. Short, wiry build, thin light-brown hair, a patchy red beard, and ruddy complexion. Horn-rimmed glasses hung from one ear. Dried blood caked the collar of his uniform and around the piano wire embedded in his neck. A patch on the uniform's left shoulder read "Prestige Security." It matched the cheap silver badge on his breast pocket. A second patch above the other pocket read "Krychek." The pants piled around his ankles were the same brown as his shirt. Attached to his belt was a set of keys, a nightstick, and a cellphone. Gitchell showed me how the piano-wire noose around the guard's neck was tied to a thin, nylon cord that ran up the back wall, through two eye hooks screwed into the translucent ceiling then attached to the inside of the outhouse door.

Gitchell's theory was that the killer set Krychek up to look like some kind of puppet. Every time someone opened the outhouse door the cord would make the body sit straight up. The movement would startle whoever it was. Then they'd close it, probably with an embarrassed 'excuse me' and move on to one of the other toilets. Gitchell scratched his cheek. "Can't say I've ever seen anything quite like it. Ingenious if you ask me."

We pulled our heads out of the door and removed the surgical masks. Gitchell nodded to the woman from the crime lab, telling her to take over. He led me around the corner into the shelter of the empty livestock barn. I asked him who found the body. He pointed toward the far end of the building at a man wearing a pair of heavily stained coveralls. He was standing next to a red tank truck with "Here's Johnny" emblazoned on the door. He looked angry and impatient as he went nose to nose with an overweight man stuffed into a rain-spattered suit. Their voices echoed through the empty barn and off the wooden sides of the stalls.

Gitchell shook his head, excused himself and trudged toward the two men. I watched as he spoke to both of them for a few minutes then came back, still shaking his head. It turned out that the man in the suit was another cop by the name of Daryl Butcher.

Remember that name, Harry. You're going to hear it again. More than once.

Gitchell described Butcher as a "good cop," but with a unique ability to piss off just about everyone he talked to.

I looked at the two men again. The angry voices had been replaced by Butcher's gestures with a small notebook and pen. His attempts at sudden patience and diplomacy looked forced. The man from "Here's Johnny" stood with arms crossed in defiance. Butcher finally walked away shaking his head.

While I jotted down notes, Gitchell gave me an expectant look and asked if this was a good story. Not wanting to disappoint him, I said it was good for today, but skipped the explanation of what little value there was in a one-day dose of the bizarre and unusual. Instead, I told him I had been at the fairgrounds on Sunday working on another story. He shrugged as if it didn't matter then apologized for bringing me back so soon.

After that came chapter and verse on Ivan Krychek. He was a twenty-five year-old graduate student at Delaney College, a small private school set in a leafy corner of southeast Portland. He'd started working part-time five weeks earlier for Prestige Security which had just won the contract to provide security for events at the fairgrounds. The owner, a guy named Buck Mather, had told him that Krychek got married a couple of months ago and wanted to earn a little extra money to help make ends meet.

Gitchell described Mather as "a real sweetheart". A militia type. Hated the ATF and the UN. Called Oklahoma City a plot to discredit true patriots. Believed the government was behind 9-11 and Sandy Hook.

Between drags on his cigarette, Gitchell said Krychek's wife's name was Anna. They lived in Beaverton, a suburb west of Portland. If he had parents or siblings there had been no time to track them down. He wrote down the wife's address, handed it to me while explaining that someone was there now breaking the news to her. I formed a mental picture of a grief-stricken, doe-like woman living in a cramped apartment and facing life without the paltry income her student-husband earned patrolling places like the state fairgrounds.

As it turned out, Harry, I couldn't have been more wrong. I'll get to that later.

When Gitchell paused to look awkwardly down at his feet, I knew what was coming. He was going to tell me how relieved he was about the verdict and that I shouldn't have been prosecuted in the first place. I waited for him to get it out, including the excuse that with all the media attention I'd received the district attorney had no choice. It was an election year and I was the latest high-profile criminal that had earned too much airtime on local TV to avoid prosecution. You're a lawyer, Harry. You know how this works. Anyway, I remembered the DA with her pinched face, permed hair and pink blouses with little bows. It was not a great memory. My consolation prize was that not long after I was acquitted, she was defeated for re-election.

"Anyway, I'm glad for your sake that it's over," he said.

I thanked him but couldn't help but add that it would never truly be over. "Two little girls are dead, Alfie," I said, "and it was my fault."

Eager to change the subject, Gitchell reminded me of his promise to buy breakfast. I glanced at the outhouse then at the two men in blue jackets and white pants hoisting Krychek's corpse into a body bag. When I said, "Rain check," he nodded in agreement.

As I turned to leave, he grabbed my arm. Now, I told you that I didn't know Gitchell that well, Harry, but I knew enough to see that he had something else on his mind. When I asked what was wrong, he got this serious look that I hadn't seen before. His words were hard to forget: "Don't blow this off, John. This was no prank. There's something else going on here."

With a cigarette firmly planted in the corner of his mouth, Gitchell waddled back out into the rain to supervise the impounding of the outhouse.

3

Zihuatanejo

Harrison Grimes drained the last of his coffee then quickly waved off another churro. They were still sitting in the bleachers overlooking the basketball court. A couple of teenagers showed up to shoot hoops with a frayed basketball and play what Itchy Donlan liked to call "Juan on Juan."

"Everyone knows what happened to you. The accident, the arrest, and the trial," Grimes said. "It even made the evening news in Seattle. I can see why it wasn't your favorite time, especially the way the newspaper where you worked treated you."

Standard shook his head. "Let's not go there. Not yet, anyway."

Standard had agreed to talk to Grimes because of Proctor Scofield, not the freak accident in which on a dark night on a lonely highway he unknowingly ran down and killed two young girls. The verdict was just something on a piece of paper sitting in a file somewhere. Former colleagues from newspapers and television stations made his life miserable until after the verdict, then quickly moved on in search of other crimes and criminals. None of that mattered. Standard would always feel guilty. Grimes bringing up his former employer didn't help.

Standard had a hard time getting over the bitterness when the newspaper he worked for refused to stand by him. He viewed the paper's management as a collection of empty suits more worried about public perception than guilt or innocence. The way he saw things it was commitment without purpose; purpose without direction; direction without leadership; leadership without commitment. An endless circle. What happened to wisdom, compassion, and common sense? What happened to work hard and do the right thing? It had all been shattered in a millisecond of ill fate. Now, everything made him hate even more what had happened. Maybe hate wasn't the right word. It was more like a deep, festering resentment mixed with the sadness that comes with killing two young girls.

Grimes gave Standard a light jab with his elbow. "So, tell me more about this stripper."

Standard laughed, grateful for the change of subject. "She had nothing to do with Scofield."

"I figured that. Still sounds interesting."

Standard had named the stripper who lived across the air shaft from his apartment Vanessa the Undressa. He guessed that she worked at one of Portland's numerous strip clubs, maybe one of the places on the eastside that attracted the occasional NBA player in town for a game.

A few nights a week during that hot summer he would sit in the dark, watching as she dropped her oversized gym bag on the couch and wiggled out of her jeans and baggy T-shirt. From twenty feet away he could easily see the sweat glisten on her brown skin with no tan lines. Blonde hair, usually worn loose to her shoulders, sat perched in a pile on top of her head. Early thirties with large, gravity-defying breasts and a hard, flat stomach. In the two months they'd been neighbors he had grown fascinated with her cat-like looks, wide smile, perfect teeth, and athletic body. She would refine her various acts in front of a mirror on the back of the bathroom door. One night she was a nurse. That was followed by a cowgirl then a cheerleader. She unknowingly entertained him with stethoscopes, lassoes and pompoms as he sat in the shadows of his apartment smoking cigarettes. Each act ended with Vanessa totally naked and staring at herself in the mirror, her face sad and quizzical. With her back to him, Standard joked to himself that he was living his own perverted version of Alfred Hitchcock's *Rear Window.* While most men would be beating down Vanessa's door, Standard could do little more than watch in sweaty fascination. No shame or embarrassment, only a sadness that matched the life his imagination had created for her.

He just didn't feel like sharing all that with Grimes.

"I'd named her Vanessa the Undressa after the character played by Rita Hayworth in the movie version of *Pal Joey,"* Standard said. "She was 'V. Michaels' on the smeared label next to the mailbox outside the front door of the apartment building."

"Did you ever meet or talk to her?"

"Eventually, just not then. In those days I didn't take much interest in my fellow inmates. My status as a child killer was still pretty raw. A low profile seemed best. If anything she became something of a muse; someone to hold imaginary conversations with about the meaning of life and how to cope with tragedy."

"Did it work?"

"Not really."

Standard explained that the events leading up to the verdict that kept him out of prison had taken its toll. When he looked in the mirror he saw another person, someone gaunt and pale with a hawk-like nose and down-turned mouth. Thick, black hair in an unruly mop curled around his ears and bunched up on the back of his neck. Hiding behind wire-rimmed glasses were the eyes of someone who'd left their contacts in too long. He even felt smaller, as if the bad times had eaten away at his six-foot frame and taken off the extra ten pounds he'd always wanted to lose. He'd escaped his marriage with little more than his clothes, which now seemed to hang on his frame like sheets covering furniture in a shut-up mansion. It was only three years later after he moved to Mexico that the person in the mirror resembled what he once was.

"Pretty weird, John," Grimes said.

Standard nodded. "I know. I felt that Vanessa and I had a certain bond that would be shattered if she ever learned who I was or that I'd been secretly watching her without making the slightest effort to say as much as hello. Looking back, it was pretty pathetic."

"But you got over it."

"Yeah, after the call from Alfie Gitchell. I remember standing at the open window, one hand clenched hard around a glass of ice water as if wanting it to shatter and slash my wrist. I imagined bleeding to death while calmly watching Vanessa slip between the sheets next to her stuffed giraffe and prop a cheap novel on her knees. All the time I was wondering if I was ever going to get the chance to make things right again, to get even with the forces that stranded me in that hell hole. Life had become like the bottom of a dry well, nothing but hard-packed sand littered with the bleached bones of small animals that had fallen in and couldn't get out. Would I ever learn that when you're at the bottom stop digging? I just wanted my fucking job back. I wanted my fucking life back."

"Including your wife?"

"More like the season tickets to the Ducks."

They went back to silently watching the two kids shooting hoops.

"So," Grimes said, "was this Krychek in some way connected to Proctor Scofield."

Standard shook his head. "At the time, I barely knew who Proctor Scofield was. I'd heard the name, of course. Knew he'd gotten his start in Portland and was one of the wealthiest men in the world. That was about it. No way would I have made a connection between him and a dead guy in an outhouse. That would come later, but at the time I just wrote it off as a bizarre murder that might earn me a few bucks."

Grimes looked up at the sun that was nearly overhead. "Let's find a bar," he said. "This story sounds like it needs to come with a cold beer."

"I know just the place," Standard said. "Follow me. We'll talk on the way."

4
Portland

So, I headed back to the city after getting Gitchell's permission to have a police photographer email me a couple of photos of Ivan Krychek perched on his plastic throne. Instead of taking Interstate 5, I pointed the car east, catching Highway 99E and following it north through the rich farmland. Bustling small towns with burger joints and strip malls offered a welcome contrast to the grotesque scene at the fairgrounds.

Sprinklers, oblivious to the rainstorm that had just passed, shot arcs of water over nursery stock. Fields of berries and hops glistened. With the window rolled down the last few drops of rain came in to cleanse the inside of the car. The smell of wet cabbage wandered in and quickly left. Traffic slowed, picked up then slowed again through Woodburn, Hubbard, and Aurora. A few more miles north, near Oregon City, agriculture gave way to industry. The Willamette River glistened to the left. Bucolic farmhouses surrendered to sprawling mansions that dotted the landscape on the far side of the river. Two lanes became four. Old became new. Slowly, I crept back to my meager existence.

I followed McLoughlin Boulevard through Gladstone and Milwaukie before crossing the river on the Ross Island Bridge and into downtown. By the time I found a parking spot three blocks from the apartment, the sky had cleared. A significantly cooler sun dried wet sidewalks. I thought about Alfie Gitchell's warning that Krychek's murder was no prank. It was hard to disagree. Anyone who took pleasure in turning dead bodies into freakish marionettes needed to be taken seriously.

I rode the elevator to my apartment on the fifth floor while taking precautions to avoid my neighbors. After getting a beer from the refrigerator, I fired up the laptop and knocked out a quick five-hundred words on the bizarre death of Ivan Krychek. Satisfied it was lurid enough to get someone's attention, I started emailing the trap-line of sleazy tabloids and disreputable websites I'd cultivated over the last six months. Meeting little success, I threw in quotes from an unidentified and totally bogus police source that the murder may be connected to a satanic cult implicated in similar murders in South Australia. I even suggested a headline, "Devil Worshippers Terrorize Pacific Rim."

The editor at the last online tabloid on my list asked about what he called "an alien angle," hinting at some connection to Roswell. I lied, telling him that I had asked about that, but my "source" seemed convinced that the satanic thing was pretty solid. He sounded disappointed but said to email the pics and copy as soon as I could. He would cut a check when the story ran. He asked about a byline. I said no. All I wanted was a check.

I hung up, thinking that what the tabloids lacked in ethics they made up for in generosity. Then I called *Inside Oregon.* If you're not familiar with it, Harry, it's the city's alternative weekly known for restaurant reviews, gossipy news about city government and lurid personal ads. When the editor Eldon Mock answered he said he'd been meaning to call me about a story idea. I cringed. Mock's last idea was a series of reviews of Portland's eclectic food-cart culture. It took me a week to recover.

Mock explained in vivid detail how he was planning a special section on Portland's topless bars, excitedly explaining that they are both topless and bottomless. He wasn't even sure the dancers wore shoes. He made some joke about why Oregon was called the beaver state then suggested stories about club owners, dancers, customers and even the police and district attorney. There was some reference to an organization called Exotic Dancers Anonymous. I knew Mock well enough to see that his idea was more about selling ads to the topless bars than a journalistic journey through the world of strippers and their customers. I looked across the air shaft to Vanessa's apartment, while Mock rattled off another half-dozen ideas on how to make naked women more interesting than they already were. Reluctant to turn down anything that might generate income, I told Mock I would think it over then pitched the story about the murder of Ivan Krychek, including Alfie Gitchell's belief that it wasn't your every-day homicide.

Disappointed at my lack of enthusiasm for strip clubs, Mock conceded that Krychek's murder sounded like good copy. He gave me his usual write-it-and-I'll-look-at-it routine then turned to a topic he'd been harping on for months: My version of the accident and what it was like to go from hunter to hunted. His argument was that there had never been a reporter who found himself on the other side of cameras and microphones the way I had.

I hung up after telling Mock not to hold his breath.

When the police photos of Krychek showed up in my inbox, I forwarded them and the copy to the tabloid. Then I sent them to Mock along with a version of the story, minus any references to satanic cults. After that, I left to catch a bus downtown to the central post office to check my rented mailbox on the off chance that a check of some kind had come in. I climbed on and took a seat across from two women in their fifties discussing their mutual affliction of Crohn's Disease. A homeless guy in a threadbare sports coat and urine-stained slacks dozed nearby. In the back, a man in his twenties with pink hair and pierced nose, tongue and eyebrow held a copy of *On the Road* close to his face. He read with lips that moved and eyes that followed his finger across the page. I thought about the story and pictures I'd just sent off, wondering if they made me any different from my fellow riders. Different or not, I had become one of them. I'd crossed the line into a simpler world, one that, unlike my old life, didn't include homeowner tax exemptions, touring Broadway musicals or tickets to sporting events.

You're probably wondering where I'm going with all this, Harry, but I want you to get a sense of what my life had become. Maybe it will give you a better understanding of why what would happen over the next few days and weeks was going to lead to either more misery or redemption. I'll let you decide when I get to the end.

Anyway, the mailbox was empty of checks but full of bills. No surprise there. Deciding to walk home, I headed up SW Broadway into the heart of downtown. I got a newspaper and a latte at a Starbucks near Pioneer Square. I took both to an empty table outside near a street preacher shouting his angry gospels to no one in particular. The story on the front page reminded me of the gun control piece still languishing on my computer hard drive.

The newspaper article featured opposing photos of two state senators, Brad Roark, and Kingsley Landis, who had emerged as the leading players in the hotly contested legislative debate over gun ownership. I really don't want to get into politics, Harry. I've always found the topic toxic and discussing it as either a waste of time or a quick way to lose friends. I felt that way when I covered state politics ten years earlier as a rite of passage for all new reporters. I feel the same way today, only more so. If there was one advantage to my new, harsh reality it was that politics and those it attracted had less appeal now than ever before.

Landis and Roark, however, were fueling renewed interest. Just not by me. I had no idea at the time how they would become major actors in what was going to happen or their connection to Ivan Krychek and Proctor Scofield. To me, they were just two politicians, who, like all modern-day pols, were eager to please and slow to offend.

Ever since incumbent governor Martin Sloane announced that health problems would prevent him from seeking re-election, Roark and Landis had been popping up at high-profile events all across the state. The media devoted endless column inches and precious airtime to the two rivals. Both were in their late thirties with carefully constructed images. Roark, the Democrat, emerged as the stereotypical liberal champion of the downtrodden. Landis, the Republican, assumed the button-down role of anti-government friend to big business. They'd played coy about their intentions to run for the state's highest office, but no one believed they would spend that much effort and then not do it. To the delight of the political press, the two wannabes had been fonts of catchy sound bites as they sniped at each other while spouting their own versions of "What Oregonians want." It all added up to an election that promised voters a clear choice. Moderates stay home.

What made the whole thing so remarkable was that the primary election was still ten months away. As entertaining as these two guys were, I shivered at the thought of such a long period of partisan-driven debate over the Second Amendment or any other issue. It took me as far as the tenth paragraph to realize the story contained nothing new about Landis, Roark, or gun control. I scanned the rest of the paper, but it was too early for any mention of Ivan Krychek's death.

Alfie Gitchell's warning kept ringing in my head. The more I thought about it the more I realized how there was something uniquely male about the way Krychek was killed and put on display. Only a man would take perverse pleasure in standing inside a cramped, sweaty outhouse turning a corpse into a puppet. There must've been people around. Someone must have seen something. Maybe the killer didn't leave immediately afterward, choosing instead to amuse himself by hanging around to watch the reactions of those who opened the door then quickly closed it after seeing a man inside with his pants around his ankles.

Curiosity and the possibility of an intriguing story pulled at me long and hard enough that I used my phone to look up the address of Prestige Security.

5

Zihuatanejo

"Harry," Standard said as they negotiated the narrow streets of central Zihuatanejo, "Before I tell you anymore, I think we need to upgrade your wardrobe. The dress-shirt-slacks-penny-loafer look isn't working. This is Mexico. Not San Diego. Follow me."

Standard guided the offended Grimes into a small clothing store two blocks in from the beach. With the help of the young girl who worked there, he traded the lawyer's Seahawks cap for a knock-off Panama with a black band. A white, light-weight cotton shirt with coconut-shell buttons replaced his button-down Oxford. Slacks were swapped out for a pair of tan shorts. Off came the loafers and on came a pair of sandals.

"Much better," Standard said, looking Grimes up and down. The lawyer gave the grateful clerk a thousand-peso note and got back a handful of coins. "Now, let's go get that beer."

~*~

Footloose was a dive bar with an L-shaped countertop, a half-dozen tables the size of pizza pans and plastic chairs with Corona logos on the back. A twenty-something bar maid with too much makeup, hot pants and a push-up bra under a baby T tried to look busy even though Standard and Grimes were her only customers. They sat at one of the tables drinking bottles of Pacifico pulled from an ice-filled bucket.

"Selling phony stories to sleazy tabloids doesn't seem like a good use of your journalistic talents," Grimes said.

Standard sighed. "You'd be surprised at the things you can do when you're working without a net."

"Still, your fall from grace, as you call it, must have been difficult. From what we could piece together, you were something of a celebrity journalist. A recognizable byline, provocative columns about the darker side of life and occasional appearances on local public affairs shows."

"Pretty much. I tried not to think about it, but it still stings a bit. So, difficult? Yeah, to say the least."

"This editor friend of yours. Mock you said his name was," Grimes said, changing the subject. "Does he have anything to do with Scofield?"

"Eventually," Standard said.

"And the two politicians …"

"Same story. At the time, though, they were just two characters in a political Kabuki that happened to conveniently fit with my gun control article. If it hadn't, I would have left them out altogether. Looking back, it was lucky for me how things worked out."

"You mean their connection to Scofield?"

"Patience, Harry. Patience."

After two beers each, Standard and Grimes walked down the street to Los Braseros, a bustling restaurant with a vast menu featuring everything from smoothies to a 72-ounce steak. Over plates of spicy tacos with more beer, Standard figured it was his turn to ask the questions.

"So, Harry. What's your real interest in this?" he asked. "A run-of-the-mill drug case seems a bit beneath you."

Grimes finished his taco then wiped his hands with a napkin. "You've been honest with me … so far. I'll be honest with you … up to a point." He leaned back in his chair. "How Scofield died has been an enduring mystery. The skimpy news release Scofield Industries put out after his death raised more questions than it answered. All it said was his death was untimely and a blow to the world-wide hi-tech industry. After that came the usual boilerplate language about his rise from humble typewriter salesman and how the company would honor his memory by continuing to innovate and serve its customers. Blah. Blah. Blah."

"I left town for a few weeks after Scofield's death, so I missed any fall out," Standard said. "What did the newspapers and television have to say?"

"Not much. Scofield's company is just as elusive, exclusive, and reclusive as Scofield was himself. All anybody could find were unnamed sources with no direct knowledge of what really happened. After that came a collection of highly dubious online conspiracy theories that muddied the waters even more. After a while, no one knew what to believe."

"Until your boy Adams."

Grimes smiled and picked up the menu. "How about dessert? I hear that flan is a favorite in Mexico."

"Okay," Standard said. "Where was I?"

"Prestige Security."

"Oh yeah."

6

Portland

Buck Mather's business was located in what could generously be called an office park. In reality it was little more than a strip mall hidden amid the used auto lots and hookers wandering along SE 82nd Avenue on the eastside of Portland. Car lots and harlots, if you will.

The address I found on the phone didn't help much, so I had to drive through the complex twice, peering through the car's fogged windows before finding Prestige Security wedged between a tattoo parlor and a payday loan store. The blinds were pulled shut on the front door. A plastic sign in the window said "Open." Next to it, a large decal read, "This property protected by Smith & Wesson." The message made me pause before parking, getting out of the car and going inside.

Colorful brochures about personal security devices littered a Formica-topped waist-high counter. On the other side was a small desk, bare except for a telephone and a black beret with a Special Forces logo on the crown. The view into the back of the office was blocked by a seven-foot divider covered with military insignias, anti-government bumper stickers and framed photos of young, stern-looking men in combat fatigues. Several of the photos were taken against a brown background that said Middle East. The room smelled like a gymnasium with too many old socks and too few windows.

When I said hello, a husky voice replied that he'd be right here. I scanned a brochure on the merits of pepper spray until the man attached to the voice walked around the partition. He looked to be in his mid-fifties and large but moved with a certain grace. A too-small, black T-shirt stretched across a massive chest and stomach. A mouth set in a jutting jaw was partially hidden by a hooked nose and a bushy moustache. He was totally bald. A thin beard started at his temples and wrapped around his chin. My first impression was of a professional wrestler who'd traded barbells for Taco Bells. When he asked if I needed help it was in a cold and arrogant tone that matched the whole military thing he had going. When I said I was looking for Buck Mather he said I'd found him.

I told him who I was then mentioned Ivan Krychek. He accused me of being—let me quote now, "One of those liberal faggots from the lame-stream media peddling fake news." Sort of channeling his inner Jesse Ventura. He crossed his tattooed arms so they rested on the top shelf of his stomach. The stance was defiant, threatening. The tattoos were mostly of skulls pierced with daggers, and mermaids with perfect breasts.

I asked him again about Krychek. He told me Krychek worked for him on and off for a few months until someone killed him. "Them's the breaks," he said. The rest of the conversation was pretty much the same. Krychek showed up when he was needed, did his job, and went home. His job apparently was little more than walking around and, if there was trouble, stop it. His work at the gun show at the fairgrounds dealt mostly with preventing thefts. Enforcing any laws or rules about gun sales was not part of his responsibility. That, Mather told me, belonged to "The Gestapo." When I picked up a brochure from the counter, he grabbed it out of my hand and told me I didn't look like the pepper spray type.

To be honest, Harry, Mather may have lacked empathy, but not ferocity. Still, it was hard not to have a little fun with him and his gung-ho-GI-Joe routine. So, just to piss him off I kept pressing, asking how he happened to hire Krychek and where else he'd worked other than the fairgrounds. According to him, he didn't use Krychek that often because he wasn't trained in security work. He guessed that if anything happened, Krychek would probably run away and that would be the last he'd see of him. As he put it, "The whole damn country is full of faggots."

I asked if he knew any reason why someone would want to kill Krychek. That drew a quick "no" and something insincere about him being a "nice kid who died in the line of duty" and that he felt sorry for him and for his family.

I pointed to the photos on the divider behind the desk and said they look like they were taken in the Middle East. When he said Afghanistan and Iraq, I asked if he'd ever killed anyone. He answered with a nod and a proud grin. The grin disappeared when I asked if he'd ever killed anyone with piano wire.

That was probably a little over the top, Harry, but it was hard to pass up. His face turned small and tight. He reached down toward his boot and pulled out a commando knife that looked about a foot long. A razor-sharp edge glistened in the light. A skull and crossbones adorned the scrimshaw handle. He stuck the knife in the countertop, where it wobbled back and forth like a depraved tuning fork. That was the only answer I got. It was more than enough.

When I asked about the last time he saw Krychek, Mather said the previous Sunday at the gun show. He'd driven down to the fairgrounds to make sure things were going okay. He wanted to check up on Krychek and let him know he could go home when the show closed for the night.

"So you were there the day he died?" I said.

He gave me a curt, "He was alive and well when I left," then pointed toward the door.

I stalled by asking about his other clients, but he kept pushing me toward the door. I picked up one of the brochures off the counter and started making notes on the back. I was still writing when he shoved me out with a brusque, "Hit the road." When the door closed behind me, Mather flipped the plastic sign from "Open" to "Closed."

I sat in the car for a few minutes before driving around to the back of the building. A white Ford van with tinted windows sat in front of a sign that read "Prestige Security. Deliveries Only." I parked five spaces down on the far side of three other cars. After a few minutes, Mather came out the back door, locked it behind him and left in the van. I jotted down the license plate number as he drove away.

With the van barely out of sight, I rummaged through my shirt pocket for the rain-spattered piece of paper Alfie Gitchell had given me—the one with Ivan Krychek's address. I hadn't learned a lot from Mather. Maybe I'd have better luck with Krychek's widow. I still had this image in my head of her as a distraught newlywed coming to grips with the brutal death of her husband. It didn't really turn out that way.

7

Zihuatanejo

"This Mather sounds like an interesting guy," Harrison Grimes said while looking around for the waiter with his dessert. "What more do you know about him?"

"I had my landlord Benny do some research," Standard said. "Turns out he was a high school dropout who enlisted in the army rather than do jail time for robbery. That was right around 9/11. Pretty soon he was in Afghanistan. Served six years. Dishonorable discharge for assaulting an officer."

"Special Forces? Something like that?"

"No. Mechanic. Helicopters. The best Benny could figure he never saw action other than running for cover."

"So the whole commando knife, black beret thing …?"

"Fake? Who knows, but it got my attention," Standard said. "Thinking back on it, I saw Mather as a future member of that crowd that broke into The Capitol wearing a QAnon T-shirt and waving a Trump flag."

Grimes' flan finally showed up along with all kinds of apologies from the waiter in Spanish. Grimes gave Standard a helpless look.

"Todo bien. Gracias," Standard told the waiter.

"You speak Spanish," Grimes said.

"I know words. Sentences are a different story, which means I get by. Fortunately, a lot of locals speak English. In a tourist town like this with all the hotels and restaurants it's kind of a must if you want a job."

Grimes poked at the flan as if unsure exactly what it was and why he had ordered it. Finally he took a tentative bite, tasted it then gobbled the rest down in a few seconds.

"You know, John, I thought that being a journalist you'd cut to the chase, so to speak, and start with real news, such as who killed Scofield."

"Former journalist, but I follow the new style guidelines of websites and click bait. Save the lead for the end so they can sell more ads."

"You leave me little choice. "I'll play the sultan to your Scheherazade." Grimes gave Standard a knowing nod. "As I recall you were off to find the widow Krychek."

8

Beaverton, Oregon

I don't know how familiar you are with Portland, Harry, but it takes a while to drive from the east side of town to the west. After that there's the perpetual traffic jam on the Sunset Highway to Beaverton. Following that was another fifteen minutes of U-turns in a confusing maze of cul-de-sacs before finding the house on Baltusrol Way.

The single-level brick home with cedar-shake roof and brick accents overlooked the fairway of a private country club. Neatly trimmed shrubs accented a small, low-maintenance yard. A boxwood hedge bordered a wide walkway of interlocking paving stones which led to the front door. The license plate holder on the shiny new Audi A-6 sitting in front of the three-car garage read, "I'd rather be shopping at Nordstrom."

If the neighborhood came as a surprise, it was nothing compared to what was ahead. I had assumed that someone who had to work as a security guard in order to stay in school would be living in student housing or a rundown apartment house like mine. Instead, one look at the house made me recheck the address. Maybe Gitchell had written it down wrong or the rain had smeared the numbers.

Confused, but satisfied I was at the right place, I parked in the street, walked to the front porch, and rang the bell. The woman who answered only added to the confusion. She looked like an extra from an early MTV video: Simply irresistible, with that air-brushed, inscrutable look of a professional model, minus the sunken cheeks. Her eyes were heavy with liner and mascara. Her nose narrow. Lips a liquid red. Jet-black hair pulled tight into a neat bun sat high on the back of her head. She was tall, maybe five-ten, and young, no more than mid-twenties. A white, knit sheath clung to a slender figure that looked more like genes than gyms. The look she gave me said "Why are you here?"

I fumbled out an apology for having the wrong address. She gave me a different kind of blank look while I told her I was looking for Anna Krychek. In a voice with a slight eastern European accent she said, "I'm Anna Krychek."

All I could do was stare at her until mumbling something about whether the police had been there, dreading that she didn't know her husband was dead and it was my job to tell her. When she told me the police had left a couple of hours earlier, I sensed neither sadness nor joy. Only a very brief and forced look of sorrow. It hit me right away. Something wasn't right.

I finally got around to apologizing for bothering her and explained why I was there. Without a word, she turned and walked away with that … pneumatic stride … that models have. I followed her, closing the door behind me. It was a nice enough house inside. Nothing special but well out of reach for a grad student with a new wife, even this wife. There was a small entry. An airy, formal living room with pink leather furniture and glass-topped tables on chrome legs. Area rugs on hardwood floors. Half a dozen recent bestselling novels—Patricia Cornwell and John Grisham mostly—looked lost and unread in the bookshelves that flanked a marble-faced fireplace. Studio photos of Anna Krychek lined the mantle. I didn't see any of Ivan. I followed her into a more comfortable-looking great room. The kind with natural leather furniture, a second fireplace and a flat screen TV. Jazz played softly on an unseen stereo system. Unlike the front room, this room appeared to have actually been used once or twice.

We sat at a round cherry-wood table in front of the French doors that opened onto a wide patio overlooking the golf course. The house felt cool and smelled of French soap and furniture polish. A Persian cat curled up on a leather ottoman in the corner by the fireplace woke up long enough to decide that I wasn't going to blow my nose on the curtains.

"You look familiar," Anna Krychek said. "Are you a television reporter?"

When I said, "No, just print," she dropped the issue with a slight shrug of her shoulders.

When I glanced around the room again, she seemed to sense that I expected something different. Without being asked, she explained that she and Krychek were married a few weeks earlier. Her parents gave them the money for the house as a wedding present. Her parents live in Palm Desert. Her family is wealthy. Ivan's is not. "He was living in a small studio apartment when we met," she told me.

Are you getting the picture, Harry? Something was odd about her, the house, and the lack of sorrow. How her accent seemed to come and go. I wanted to be generous, but the whole scene was making it hard. My only option was to play it out and see what happened.

The more we talked the more I realized that the only thing consistent about her was how she pronounced Krychek's first name. It wasn't I-von, but Ee-vahn. I sat there mesmerized while she explained how she'd been a student at Delaney College, and that Ee-vahn was a graduate assistant in the political science department. They met earlier in the year at a seminar on the global implications of Russian meddling in U.S. elections. She said her parents were from Prague so she'd been there several times. Ee-Vahn visited there last summer. They traded stories about restaurants and shops. In her words things sort of took off from there. She described her late husband as a smart man and brilliant researcher who was working on his doctorate and wanted to be a professor.

I couldn't shake the idea that she was reading lines from a script. Plenty of information, just not much emotion. In fact, none at all. I played along, saying it must be hard losing him so soon after the wedding but that she seemed to be taking it pretty well. She coaxed a single tear from one eye. It ran down her cheek, bringing tiny bits of mascara with it. She reached across the table to gently lay a soft hand on my arm. I would've ignored it as the gesture of a grieving wife had she not started drawing circles on the back of my hand with a long, perfect fingernail. A second tear chased the first.

"Forgive me," she said, explaining that it was not her nature to show grief in front of strangers. She slowly pulled her hand away, adding that she would deal with Ivan's death in her own way and in private. My first thought was, Cut. Print. Next scene.

I played along by apologizing if I sounded cynical and suspicious, adding that it came with the territory. She pursed her lips and undid the bun on the back of her head. It turned into a ponytail. When she swung her head, it wrapped around one shoulder like a pet ferret.

When Anna Krychek went to the kitchen to get us something to drink, I asked to use the bathroom. She pointed down a hallway that led to the opposite end of the house. On the way, I quickly opened two doors, but saw nothing that looked unusual. Just a spare bedroom and a den. In the bathroom, I killed a few minutes checking the medicine cabinet and flushing the toilet. On the way back, I checked two more rooms, including the master bedroom. The king-size bed and headboard looked like a furniture store display. I closed the door, thinking that the house had all the charm and personality of the best room at a Holiday Inn Express.

Anna was back at the table. Two glasses of what looked like tonic and lime sat on granite coasters. She was looking out the window at two women driving by in a golf cart. I asked if she played. When she said no, it only added to my confusion about who she really was and why she was living in a house on a golf course. Instead, I asked why, if she came from a wealthy family, Ivan was working as a security guard. What I got back was another well-rehearsed answer about how he was a proud man who wanted to work and earn an income to support his new wife. Being a security guard, she said, allowed him to earn a little money. The work schedule was flexible enough he could continue with his classes and his research. "It was very cute, but unnecessary," she said. "I have plenty of money."

The same thought hit me again: Cut. Once again, Anna. This time with feeling.

While I started believing that the whole thing—the house, the marriage, her—was an elaborate charade, I couldn't figure out what the point was. So, I pressed on, asking if she had reported her husband missing. The answer was as well rehearsed as all the others: She had been in California visiting her parents. She got back around ten the previous night. She wasn't surprised that Ivan wasn't home. He sometimes worked all night either as a security guard or on his research.

When I asked what kind of research, she said she wasn't sure. Apparently, Ivan was very secretive about his work, even keeping his wife in the dark. She guessed that it had something to do with politics since he was studying political science. Other than that all she knew was that he wanted to get his doctorate and be a professor of political science at Delaney College.

I got the feeling that she knew what questions were coming before I asked them. My role, it seemed, was to keep feeding her lines and getting back well-rehearsed answers. Maybe sooner or later I would ask one too many and trip her up.

"Any idea why someone would want to kill your husband?" I asked. She slowly shook her head. They hadn't known each other for long before being married, but what she did know didn't make her think he was in any danger. The police who came to the house didn't offer any theories. They just wanted to know where she was on Sunday afternoon. She gave them the contact information for her mother and father.

I smiled for no other reason than to break the moment then asked if there was someone at the college I could talk to about her husband. When she shook her head no, the ponytail whipped around the back of her neck to hang over the other shoulder. When I said I found that odd since they were students in the same department, she looked flustered for a moment. Finally, I thought, I had forced her off script. She quickly recovered, suggesting I talk to the dean of the department, whose name she couldn't remember.

Cut. That's a wrap.

I thanked her, said I would show myself out and left her sitting at the table with her tonic, lime, and stoicism. While winding back through the upscale homes with perfect lawns searching for the elusive exit, I decided that Anna Krychek had come across only slightly less convincing than Buck Mather's macho-man routine.

Heading east into the city, I pulled over to scribble more notes about what Anna Krychek and Mather had told me. I remember thinking how good it felt to care about something again.

9

Zihuatanejo

Harrison Grimes polished off the second flan then ordered coffee from a passing waiter. Empty plates and a half-full basket of tortilla chips littered the table. Standard ordered another beer and watched the street outside Los Braseros fill with taxis and delivery trucks. The city was breaking out of yet another monsoon season. The tourists were returning, breathing life back into all things Mexico.

"Buck Mather and Anna Krychek? Did they have any connection to Proctor Scofield?" Grimes asked. The look on his face was of someone eager to get to the real reason he came to Zihuatanejo.

"Like everything else at that point, I had no idea. All I could figure out was Mather and the widow Krychek seemed like little more than bit players in a larger production. The question was what production. Both of them acted too odd not to be involved in something important. If they were, then who was calling the shots and why? All I'd gotten from the two of them was suspicious. A security company run by an uncaring, anti-government zealot. A doctoral candidate moonlighting as a security guard. A princess-and-the-frog marriage. None of it added up."

"Should I assume that their names will pop up again?"

"Definitely."

After Grimes paid the check, they walked along the crowded sidewalks back to the bay front. Waiters stood in the street holding menus and offering the best food in town. When Standard smiled and said, "*Mas tardes*," the waiters grinned. A few of them said, "*Sí, mas tardes*, Señor Juan. Maybe soon? Okay?"

"You seem to be something of a local celebrity," Grimes said.

"They all got pretty excited when they found out I was from Oregon. Turns out they all have relatives there."

They walked past the *Museo Arqueologico de la Costa Grande*, fought off a few more menu-wielding waiters and crossed a bridge over the mouth of a fetid canal filled with plastic water bottles and soiled diapers. They cut over to the concrete path that led around a rocky point on the edge of the bay to Playa la Madera. Halfway along the path they found a bench, sat down and watched the sailboats bobbing idly offshore.

"Where does Benny Orlando come into the picture?" Grimes asked.

The question caught Standard off guard until he added things up. "I was going to ask you how you knew I was in Zihuatanejo."

"Don't blame him. One of the associates from our Portland office went to your apartment building. When she asked where you were he sort of blurted it out without thinking. He felt pretty bad about it, but she assured him that we meant you no harm. Just needed help with a case."

"Was this associate of yours young, attractive and with a strange fascination for former circus midgets?"

"I can attest to the first two," Grimes said with a scowl. "I'd rather not think about the third."

"Don't worry about it," Standard said, "Benny is charming, but harmless when it comes to women."

"So how does he fit into all of this?" Grimes asked.

"Benny's my landlord and a good friend. He knew my story when I showed up on his doorstep looking for a place to live. He rented an apartment to me when no one else would. Knowing I was broke or close to it, he even waived the first and last month's rent plus deposit."

"What's his story?"

"He spent half his life as Baby Benny, wearing baggy diapers and chasing other clowns around a circus ring while brandishing an oversized plastic baseball bat. He learned most of his life lessons from male lion tamers and female contortionists. He's easy to take for granted, but he's no one to fool with. I've seen him in bar fights. You haven't lived until you've seen him hit a grown man in the balls for making one too many short jokes. Even the women cringed. He's also turned himself into a top-shelf website designer."

"And computer hacker, I hear."

Standard laughed. "Just don't tell anyone. His skills are formidable, but nothing compared to his extensive network of other hackers, pimps, whores, disaffected cops, and passive-aggressive government workers. If you need to know something, Benny will find it for you. Just don't ask how."

Grimes pulled the tube of sunblock out of his shirt pocket, squeezed some out and rubbed it on his arms and legs. “So,” he said, now that he was all greased up. “What’s next?”

10

Portland

When I got back to town, I picked up a roast beef sandwich to go from Cosmo, the Greek immigrant who owned the small deli across from my apartment building. I also grabbed a six-pack of beer from the small cooler, all of which Cosmo put on my growing tab without asking for the money he knew I didn't have. I ate half the sandwich and drank a beer in the time it took for the decrepit elevator to arrive from the fourth floor and deliver me to the fifth. The windows had been open all day, so the apartment smelled better than the musty lobby. Across the air shaft, Vanessa was heading out the door. It was Tuesday. That meant the gym bag hanging from her shoulder contained the nurse's costume with the little white hat, tear-away candy-striper dress, and stethoscope.

I stood in the kitchen eating the other half of the sandwich. When it was gone, I opened a second beer. That was when Benny called. He said to come down and bring the beer with me.

I don't know what your associate told you, Harry, but Benny always kept a vigilant eye on who comes and goes from the building. His apartment sat atop the building's front entrance overlooking the South Park Blocks. From his front room, he had a clear view of the daily parade of students, homeless, and office workers who occupy the benches or sit on the thin grass across from the First Christian Church.

I took the stairs down to the second floor, knocked on Benny's door and went in without waiting to be invited. I followed the din of calliope music down the narrow hall to the back of the apartment. As usual, Benny was perched in front of one of his computers. His tiny feet on short, fat legs dangling from his custom-designed chair. Sausage-like fingers flew around the keyboard. His eyes never left the screen as he created electronic works of art for people he'd never met, who sold products or services he'd never buy or use. The air conditioner set into the window rattled. Water dripped into a plastic bucket on the floor. The AC was there for the benefit of the terminals, processors, printers, and modems. It made the cramped room feel more like a meat locker than a cozy respite from the summer heat. The windows were covered with aluminum foil. The only light came from a hanging lamp and the blue glow of computer screens that never went dark.

For reasons even Benny admitted he didn't fully understand, he had an affinity for computers. The software necessary to create Internet web pages and online ads came to him naturally. He didn't read the manuals. He didn't have to. He just seemed to know what to do. His client list included the last of the traveling circuses, two small casinos in Nevada, and theme parks in five southern states. His hacking skills, while formidable, were a sideline that I had yet to take advantage of. That would eventually change.

What Benny lacked in height he made up in density. A thick chest and square head set on a massive neck. He had this thick, black hair that dangled around the edges of his face. The dimly lit room created shadows that made his eyes seem like unlit charcoal. He had to turn his whole body to nod toward the corner of the room. He introduced the girl painting her toenails with purple polish as Ivy. She pushed goggle-shaped dark glasses up into a tangle of unevenly cut, multicolored hair. Blue eyes set in a deeply tanned face darted between me and her big toe. She smiled with the passionate apathy of a twenty-something then emitted a squeak that resembled hello accompanied by the glint of the metal stud in her tongue. When she quickly turned her attention back to her toenails, I looked at Benny. He met my gaze with a wink then asked if I was there to pay the rent.

As much as I liked Benny, I hated having to explain another late rent check. Instead, I gave him a vague explanation about the Krychek story I sold to the tabloid and that the gun control article I was doing for the magazine in Philadelphia would be done this week after one more trip down to Salem.

Finished with her toes, Ivy slipped into a pair of clunky sandals and got up to leave. Her bare midriff revealed a navel pierced with two gold rings. A tattoo of a gecko peeked out above low-rise jeans. She told Benny she'd be back then said it was nice to meet me and left.

"Ivy looks a little young," I said. When he said they had a lot in common, I resisted the urge to ask if she'd been a circus clown as well.

For the next half hour we sipped beer while I described the scene at the state fairgrounds and my visits with Buck Mather and Anna Krychek. Benny swung his stubby legs back and forth while listening to my explanation of the odd feeling I took from the two interviews.

"You think one of them killed this Krychek guy?" Benny asked.

The thought had crossed my mind. Spouses are always suspects, but Anna Krychek's alibi would be easy enough for the police to check out. Besides, she didn't look like the type to turn her husband into a macabre puppet. Mather was a different story. His attitude was enough to get him on a list of suspects for any of the city's unsolved crimes.

Benny hopped out of the chair to turn the air conditioner up a notch. The rattle got louder and the drips came faster. One of the computers beeped with another email message from Benny's world-wide network of circus freaks and hi-tech nerds.

"You might want to check that one," I said. "Maybe the bearded lady needs some advice about opening an electrolysis business."

Benny coughed out a short laugh then waddled over to the stereo. Soon the soundtrack of "*The Greatest Show on Earth*" replaced the calliope music. Back in his chair, he asked what I was going to do with this Krychek story. I didn't have to tell Benny that not having a newspaper job anymore just made everything that much more complicated. He'd heard me complain about finding plenty to write about, just no one to publish it. I sank into the chair and rubbed the cold beer can against my cheek.

I was surprised when he asked me if the story was big enough to get my old job back. The possibility of using the Krychek murder as a way of getting back into the good graces of the editor who fired me was a non-starter. For good reason. That bridge was burned and still smoldering.

After the executive editor told me that I was a liability and the paper no longer needed my services, I pretty much destroyed her office and, with it, any chance of redemption. I turned over her desk and file cabinets. Threw her laptop out of the fifth-floor window into the middle of SW Broadway. The glass showered down onto the sidewalk, narrowly missing a group of third graders on a field trip to the newsroom. I was still ranting and raving when three security guards escorted me out the back door.

I started explaining all this to Benny when he turned away to start idly tapping on the keyboard of a turned-off computer while muttering "Blah. Blah. Blah."

I didn't answer. We'd been over the same ground a hundred times. Staying up late into the night drinking Corona and arguing over how long I was going to feel sorry for myself. Benny would pound the arm of his overstuffed chair, demanding that I get on with life. He said

I should move away. Get out of the rain. Forget all of my so-called friends who treated me like O.J. Simpson.

I left and went back to my apartment to tinker with the gun control story. I knew that the final touches would have to wait until the issue came up before the state legislature. Working on it at least made me feel useful. A call to the state capital confirmed that debate on the gun-control bill was the next afternoon in the state senate. Then I emailed the editor in Philadelphia to let him know he'd have everything ahead of schedule.

Not wanting to spend the rest of the day sitting in the apartment, I left the building through the back stairs that opened onto an alley. I walked up SW Tenth Avenue to Powell's Books on West Burnside. On the way I stopped at Jake's Famous Crawfish but left after one beer. The affluent-looking people inside laughing and drinking reminded me too much of my old life. A hot dog and a bottle of water from a street vendor suited both mood and budget. The rest of the afternoon was spent wandering through the endless maze of bookshelves that made Powell's a Portland landmark. Somewhere in the stacks of new and used books were the answers to everything. How to make an omelet. The best golf courses in Scotland. How to write a screenplay. It was a perfect place to grab a few hours away from my new reality and the memories of my old one. I eventually wandered into the journalism section where all my heroes—Cronkite, Woodward, Murrow, Halberstam, Theodore White—stood in judgment, leaving me wondering what they would think of their profession today. Would they cringe at what they saw? If they didn't, I could do it for them.

After spending a few bucks on a used biography of Art Buchwald, I walked up Burnside toward Providence Park, home to the Portland Timbers soccer team and little else. Scanning the book over a beer in a tavern near the stadium, I noticed two people sitting at the bar looking over their shoulders at me and whispering to each other. I'd seen this before. I drained my glass and left. I covered the last three blocks on the walk home thinking of a cold shower and an even colder beer.

It never happened thanks to the large man in the sweat-streaked, gray suit waving at me from a park bench across from the apartment building. It took me a few moments to recognize him. Spread out across the tiny bench, he looked larger than he did in the expanse of the animal barn at the state fairgrounds. I sighed, walked between two cars, and crossed the street.

Without getting up, he introduced himself as Sergeant Daryl Butcher, Homicide, Oregon State Police. He apologized for not getting a chance to meet me the other day at the fairgrounds. He talked while shoving a red swizzle stick into the corner of his mouth. I asked if he was there to see me, although I couldn't figure out why he would be.

"As a matter of fact I am," he said in sort of this good-ol'-boy drawl. "I've got this homicide on my hands and was thinking maybe you could help me out." He hauled himself off the bench and turned full circle to survey the park. Beads of sweat had collected on his forehead and dripped down his cheeks. Thin hair tinted orange to hide the gray hung in wet strands over the back of his shirt collar. Fleshy cheeks made his eyes little more than slits. The wrinkle where his eyebrows and the bridge of his nose came together looked deep enough to hold a silver dollar. He pointed to the park and described how in the last twenty minutes he'd counted, quoting now, "Two drug deals, four homos and a couple of dykes."

When he said he was better at talking shop over a plate of food, I suggested the Virginia Café on SW 10th Avenue. Butcher shrugged and we headed off. Watching him walk beside me was like watching a grizzly on the way to the dump. That's the only way I can describe it. His huge body tilted forward as he struggled to keep pace while panting and smoking a cigarette. His momentum made me wonder if I should stop him when we got to the restaurant or just let it carry him down the street into the Willamette River. Instead, he followed me inside. We settled into a corner booth and ordered. After Butcher caught his breath, he fed me some BS about how reporters are smarter than everybody else and that I might have a theory about who murdered Ivan Krychek. He winked at me while shedding his coat.

"All I know is what Gitchell told me," I said then suggested he check out an on-line tabloid reporting that Krychek was killed by either a satanic cult or aliens. That didn't go well after that, Harry, especially after I told him that he must be in big trouble if he was coming to me for help. He quickly reminded me that I was an ex-reporter, which only made him appear even more desperate for answers.

Butcher changed the subject to Ivan Krychek's wife and if I found it a little odd that Krychek would be, in his words, "Humping an uptown twist like that." Rather than tell him that I'd already talked to her, I listened while thinking that my estimation of Butcher couldn't go much lower. I was wrong. Very wrong.

We sat in icy silence until the waitress showed up with my dinner salad and a bowl of chili. Butcher had opted for a platter of steak and mushrooms. He dove in, holding the fork in his fist and shoveling the food into his mouth. He didn't let eating interrupt his talking. Between mouthfuls, he brought up that I was at the gun show at the fairgrounds the day Ivan Krychek was killed and asked if I'd run into him.

When I told him I'd already explained all that to Alfie Gitchell and suggested the two of them compare notes, he ignored me in favor of scraping his empty plate with a fork then pushing it aside and belching. He leaned forward so both elbows were on the table. Beads of sweat were still attached to his forehead. His breath came in short gasps. "How do you feel about guns?" he asked.

"I'm not a fan," I answered.

"What are your thoughts on piano wire or is your favorite weapon a car?"

The question came out of the blue. That night on the highway had cost me a career, a wife and all that went with it. I had no intention of explaining anything to Butcher about an accident, a trial, and a not guilty verdict. I called bullshit and started to get up and leave.

That didn't stop him. He went on a rant about what better place to start a homicide investigation than with someone who was at the scene and had already killed two people. That morphed into a harangue about idiot jurors and the false claim that I had been drinking the night of the accident. In his words:" Once a killer, always a killer."

He said he didn't like people who got away with things because of who they were or what they did for a living. In his mind, if some poor son of a bitch who just got off work at a lumber mill had killed those two girls, he'd be in the state pen making furniture and taking it up the ass from some body builder. But a yuppie reporter like me mows down the same two kids and all I end up with is a shitty apartment in downtown Portland.

I didn't know what to say, Harry. I thought it was some kind of joke. Like those guys in gorilla costumes who bring singing telegrams to birthday parties. I finally asked him if he had anything as exotic as a motive. Butcher pulled another plastic swizzle stick from a shirt pocket, started digging at his back teeth and telling me that if he did, I'd already be under arrest and sitting in a jail cell.

You're a defense attorney, Harry, so you know that there are cops out there who always want to take the path of least resistance. Pin it on the person who has the weakest alibi. Play the odds. I get that, but what scared me about Butcher was not being accused of murder, but that he was too stupid to find out who really killed Krychek. That meant there was a killer walking around free while he wasted time trying to make my life miserable.

When the waitress brought the check, I picked it up, telling Butcher that I didn't mind being accused of murder, but I wouldn't want to be a bad host. What came next scared the hell out of me. It went something like this: "You're pretty smart aren't you, word man? You think Daryl Butcher here is just an old boy blowing smoke up his own ass. Well, I could pin this thing on you whether you did it or not. I could even haul your butt in for questioning and turn you over to those boys we got locked up downtown. You could have a whole different sexual orientation before your buddy Gitchell even found out you were in jail."

That did it for me. I started for the door again when he grabbed my arm and pulled me back down into the seat so hard it rattled the dishes and silverware. A middle-aged couple sitting at a nearby table stared at us then moved their chairs a few inches away. Butcher ignored them, his purple face within inches of mine. His breath smelled like cigarettes and mushrooms. The swizzle stick between his teeth snapped.

He said he couldn't prove I killed Krychek, but he would. In the meantime he might leak my name to a few reporters. Let the world know that I was suspected in another death. His theory was that most reporters probably already thought I was guilty of killing those two girls. It won't be hard for them to think I'd kill again.

He had my arm pinned to the table. His fingers tightened for a moment before easing enough to get free. I rubbed my wrist while watching the middle-aged couple gather up their plates and move to another table. When I left, Butcher was ordering dessert from the waitress.

It took most of that night to fight back the panic. I'd felt that same way the day police arrested me, while sitting through the trial and the agonizing two days before the verdict came back. Now, along came Daryl Butcher armed with baseless accusations that made me feel like I'd swallowed a live rat. Only this time I hadn't killed anyone.

I sat in my broken down armchair, smoking, sipping at glasses of cheap scotch and watching the dirty curtains flap in the breeze that wandered up the air shaft. The image of Butcher's face hung just out of reach like a gun pointed at my head. I was still sitting there when Vanessa came home a little before three a.m. She went through her routine: Drop the bag on the couch. Take off her clothes. Look at herself in the mirror. Sigh.

It was Wednesday, which meant the bag containing the cowgirl outfit with the white hat, rhinestone vest and tear-away chaps. I watched her, thinking she could've been anything—a barista, a computer analyst, a grocery store checker. Anyone who gets up each day, goes to work then does it all over again without complaint. Nothing ever goes wrong or right. Things stay the same, day after day. She'd probably never killed anyone or been accused of it. She might think that her life was boring, but I watched her with an odd sense of envy. Maybe her life was outside the ordinary, but at least it was predictable. If only things could be as simple as going to work each night, dancing naked for a few hours in front of strange men then going home with a purse full of fives, tens, and twenties.

Butcher's determination to blame me for Ivan Krychek's murder might be a personal thing. Maybe I looked like an easy target for a lazy detective with a deep dislike of defrocked reporters. He obviously resented the fact that I wasn't convicted and wasn't satisfied that I had lost everything in the process. He probably didn't believe in accidents or that people could fall asleep at the wheel and not realize what they'd done.

Rather than relive the past, I went to bed after watching Vanessa slip between the covers next to her stuffed giraffe. Lying face up, I felt the yellowed wallpaper and peeling ceiling paint close in around me.

11

Zihuatanejo

Grimes and Standard were still on the bench overlooking the bay. The sun was disappearing behind the hills to the west, turning the underside of the thin clouds a dusty rose. The foot traffic along the path was a mixture of locals and tourists, all heading into the town from Playa la Madera.

"This Butcher sounds like he could be a problem," Grimes said.

"He was. At one point he suggested that I was having an affair with Anna Krychek and that we conspired to kill her husband."

Grimes shook his head then put a hand on Standard's shoulder. "I know that's all in the past now, but I can tell what Butcher said still bothers you. So, let me give you a little perspective. After thirty years of representing labor unions, including a couple of police unions and the occasional accused criminal, I've learned a few things about people and what they do for a living. It goes like this. There are good carpenters and bad ones. There are good bricklayers and electricians and there are bad ones. The same goes with cops. Some are good at their jobs. Others not so much. Sounds like Butcher falls in the second category."

"It gets worse," Standard said, "but I'll get to that later."

Standard suggested they walk back into town and grab an early dinner at Mango's, an upscale restaurant in the center of town favored by American expats who had either moved to Zihuatanejo permanently or wished they could.

"The problem with Butcher," Standard said as they negotiated the narrow path along the bay, "is that he kept popping up. Part of it was my fault. I kept showing up at the wrong places at the wrong time. Still, he just wouldn't let it go. He was determined to hang Krychek's murder on me, apparently for reasons I didn't know about at the time."

"Like what?"

"I found out later from Alfie Gitchell that a few years earlier Butcher's wife and only son were killed by a drunk driver who turned out to be a wealthy hedge fund manager on his way home from a business dinner. He lawyered up and walked on a technicality. Butcher's had a hard-on ever since for anyone he thought was getting away with something. Gitchell said he talked to Butcher about it, but that he was a hard man to reason with."

It was late afternoon. Enough of a breeze came up to cool things off a bit. A few tourists walked the streets or sat in sidewalk bars drinking beer. The men wore tank tops, shorts, and sandals. The women wore pretty much the same except for the occasional muumuu. Most were sunburned. All were happy.

At Mango's, Grimes and Standard hit the bar first, ordered drinks and waited to get a table for dinner. After Standard talked to the head waiter for a few minutes, they were led to a table in the corner that looked out over the dining room. When they sat down Standard told the waiter to take away his knife. Grimes gave him a what's-up-with-that look that Standard ignored. He didn't like sharing his phobias with strangers.

Over plates of grilled snapper and *carne asada*, Grimes asked how Standard ended up in Mexico.

"It's a long story," Standard said. "Let's just say I got tired of Portland and Portland got tired of me."

"What about journalism?"

"Same story."

Grimes took the hint. "What about your girlfriend? I think you said her name is Emma. How did the two of you meet?"

"I came down here on a whim last December with no place to stay. A taxi driver who brought me into town from the airport said he knew an American woman with a house for rent at the end of Playa la Ropa. I didn't know where that was, but said sure, let's go. Emma seemed nice and so did the house, so I rented it for a couple of months. She lived in the other house on the property. The rest you can guess."

"How's it working out?"

Standard waited a while to answer. Emma Parrish was the best thing that ever happened to him, but there had been some difficult times. His penchant for attracting trouble had followed him from Oregon to Mexico. That meant it ended up involving Emma as well. At one point it had made her think twice about why she was living in Mexico at all. The troubles passed, but that didn't mean they wouldn't return. All Standard could do was hope for the best.

"Pretty well," Standard finally said.

"So, are you going to stay here? Is this your home now?"

"That's what I'm thinking. We'll see how it goes."

"Can you make a living down here?"

"You'd be surprised," Standard said, then suggested a night cap followed by home. "I'll drop you off at your hotel. It's on the way to my place."

Grimes looked at his watch. "It's early and I have this feeling you're getting closer to Proctor Scofield."

Standard agreed and they ordered two glasses of Amaretto straight up.

"Are you familiar with Delaney College?" Standard asked.

"Not much other than it's where Ivan Krychek went to school?"

"Yeah, but it plays a bigger role than that."

"Let's hear it."

12

Portland

The day after my encounter with Butcher I got up early, got coffee from Starbucks and headed for Delaney College. I was armed with a latte, what little I'd picked up from Krychek's widow and a nagging sense that there was more going on than a dead guy in an outhouse.

I'd never been on the campus of Delaney College, only driven by the ivy-covered entrance gate a few times. All I knew was its reputation. Private school tucked into a leafy enclave of southeast Portland. Founded in the late 1800s by a long-forgotten religious order. Grew into a small but highly acclaimed school willing to forego its saintly roots for the worldly pursuits of high-priced tuition and aggressive fundraising from wealthy alumni. The small campus was a mixture of buildings that tracked the college's evolution from the late nineteenth century to early twenty-first. Stately brick and ivy mixed with the architecturally tone deaf concrete and glass. The combination produced a cloistered atmosphere filled with the trappings of higher learning, but devoid of the realities of living in the real world. In other words, a typical American college.

I wasted fifteen minutes wandering around the campus trying to find the Political Science Department. The clock on the front of a large, brick building announced in Roman numerals that it was a little after ten in the morning. That meant plenty of time to find out what I could about Krychek before driving down to Salem, dreading the thought of listening to a gun control debate. I stopped two girls with backpacks and Birkenstocks. The Political Science Department, they said, was in the basement of Mayfield Hall. One of them pointed to a three-story, ivied encrusted building with steep stairs leading to the main entrance. From a distance, the tower looked like a church steeple. Inside, it smelled of chalk blackboards, erasers, and floor wax. Halfway down a long, narrow hallway, past classrooms with the doors closed, was a sign that read "Political Science Department, Jasmine Grant, Ph.D., Dean." An arrow pointed down a set of stairs. At the bottom was a lost world of cramped offices, closets, water fountains and yellowed linoleum. Small, white cards in copper frames on each of the office doors had the occupants' names and office hours. Yellow police tape stretched across one door. The card in the small frame read: Ivan Krychek.

The door at one end of the hallway led outside to a stairwell under the steps of the building's main entrance. I remember a janitor emerging from a small closet with a mop and bucket that rattled across the floor. At the other end of the hall, a half-dozen people milled around outside a lecture hall. I joined them, slipping inside to stand against the back wall. The room was your typical lecture hall. Descending tiers of seats arranged in a half circle. At the bottom was a small platform with a podium, library table and portable blackboard. Scattered around the room were men and women ranging from late twenties to early sixties. They all stared at a woman standing at the podium. She appeared to be just finishing up whatever she'd been telling them. The mood in the room was dark, somber, and sad.

The woman at the blackboard was in her mid-thirties and dressed in the casual clothes of summer term at a college—sandals, colorful print skirt, loose-fitting peasant blouse. What got my attention were the wisps of black hair escaping the plastic clip on the back of her head. The strands dangled around a face with soft, Asian features. She constantly brushed at her hair with long, graceful fingers with manicured nails, but no jewelry.

I could see that she was trying her best to hold herself together as she explained how some of them may be questioned by police, if they haven't been already, about the death of Ivan Krychek. She urged them to cooperate, be honest and tell the truth. After that everyone started to get out of their seats and head for the door. They stopped when she made one last plea to keep Ivan Krychek and his family in their thoughts. She seemed about to add something else but stopped when tears filled her eyes.

Taken individually, her unkempt hair, slight overbite, angular nose with the small bump on the bridge and Haight-Ashbury wardrobe were not that attractive. Collectively, though, they created a kind of innocent beauty. I don't want to go all poetic here, Harry, but she gave off a kind of vulnerability out of sync with the times if not the place. How can I say this? She seemed authentic in a way that made her way more alluring than the well-rehearsed and … plastic beauty … of Anna

Krychek. The absence of makeup meant there was nothing to smear or streak when the tears that filled her eyes flowed down her cheeks.

Finally, someone willing to shed an unforced tear for the late Ivan Krychek.

I leaned against the back wall to let the twenty or so people get by. When the room emptied, I walked down toward the podium where the woman was gathering up papers from the library table. I gave her my name and told her I was a freelance writer doing a story on Krychek's death. She gave me a weak smile and said her name was Jasmine Grant followed by a look that made it clear she had no intention of helping me. She went back to gathering up papers and stuffing them in her backpack.

"I'm sorry," she said, but in a way that made it clear that she'd told the police everything she knew and didn't want to talk about it anymore. I pressed her, gently, just a little more. She stopped fussing with her papers long enough to give me a pleading look then sort of surrendered. Too tired to fight, I guessed. She and Ivan had worked together for several years. He was her student then her graduate assistant. The tears returned when she told me that they had become close friends.

I told her most of what I'd heard from Buck Mather and Anna Krychek. If any of it registered with her, she didn't show it. I asked what kind of person Krychek was and if she could give me some insight into the research he was doing. That seemed to break the ice a bit. She eagerly described him as a "dedicated and resourceful researcher with an unquenchable thirst for the truth." Then she asked if that was a good sound bite. We shared a smile at the expense of journalism's love of cheap quotes. I needlessly, but dutifully, scribbled notes.

We sat in office chairs at opposite ends of the library table. She seemed more relaxed, relieved, more willing to talk. She explained that Krychek had been working on a doctoral dissertation that had something to do with the polarization of American politics. The conservative right versus the liberal left. Talk radio meets public broadcasting. Fox versus MSNBC. Right wing websites versus Google and Facebook. Conspiracy theories versus the truth. He'd started work on it the previous year, she said, but about three months earlier became very secretive about the project. She'd asked him several times how things were going. Each time he said everything was fine but made it clear that she would have to wait until he finished.

When I told her Anna Krychek had described her husband's research the same way, she suddenly went quiet. It wasn't a question so there was no need for her to answer. She didn't have to. Jasmine Grant would make a terrible poker player. Anyway, I let it pass, but the change in her demeanor was hard to miss—Anna Krychek was a sore subject.

As someone with a bachelor's degree in Liberal Arts, Harry, I'm only vaguely familiar with the dos and don'ts of a graduate student's research, but it seemed like an advisor should know something about it. When I asked her why she knew so little, she swatted again at the unruly strands of hair that had escaped the clip. She agreed it sounded odd, but she and Ivan were friends. She trusted him. Didn't feel the need to check up on him. Knowing the general nature of his research was good enough. She would find out sooner or later.

I brought up Anna Krychek again and her explanation that Ivan was working part time as a security guard to support his new wife. Grant's response was a catty comment about believing anything Anna said then went back to stuffing more papers into her backpack.

I couldn't let that pass. I said they made a strange couple. She's beautiful and he was, well, not.

It didn't take her long to answer. "I have no insights into Ivan's personal life," she said. All she knew was that he married her shortly after they met. It all happened very fast and unexpectedly. Was she surprised? To say the least. She grudgingly admitted that Krychek never talked to her about Anna or getting married. There was no wedding that she knew of, but she'd been in Hong Kong on sabbatical for two months. The pleading look that crossed her face told me she was done talking about it.

I changed the subject to whether the police had found anything in Krychek's office. She shook her head no then went back to stuffing her backpack and erasing the blackboard. I remember her delicate arms making angry arcs across the surface. I wanted to ask more questions just to watch her talk. She was someone easy to be honest with. A generous heart in an ungenerous world. It was time to come clean. I guess I blurted it out, "There are some things about Krychek's death that don't add up."

When she stopped erasing and turned around, I let it all out. Someone went to a lot of trouble just to murder a lowly security guard. The guy who owns the security company doesn't seem too upset about it. Neither does the widow. Why was he working as a security guard in the first place? I think the whole marriage, moonlighting thing looked a bit phony.

She went back to wiping the clean blackboard over and over. She politely and diplomatically told me that what I said was fascinating, but she needed to get ready for an afternoon faculty meeting. She snatched up her backpack and headed up the aisle toward the double doors. She had this unique walk—purposeful, her body bent slightly at the waist. Her right arm pumping across her slender body as she negotiated the wide, low steps. The faint odor of patchouli hurried along behind her.

Then I did something that I hadn't done in years—I asked if she would have dinner with me that night. It just sort of came out as if some force inside wanted companionship worse than I did. Before she could say no, I suggested an Italian place in the Pearl District called Angelina's. When she hesitated, I told her the people who go there sniff the wine before drinking it. That brought a smile and a few seconds of hesitation. She said she knew the place and would meet me there at seven. After that she was out the door.

I left for Salem still surprised that I had asked Jasmine Grant to dinner. More surprised that she had accepted. It had been six years, Harry, since I'd been on anything that resembled a real date—five years of marriage to Christine and one year of not caring one way or the other. So, when I got to Salem, parked, and walked to the capitol building, I wondered what made her say yes and hoped it didn't have anything to do with my infamous status. Either way, I had something to look forward to for a change.

13

Zihuatanejo

Grimes pushed his plate away and looked out across the restaurant. The circular bar was full. The dinner tables were set and ready for diners who had spent the day in the sun.

"Nice place," he said.

"Best in town. Emma's late boyfriend used to own it," Standard said.

"Late?"

"Died in a SCUBA diving accident. Emma seldom comes here. When she does it's like a royal visit. Lots of hugs and air kisses."

"Let's get back to Jasmine Grant. It sounds to me like this is a renewal of your love life, but I sense that something happened before your date."

"You're right. It's what you've been waiting for."

"And?"

Standard had covered the state legislature ten years. For some reason his editors were captivated by state government. He, on the other hand, didn't find it all that enlightening, but it earned him plenty of bylines about issues that were seldom resolved. The capitol building itself was more interesting than what went on inside. It had been described as either a testament to New Deal architecture or the world's largest bowling trophy. It had a flat-topped dome with a gold man on top. Inside was a vast, marble-floored foyer. Depression-Era murals covered the walls. Brass stands with red velvet ropes surrounded an ornate state seal embedded in the floor. Two wide sets of marble stairs lead to the second floor. House chambers on the right. Senate on the left. The chatter of legislators and lobbyists echoed off the walls.

Grimes leaned back in his chair. He gave Standard the sly smile of someone who knew that there was more to the story than what he'd heard so far. "I think we're getting closer to why I'm here," he said. "How about a night cap?"

Standard could sense Grimes's growing impatience about getting to the punchline but didn't care. He'd signed on to hear

Standard's whole story. Standard was going to hang to hear all of Grimes's.

"Good idea," Standard said and waved to the waiter.

14

Salem, Oregon

To be honest, Harry, I was not excited about coming back to the capital. I'd done my time there, made my mark for what it was worth and moved on. It was what happened to me later that made me nervous. Afraid someone would remember me, I kept my head down and ducked past lobbyists standing in front of a closed-circuit television showing the proceedings on the Senate floor. At a table guarding the entrance to the chambers, I got a copy of that day's Senate calendar. Debate on the gun control bill was still at the top of the agenda.

I walked around the corner and took the stairs to the third floor. The Senate gallery occupied three sides above the chamber like balconies in an Elizabethan theater. Most of the seats were empty, except for a dozen men dressed in paramilitary garb sitting in the front row of the center section. They were leaning over the brass railing like kids at a Saturday matinee. I hunkered down in a front row seat on one of the smaller side galleries. The senators moved through the routine business of the day. I spotted Brad Roark on the far side of the chamber holding forth with a wire service reporter. Ten feet away, Kingsley Landis was doing the same with a television reporter. Within a few hours their faces would be all over the evening news in what would be billed as a preview of the gubernatorial race. I took a deep breath and told myself it would all be over soon.

The routine business of the Senate dragged on until the presiding officer, an elderly man with an ice cream suit, banged his gavel and droned through an official script before yielding to Brad Roark. I pulled out my notebook and pen. The television lights on the other side of the gallery switched on. Roark stood up behind his desk. He looked about the same as in the newspaper photo from a few days earlier. Black, stylishly long hair mussed in a way more intentional than natural. Coatless with a slightly wrinkled white button-down collar shirt. Sleeves rolled up. Tie loose. Baggy khaki pants. His speech was a litany of carefully crafted sound bites. I still remember some of it: "I rise today on behalf of the thousands of innocent people who have been slaughtered in this state and this country because of some people's overwhelming and all-consuming fascination with guns. The ease with which criminals and criminals-to-be obtain handguns, assault rifles and other deadly weapons has left behind a legacy of lost hope, lost dreams and lost lives." He paused for effect and a well-timed choke in his voice. "There is enough blood in the streets."

The end of his speech was greeted by hoots and catcalls from the boys in the military suits seated in the gallery. They were immediately gaveled down by the man in the ice cream suit and admonished by two uniformed guards. Their protests stopped, but not without mugging for the television cameras and grumbling about infringing on their right of free speech. It wasn't until the ruckus died down that I noticed the uniforms worn by the security guards. They looked familiar, but I couldn't remember where until one guard turned toward me. The emblem over the shirt pocket read: Prestige Security.

A few days earlier, Harry, I thought Prestige Security was nothing but a low-rent operation run by a right-wing macho man doing business out of a strip mall. Now, men sporting Prestige logos were rousting gun nuts in the gallery of the State Senate. I was clearly missing something.

At the same time, the presiding officer recognized Kingsley Landis. He stood up behind his desk looking like he'd spent the night locked in a Brooks Brothers store. His speech was about as well starched. Each line was straight out of the anti-gun-control playbook: "Making guns illegal won't make criminals more honest or crazy people saner. Guns don't kill people. People kill people."

More interested in why a private security company was guarding the capital and convinced I was not going to learn anything new about gun control or efforts to stop it, I left to find the security office. I wandered the halls until I found a single door at the dead-end of a dimly lit hallway. The word "Security" was stenciled on opaque glass. I knocked then tried the knob when no one answered. It was open.

The inside was pretty much what you'd expect. A cramped office. A bank of small monitors showing grainy, black-and-white pictures of the house and senate chambers and a half-dozen other places. A uniformed guard sitting behind a desk was wearing headphones and flipping the pages of a magazine. He looked to be in his twenties, whip thin and a cold sore on his lower lip the size of a roasted marshmallow. His face was a permanent mask of boredom. Even sitting down, his pants and his shirt looked two sizes too big. To be honest, the kind of guy that looked like he couldn't secure much more than a paycheck.

The patch above the guard's shirt pocket read "Parchman." I was just about to reach out and tap him on the shoulder, when he jumped up, startled, and reached for the gun on his hip. I backed up, hands in the air. He pulled off the headphones and tossed them on the desk.

"Sorry," he said. He didn't get many visitors and I'd scared him. It still took him a few seconds to take his hand off his gun. When I asked him how long Prestige has had the contract to provide security at the capital, he looked confused. Probably unsure whether to answer. Finally, he said about a year, which is how long he'd been working there. "Retired state cops used to do this, but the legislature decided to turn it over to private industry," he said. "Politics, I guess."

I asked if he knew Ivan Krychek. He said they'd worked together then asked if I knew he was dead. It was my turn to nod.

It turned out Parchman and Krychek became good friends working the capital together a couple of nights a week. Their shift started at eleven p.m. and ended at six a.m. Krychek spent most of his time patrolling the wing of the building that housed the senators' offices. Parchman worked the house wing. Sometimes after their shift they would have coffee or breakfast together in the capitol cafeteria. One day Buck Mather showed up and told Parchman that Ivan wouldn't be working in the capital anymore. The next thing Parchman knew Krychek was dead. He didn't know anything about Krychek's research, other than it had something to do with politics, which is why he took the job at the capitol.

All this made me wonder why Mather hadn't mentioned that Krychek worked at the capitol building. Neither had Krychek's wife. Then there was the obvious question: What did Krychek hope to learn about politics by patrolling the state capital at night. Parchman never met Krychek's wife. When Krychek showed him a picture of her he wondered why he was working a graveyard shift.

We talked a while longer. I learned that Mather frequently stopped by. He and Krychek seemed to get along as well as could be expected given their different personalities. G.I. Joe meets The Big Bang Theory, in Parchman's words. He said he got the impression that getting the contract to provide security at the capital and other government buildings was a big deal for Mather. He wanted everything done just right. When Parchman whispered that Mather wasn't exactly boss of the year material, we shared a quiet laugh.

I reassured him that his secret was safe with me, then wrote my name and telephone number on a yellow sticky note from Parchman's desk. He agreed to call me if he thought of anything else that Ivan might have told him about his research. He looked at the note then at me. I left after he said that Krychek was his friend and he would do anything to help. I thanked him and left after suggesting he not tell Mather we talked.

The gun control bill passed by two votes in what was either a victory over senseless violence or a mortal blow to the Constitution. I went back to the Senate gallery for a few angry quotes from the militia boys. Then, I reluctantly headed downstairs to the basement. I cringed at the thought of showing my face in the press room, but worth it if hearing what Roark and Landis had to say about the gun control vote adding something to my article.

By the time I got there a gaggle of reporters were surrounding Roark. For the first few questions they fired at him Roark remained calm and glib. Then he gradually began to look nervous. The more uncomfortable he appeared, the more pointed the questions. The only way I can describe it, Harry, is that the well-oiled figure from the senate floor had turned into a rusty tin man. Finally, he held up his hands to signal surrender and quickly left.

In the hall outside the press room he stopped to talk to this slick-looking guy with moussed hair and a tan. He wore gray slacks, a dark double-breasted blazer and a bright-white shirt with a tab collar and striped tie. They spoke for a few seconds. Roark nodded to whatever the man whispered to him then headed out the door.

Just as Roark left, Kingsley Landis arrived. Reporters quickly hit him with the same barrage of questions. Like Roark, Landis appeared comfortable with questions for the first five minutes. Then he, too, began to ramble and squirm. Leaving the room, he walked down the hall and stopped to talk to the same slick-looking man.

The woman standing next to me was typing into her smartphone. She had the fresh-faced, harried look of a young television reporter. I pointed out the door and asked her if she knew the guy talking to Landis. She glanced over her shoulder. "Mitchell Penroy, lobbyist for Scofield Industries," she said then rubbed her fingers together in the international sign for money.

There it was, Harry. The first time Scofield's name had come up in any of this. Obviously, it wouldn't be the last. But like I told you, at the time what I knew about the reclusive billionaire was pretty much common knowledge. That he lived in Portland only added to the city's reputation. His wealth and influence made him a target for every politician in the state looking for money and an endorsement. No surprise that both Roark and Landis stopped to kiss the ring of his representative.

Any mention of Proctor Scofield and Scofield Industries was an added dimension to any story. Why not gun control? So, I followed him out a door into the basement parking garage. When I gave him my name and told him I was a freelance reporter, he stared at me without saying anything. It was almost like I wasn't there.

I asked if Scofield Industries had an interest in gun control and what was his reaction to today's vote? He rattled off something about a corporate commitment to safe-and-sane gun laws without infringing on The Constitution then started walking away. I tried again, asking what role did he think gun control would play in the governor's race. Does Scofield Industries have a horse in that race?

He turned toward me and paused, measuring his words. "The involvement of Scofield Industries in local politics is minimal," he said then started to walk away. I said I'd like to talk to Scofield about gun control and politics in general. Could he arrange it?

As you would expect, Harry, that pretty much ended it. Penroy stopped long enough to put on a pair of dark glasses with small, round lenses then started walking away again. He crossed the concrete floor to a dark blue Lincoln Town Car with tinted windows. He backed out of a space with a sign on the wall that read "Legislators Only." As the car drove away, I caught the license plate number and wrote it in my notebook.

I drove back to Portland, eager for my dinner with Jasmine Grant, but struck by the images of Prestige Security guards in the capital, but more by Mitchell Penroy and his boss, Proctor Scofield.

15

Zihuatanejo

"Finally," Grimes said as he finished the last of his second amaretto. "Proctor Scofield's name comes up. It took a while, but it was worth the wait. This is a fascinating story, John. I'm just not sure where it's going."

The restaurant was half full of diners, but the bar was doing a box-office business. Standard had seen most of the drinkers and thinkers before, but not since the previous spring when they left town. Only now were they starting to drift back to spend a few weeks or a few months. There were a lot of hugs and air kisses among the women, handshakes and back slaps for the men. This was mostly Emma's crowd. She was the queen bee of the ex-pat community. Her rare appearances at Mango's only added to her exalted status, which did not extend to Standard. They either tolerated him because of her or resented him because he had won what they—both men and women—had coveted.

"So you were starting to connect the dots," Grimes said.

"Dots, yes. Connect, no. I could put Scofield, Penroy, and the two politicians in one basket. That left Mr. and Mrs. Krychek. I considered Mather little more than hanging chad. All I had was a vague sense of Proctor Scofield looming in the background somewhere. I remembered Alfie Gitchell's warning that Krychek's death was not your garden-variety murder. As it turns out he was more right than I imagined."

When Grimes stifled a yawn, Standard was about to pay the bill and call Arturo, his favorite taxi driver. That's when Itchy Donlan showed up looking like he always did: Needing a drink and someone to buy it for him. He was dressed in Topsiders, baggy shorts, a faded Tommy Bahama shirt and a pork-pie hat. Spotting Standard, he walked over and pulled up a chair.

"I believe you know Mr. Grimes," Standard said. "He gave you five-hundred pesos to tell him where to find me." Standard turned to Grimes.

Donlan looked at Grimes then gave Standard a perplexed stare. "Did I do something wrong?"

Standard let Itchy stew for a few seconds before laughing. "Everything's good, Itchy, but if you're going to tell people we're partners you need to be a little more loyal."

Duly admonished, Itchy shook Grimes' hand while ordering a margarita from a passing waiter and giving Standard a sheepish grin.

"Sorry, John. Things are a little slow right now." Then he turned to Grimes. "You must be here on vacation, so if you're interested in deep-sea fishing, SCUBA diving, or a sunset cruise on a catamaran, I'm your man."

"You're a little late, Itchy" Standard said, seeing the look of helplessness on Grimes' face. "Harry is just here on business. He's leaving soon."

At the mention of business, Donlan looked suspicious then turned excited. "Business? You mean you're on another case? Right, John?" Donlan looked around to make sure no one was listening then leaned towards Grimes. "John and I are a team, you know. We've been on several cases together. Sort of like Spade and Archer."

"Itchy, stop it," Standard said then looked at Grimes and shook his head. "We are not a team, Harry, and there were no cases."

Itchy started to protest. "What about …?"

"Itchy," Standard said. "Stop it. Why don't you go to the bar while we finish our business? Order another margarita on me."

Itchy looked hurt but stood up. He told Grimes it was nice to meet him and headed off across the dining room to the bar.

"What was that all about?" Grimes asked.

Standard sighed. "Itchy came down here about five years ago with his wife and two sons. They left. He stayed. He makes a meager living steering people toward dive trips and catamaran cruisers and bilking the occasional divorcee or widow dumb enough to fall for his bullshit. He's harmless. Just sort of a fixture around here."

"How so?"

Standard thought for a moment. "Someone once described Itchy as like a saxophone in fifties rock 'n roll—annoying but necessary."

Grimes looked confused for a few seconds then slowly nodded. "I get it."

By the time Arturo showed up, Standard and Grimes were waiting outside the restaurant. They climbed in the back of the taxi.

Arturo weaved his way through traffic and out of town toward the hotel district overlooking Playa la Ropa.

"Tomorrow, then?" Grimes said when they pulled up at his hotel.

"The Tortuga. Ten a.m.," Standard said.

"I take it that's your favorite hangout."

"You've seen one beachfront Mexican restaurant; you've seen them all." Standard said before they drove away.

"You have a new *amigo*, Senior Juan," Arturo said as they headed toward the turnaround at Playa la Ropa. "A *norteamericano*. Someone from home?"

"Sort of," Standard said.

Standard still wasn't sure what to make of Harrison Grimes. He'd been coy about the reasons why his firm took on the case of Nico Adams. While Standard was sure it had something to do with Proctor Scofield and Scofield Industries, it was just another dot he couldn't connect, unless, of course, it was money. Suing large corporations was nothing new for lawyers. But sue Scofield Industries? For what? Figuring he'd find out sooner or later, he remained determined to drag his story out as long as possible. The number of people who knew the truth about how and why Proctor Scofield died was small. He had promised one of those people that he would take care of everything then remembered he'd also promised to check in. He looked at his watch, given the time change it was not too late to call.

After Arturo dropped him off, he stopped by a beachfront restaurant called Rossy's for a beer then walked home. He turned on all the lights, poured a shot of Patrón, and dialed the number. The answer came on the second ring. He gave a short update, ending by saying he knew where he wanted things to go, but unsure if he could get there. He hung up after the voice on the other end said, "I trust you."

~*~

Standard was drinking coffee and reading a two-day old *USA Today* when Grimes arrived at The Tortuga the next morning. They ordered breakfast from the long-suffering Pablo and chased away a few beach vendors selling cheap jewelry and hand-painted plates. Grimes bought a couple of bobble-head toys to take back to his nieces and nephews.

"I'm starting to like this place," Grimes said. "Maybe I can convince my wife to come down here. I just have to convince her that it's safe."

"Let me know. I'll have Itchy hook you up with some deep-sea fishing or a tequila-fueled catamaran trip at sunset."

"Done," he said. "Now, where were we?"

"Jasmine Grant."

"Ah, yes. You resurgent love life."

16

Portland

I was early for dinner. Jasmine a little late. We got a table in a dark corner of the bar and by six-thirty had ordered dinner and drunk half a glass of Chianti each while fumbling with the awkwardness of what I stubbornly insisted on calling a date.

In between the focaccia bread and the salad, she told me about growing up in San Francisco, the child of tie-dyed sixties radicals with stories of hanging out with Angela Davis and Eldridge Cleaver, going to demonstrations in Berkeley and epic concerts at The Fillmore. She lived in Hong Kong for five years after her parents died, returning to California to get a master's degree then a doctorate in political science. She'd been at Delaney College for eight years, two of those as dean of the Political Science Department. There was a brief marriage she didn't want to talk about and, best I could tell, no one who inspired enough interest to qualify as a boyfriend. Once again, I found myself asking questions just to watch her talk. She had this infectious optimistic attitude toward life and politics. It was refreshing to meet someone who could understand both and not be poisoned by either. She was nothing like my ex-wife with her ceramic personality that could shatter into a million pieces at a word or phrase said the wrong way or at the wrong time. Jasmine was playful and mischievous. Durable.

At one point, she stared over my shoulder at a man sitting alone at a table against the back wall of the restaurant talking on his cellphone. He looked to be in his mid-fifties with dark glasses, a diamond earring, silk shirt open at the neck and thin black hair pulled tight into a greasy ponytail. She looked embarrassed when I asked if she knew him. She apologized then giggled and leaned forward, confessing to being a shameless people watcher. She pegged the guy as someone who owns a warehouse full of toxic waste. I saw him as a salesman, probably carpet or linoleum.

We shared a laugh, then ordered more wine and bread. When she said she wanted to ask me something, I nodded but already knew what was coming.

"You're the reporter who was in that ... accident ... with the two little girls," she said, pausing over the word accident as if unsure it was the right one. When she'd read about it at the time it reminded her of a Greek tragedy. The kind where a good man leading a good life commits a heinous act through no fault of his own. It forever changes the course of his life, but in the end, though he is found innocent, he couldn't escape his own guilt. That seemed a bit obscure for me, but she was the academic so who was I to argue. Instead, I fingered my linen napkin with one hand and twirled the wine glass with the other. It was hard not to marvel at how she had depersonalized the whole event without offending me or making me feel like she was prying into areas that were better left forgotten.

I told her I appreciated her assessment but searched for a polite way to change the subject. She persisted in a charming way that made it hard to tell her to stop. She asked about my life before it happened. I said it was like my name—typical and normal.

"And after?" she asked.

"Anything but."

When she asked if I'd learned anything from what happened, I waited to answer while silently reliving the past year. "I learned that I don't have an addictive personality so I couldn't become an alcoholic, at least not yet. Mind-altering drugs are too undependable. Painkillers are hard to come by, but best taken on an empty stomach."

When she kept at it, I offered her more wine with a smile that I hoped would tell her to slow down. When she got the message, an awkward silence replaced the topic of my past. Over the main course of salmon-stuffed tortellini and more Chianti, I finally broached the subject of Ivan Krychek. The wine had taken the edge off her emotions. This time she didn't balk or turn sad when his name came up.

It turned out that Krychek came to Delaney as a freshman, graduated in three years, got his master's a year later and had been working on his doctorate for about a year. His goal was to finish his dissertation by next spring, hoping to get his doctorate in time to become a political science professor at Delaney the following fall. They had talked about what it would be like to teach together even though there was no guarantee the college would hire him. The problem, she said, was not the future, but the present.

She confessed that what she'd told me earlier about Ivan being a dedicated and talented researcher wasn't quite true. He was dedicated all right, but not particularly talented. He wasn't stupid or lazy. In fact, just the opposite. The problem, as she saw it, was that he had strong opinions and a tendency to believe things that supported those opinions while discounting things that didn't. I watched her as she explained how Krychek would manipulate the facts to take him to where he wanted to go rather than the other way around. She had tried to coach him, but in the end, he always came up short. When he started work on his doctorate, he'd already reached a conclusion about the evils of a politically polarized nation with a growing segment of society falling prey to conspiracy theories. She knew those conclusions would be seriously challenged when it came time to deliver his dissertation.

With one long swallow, her wine disappeared. She either didn't notice or didn't mind when I ordered another for both of us. We concentrated on the food for a few minutes before I asked about Anna Krychek. She apologized for her catty remarks earlier, admitting that she'd only met Anna once and it was unfair to jump to conclusions. While Anna seemed nice enough, Ivan running off and marrying someone like her was out of character. She never thought of him as a risk taker or prone to rash behavior. After hearing about the marriage she felt disappointed and a little betrayed. Her looks only made Jasmine that much more disappointed in Ivan, as if he had chosen style over substance. What made it even odder was that Ivan was always uncomfortable around women. Yet she seemed like the aggressor. Out to get Ivan even though he wasn't much of a catch.

At one point, sensing that I was digging for something, she made it clear that she and Ivan were never involved. She always believed that he would end up with a stronger, more intelligent woman. Instead, he chose a Barbie doll. When I said, "A wealthy Barbie doll," she raised her glass in a mock toast to beauty and money over strength and intelligence.

Over coffee I asked about Krychek's part-time job at Prestige Security. That, she said, baffled her. Ivan's family wasn't rich, but they had enough money to keep him at Delaney for five years, which isn't cheap. He'd never worked before other than a little work-study, so she couldn't understand why he felt the need to work now. From what she knew of Anna, she doubted that he needed to work at all.

She sipped her coffee, seemingly to give herself more time to think. She was convinced that job had nothing to do with supporting his wife. So, it must have had something to do with his research. One thing she'd learned about Krychek was that he didn't do anything that wasn't in some way related to his doctoral studies and his desire to become a professor.

I asked if she'd talked to the police. She had. Of course it was Butcher. No surprise that he came off as belligerent. After he left, she felt like a suspect. I told her not to worry about it. Butcher thought everybody was a suspect. I didn't mention that he included me.

When the topic of Krychek's killer came up, she shook her head. Her only guess was that it was some monster determined to kill someone in a bizarre fashion. Ivan just happened to be in the wrong place at the wrong time. What else could it be? She refused to believe that he was involved in something so sinister that someone would want to kill him. Politics may have become blood sport but surely it hasn't gotten that bad.

When she excused herself to go to the restroom, I paid the bill and sipped coffee. When she returned, she walked to my side of the table, leaned close and in a soft voice that made my skin tingle said it was time to go.

Her mood had changed. Either a slight lustiness had emerged thanks to the wine or my imagination was working overtime. Still, there was something in her voice, her eyes, and the way her hand gently brushed my shoulder when she moved away. I followed her out the door, unsure what to do next. Once outside, I asked what made her decide to have dinner with me. Apparently, she just wanted to know more about me, saying it while looking at me in a way that said she was being serious.

Suddenly she kissed me on the cheek, thanked me for dinner and walked toward her car at the opposite end of the street from mine. I stood there watching her. Halfway down the block she turned around and walked back. She told me she had a meeting the next day at Portland State, but was free from noon on. Would I like to have lunch? It was the right invitation at the right time. I gave her my telephone number and watched as she entered it into her cellphone.

I drove home fully convinced that Jasmine Grant represented a new beginning and that maybe the dark days were over. I hoped it was true, but past events told me not to get too far out ahead of myself.

Later that night, I finished the gun control article. After running it through the spell-checker one more time then reading it out loud to make sure nothing had been overlooked, I added the photos and a cover letter and emailed the whole thing to the editor in Philadelphia.

After two glasses of wine and a quick replay of my dinner with Jasmine Grant, I went to bed feeling disappointed that Vanessa's apartment was dark, meaning she probably had the night off. Thoughts of Jasmine and the anticipation of lunch the next day had stirred something inside that would make Vanessa's nightly act more interesting than usual.

I slept until ten the next morning then showered, dressed, and went downstairs to have coffee with Benny. Ivy was rattling around in the kitchen trying to figure out the coffee maker. She looked exactly like she did the first time I saw her, which made me wonder if she'd spent the night with Benny. That triggered more thoughts about my upcoming lunch.

Benny put down the newspaper so he could listen while I described my new status as a murder suspect and meeting Jasmine Grant. In his mind I was leading a pretty interesting life for someone who's been doing everything possible to make himself invisible.

"Being accused of murder doesn't meet the definition of an interesting life," I said.

"I was thinking more about the professor." Benny scowled at me. "Technically, you're still married."

Ivy plopped down parrot-like on the arm of Benny's chair, her pale arm snaking around his back and coming to rest on his shoulder. Benny watched my face then started slyly humming Gene Autry's "Back in the Saddle Again." When I refused to rise to the bait, Benny asked about Daryl Butcher.

We talked about what to do, finally deciding that I needed to call Alfie Gitchell and ask him to get Butcher off my case. Gitchell got me into this by inviting me down to the fairgrounds. Maybe he can get me out of it by dragging some other red herring under Butcher's nose.

Two cups of coffee later, Benny disappeared into his computer room. Ivy went back to painting her toenails another shade of purple. I returned to my apartment to wait for Jasmine's call. It came a few minutes after eleven. She was a few blocks away. I told her to drive north and meet me in front of the Portland Art Museum on SW Park Avenue.

Ten minutes later I was sitting in the air-conditioned comfort of her Volvo. The giant hair clip had been replaced by two large oriental needles that seemed to be doing a better job holding everything in place. Her clothes were the same as the day before, but with different designs. Her skirt was pulled up and tucked under her legs so I could see her thighs. The curve of her breast was just visible through the side of her sleeveless top. Her smile made me feel five years younger.

When she asked, "Where to?" I suggested Dan and Louie's Oyster Bar on SW Ankeny Street, but she insisted on someplace with outside seating. We agreed on Papa Haydn's in Northwest Portland and headed over to West Burnside and turned right on NW 23rd Avenue. After fifteen minutes of driving along crowded residential streets, we finally found a place to park, got out and walked to the restaurant. At a table on the street under the shade of a pinwheel-colored awning we ordered wine and sandwiches. By the time the tables on either side filled up, we had once again gotten past the awkward small talk.

She asked where I lived and why I didn't want her to pick me up there, jokingly asking if I was married. The art museum was easier to find and my place wasn't exactly something out of *Town and Country*, I told her. When she waited for an answer about my marital status, I said, "Separated. About a year."

Jasmine sipped her wine and delicately pulled a slice of bread from the half loaf wrapped in a calico napkin. I could tell there was something on her mind. It took a few more sips before she got around to it. She explained that after she got home last night, she searched the Internet for some news articles about what happened to me. She couldn't find anything about my side of the story or that I'd testified at my trial. She wanted to know why.

"Not much to tell," I said, explaining how the lawyer I'd retained on the cheap said there was no reason for me to take the stand. It was an accident, pure and simple, and the jury was either going to convict me for an accident or they weren't. I'd already publicly expressed regret and doing it again on the stand wouldn't change anything.

She acted amazed that I didn't get my day in court. I told her I never wanted my day in court because I never wanted to be in court. Anyway, it wasn't much of a story. I fell asleep at the wheel. I thought all I did was wake up in time to keep the car from going into a ditch.

I swirled the wine in my glass, wishing for something stronger. Jasmine stayed silent, waiting for more to come. I hated talking about it, but not to her. She was one of those rare people who liked to listen. I can never remember her starting a sentence with "I."

I described how I'd spent the next few days mowing the lawn, trimming the hedge, and taking my wife out to dinner. Everything was great until the state police showed up. Someone had seen a car like mine and phoned it in. The police did what police do and they ended up at my front door.

She leaned forward, elbows on the table, ivy-green eyes focused on my face. I knew she'd read all of this in the news clips about the trial, which made me curious why she wanted me to tell her. Turns out she just wanted to hear me say it, watch my face while I talked about it.

"So how do you get past this?" she asked. "Even a political science professor from a Podunk college can see that what happened that night is right under your skin. Why not throw in the towel? Give up? Leave town? Start over somewhere new?"

She seemed to be reading my mind. There was a time when I almost did go somewhere else to start a new life. After my wife left and the paper fired me, I was too drained to do much beyond feel sorry for myself. I couldn't find the energy or the desire. So, I stayed put. Then there were the questions of money and where I would go. Hell, Harry, it took me six months to get up the nerve to drive at night. I still don't like it.

She asked if I'd gotten any help. In other words, a psychiatrist. My lawyer had ordered an evaluation in case things got so bad I had to fall back on a mental incapacity defense or some other nonsense. Anyway, the outcome was deep depression with self-destructive tendencies. In other words, suicidal. Only I wasn't.

I gazed over her shoulder at the stop-and-go traffic crawling along NW 23rd Avenue. Noon-hour shoppers walked through trendy shops on the east side of the street. A block away, teenagers sat in front of a coffee shop smoking cigarettes and laughing. Honking horns and motorcycle engines were the perfect distraction. She dropped the whole accident thing and asked about my interest in Ivan Krychek. I told her about the telephone call from Alfie Gitchell. She stopped eating when I described Mather and what he told me. She sat in stony silence when I described my visit to Krychek's house. Her eyes turned dark and angry with the news that Mather and Anna Krychek had failed to tell me about Ivan's stint as a night watchman at the capitol building.

We ordered coffee and shared a slice of New York-style cheesecake. Jasmine insisted on paying the tab, despite my weak protest. We walked slowly back toward the car, stopping in the off-beat stores along the street before going into the Nob Hill Bar and Grill and getting a table in the corner. We both ordered a beer and glanced at the Cubs-Giants game on the big-screen television in the corner near the front door. Turned out she was a Giants fan.

I knew there was one question I still hadn't answered: How was I going to get over all of this and forget what happened?

17

Zihuatanejo

Harrison Grimes tasted the coffee, grimaced, and asked if Zihuatanejo had anything that resembled a Starbucks. Standard said maybe in Ixtapa, the pop-up resort area north of town, but he seldom went there.

"That bad?" Grimes said.

"It's fine if you like faux Mexico and a beach lined with high-rise hotels," Standard said. "This place suits me fine."

Grimes looked around at a scene that he seemed to be growing more and more fond of. Standard could tell that sitting in the shade, feet in the sand, overlooking the beach and the parade of people walking by were having a positive effect on the lawyer. It had done wonders for him. No reason it wouldn't do the same for Grimes.

When Standard first arrived in Mexico, the events that brought him there felt like they were tearing him apart. After a few days in the sun and nights in the palapa house on Emma's property, he began to feel his load lighten a bit then, over time, disappear … almost. Things that once seemed important faded away, replaced by a serenity steeped in warm, lazy days and cool, exotic nights. He was getting the sense that Grimes was starting to feel the same things.

Grimes asked Standard to tell him more about how he ended up in Zihuatanejo.

"This is not the time to get into details, Harry," Standard said. "Let's just say that after the accident and what happened with Proctor Scofield, I got lucky, made some money then ended up in the hospital. When I got out, I decided it was time to go. I found Zihuatanejo on a poster in the window of a travel agency."

"I'd like to hear those details some time."

"Sure," Standard said, not meaning it, then waited for Grimes to get back to why he was there.

"So, did you know yourself how you were going to get past what happened?" Grimes asked. "Did you tell her about it?"

Standard once had his own ideas about how to get over it, but hadn't shared it with anyone, not even Benny during their late nights of drinking and soul searching. Maybe it was the wine with lunch or the sleepy glow from the beer, but Jasmine Grant had changed all that. Her laid-back confidence had given him the feeling that all he had to do to make things right again was tell her everything. Bare his soul to someone he'd just met with no idea if it would help him or not. Maybe it was even simpler than that. Maybe he was like a stray cat hanging around the back door of anyone who showed even the slightest bit of affection. Whatever it was, it didn't make any difference. He didn't want to keep it all inside anymore, so he let it all out at one time, afraid to stop for fear of not finishing, grateful that Jasmine had the patience to listen and not interrupt.

"Let's put it this way, Harry," Standard said, finally. "I told her that I felt I owed a huge debt. Not in terms of money or legal bills, but more important than that. Two little girls were dead. No jury could wipe the slate clean, no matter how strongly they felt that it was just an accident and not a crime. Somewhere, someplace, I needed to find a way to make amends for what I'd done."

"And she was the type of person who would pick up on that right way," Grimes said.

Standard nodded. "She knew immediately that this was bigger than simply going to the girls' family and begging forgiveness or sending them money. She knew there was a debt against my soul, a debt I'd incurred by fate, by some force that put me and those two girls in the same place at the same time. She believed it would be fate that would allow me to repay that debt in full. Anything short of that was just a token payment. Pennies in a beggar's tin cup was the way she put it."

"She sounds like quite a woman," Grimes said. "I don't suppose her being part Asian had anything to do with it."

The comment surprised Standard. He had Grimes pegged as a buttoned-down lawyer who read nothing but briefs, case law and the bar review. Apparently, he was wrong.

"Don't tell me that in addition to labor law you're also an expert in eastern mysticism."

"Far from it," he said. "Just someone with an undergraduate degree in liberal arts."

"So you're familiar with Tao Teh Ching, one of the sources of a religion, Taoism? The I Ching? Tai Chi? All of that?"

"Probably not as much as your Ms. Grant."

Standard remembered Jasmine's eyes lighting up as she explained how Taoism was more of a way of life than a religion. How Tao translated to the path, the way. Teh was virtue. Ching was laws. Tao Teh Ching: The Law of Virtue and its Way. Lao Tse, an early contemporary of Confucius, wrote that misery may yield happiness; happiness may conceal misery; who can say which will be for the best?

Standard could still hear Jasmine's voice and feel her breath on his cheek when she spoke. How he let her words wind around him, pulling him closer until their faces were inches apart over the table and he was answering her in the same intimate way that she talked to him.

"It all made sense, up to a point," Standard said. "I told her there were times when I couldn't get comfortable. Wherever I was, I wanted to be somewhere else. Whatever I was doing, I wanted to be doing something else. I told her that I thought it was because I never saw a chance to determine my own fate, to jerk the steering wheel the other way even if it meant killing myself. After that, nothing was the same."

"And finding Ivan Krychek's killer would change all that," Grimes said. "Repay the debt you felt you owed."

"I guess. All I wanted to do was break even. If that worked then fine. If it was something else then that would be fine as well. But for the time being all I had was trying to unravel the mystery of who killed Krychek and why."

"So she dropped it there?"

"No. She brought up Lao Tse again and what he wrote about fate. I remember every word of it: 'Fate does not contend, yet all things are conquered by it; it does not ask, yet all things answer to it; it does not call, yet all things come to it; it does not plan, yet all things are determined by it.'"

"In other words, fate will make things even again," Grimes said. "Pretty heady stuff."

"It was, particularly for someone like me whose profession preached who, what, when and where, a little bit of why and little else. Or at least it used to. If she was right, would I get the chance to right the wrong, would it be unequivocal and would I even recognize it when the time came, if it ever did?"

Standard thought back to how she moved around the table to sit next to him and, in soft tones, explain how Taoism supports the concept of non-action, yet nothing is left undone. Things will develop naturally. In other words, she said, "Patience, John Standard, patience."

"Sounds like the two of you hit it off," Grimes said. "How did things go after that?"

He wasn't about to tell Grimes how she said no when he suggested another beer. How she passed on a chance to check out some of the shops along the street. How she gently squeezed the inside of his leg and told him without hesitation how badly she wanted to see the inside of his apartment. How, when he asked if she was one of those take-a-loser-to-bed freaks, her eyes turned a shade darker and slightly more exotic as she said, "Would it matter?"

"Let's put it this way," Standard said. "This is when things started getting really weird."

"So you're getting closer to Scofield?"

"In the end, all roads lead to Proctor Scofield."

18

Portland

There's nothing more pathetic, Harry, than a lonely man waiting for a woman to call. But there I was, hanging around the apartment hoping Jasmine would phone me and debating whether to call her. During our night together she asked what I liked. When I told her all I wanted was to forget for a while, it was all she needed to know. She'd been both soft and passionate, playful and serious, exotic and conventional. Memories of last year disappeared. The sad surroundings of my bedroom had become a playroom full of dark, mysterious places to explore and hide from the world. Remembering it brought back the urge to call her. It had only been a few hours since we'd walked together to her car, and I'd watched her drive away, waving at me through the Volvo's sunroof as she disappeared into traffic. When I got back to my apartment, I found the note she left attached to the bathroom mirror. It was written on a piece of paper in perfect block letters. It read: "All that ever stays the same is change. And I Dream. I Wander - Lao Tse." I read it three more times before carefully folding the note and placing it in the top drawer of the bureau in the bedroom.

I fired up my laptop to check my email, wanting to make sure the magazine in Philadelphia received the gun control article and the attachments. There was a note from the editor saying everything looked great and he would get back to me with any questions. I started feeling that things were brightening a bit. When I got to the post office, I even found a check from the tabloid for the story of how Ivan Krychek died at the hands of a satanic cult.

Feeling happy and flush, I walked down SW Broadway to one of the last Chinese restaurants in Chinatown for a dim sum lunch and a chance to read the morning paper. Roark and Landis were still on the front page as the featured acts in the aftermath of the gun-control debate. I read the story with a sense of relief that I was done for good with both of them. Or I thought.

The walk back uptown after lunch cleared my head of everything except Jasmine and the lingering uneasiness about being a target of a murder investigation. After spending the night with Jasmine, my status as Daryl Butcher's prime suspect seemed more like a bad dream. Except it wasn't. I couldn't lose the feeling that he or someone like him was following me around town. I shook it off and cruised through Nordstrom but resisted the urge to buy anything new despite the deplorable condition of my so-called wardrobe. Patience, I told myself; wait until the check from Philadelphia shows up. Maybe then I could afford a small upgrade.

When I got home, I called Alfie Gitchell, who listened without comment while I described my lunch with Butcher and his half-baked ideas about how I killed Ivan Krychek. Gitchell promised to talk to him, but quickly pointed out that Butcher was just doing his job and, after all, I was there the same day Krychek was killed. When I pointed out that thousands of gun nuts had been there as well, it didn't go over well. They were also suspects, Gitchell said, but none of them have the reputation I did. It sounded to me like he had bought into the gospel according to Daryl Butcher: Once a killer, always a killer. He made a few more excuses for Butcher, the last one being that he would eventually figure things out. I needed to be patient. There was that word again.

I let it go and asked what else he had learned. Turned out not much. Still no motive. The rope, hooks and piano wire found in the outhouse were available in any hardware or music store. Anna Krychek's story checked out. The airline and her family in California confirmed everything. In other words, she was nowhere near Salem the night Krychek died. Mather was way down on the investigation's list of priorities.

I hung up still feeling uncomfortable about being a suspect, but helpless to do anything about it.

So, with the gun-control article finished, I needed to start beating the bushes again for more work. I called the Reuter's bureau in Seattle to see if they needed someone to cover the U.S. Women's Open golf tournament, which started in three weeks at a course west of Portland. The bureau chief appreciated the reminder. He said to check into getting press credentials then get back to him before the tournament started. Before hanging up he asked if there were any new angles on the legalization of marijuana. I hung up after mumbling something about looking into it. I got on my laptop to pitch a few ideas to *The Huffington*

Post and *Politico*, not that either one of them paid anything more than beer money when I needed rent money.

I was still thinking about calling Jasmine when Verizon escorted Christine back into my life. The last time I saw her she was frozen in horrified silence while the police questioned me in the living room of our house. One look at her face and I knew I had something else to worry about besides a hit-and-run charge. Within hours she was on a plane back to Scottsdale and her parents. Now she's on the phone telling me her attorney says she's not supposed to talk to me. I told her I thought that was a great idea and started to hang up. That's when she said she had news for me.

I don't want to dwell on this, Harry, but what happened after I was arrested was not pretty. Photographers took pictures of her, shouted questions at her and looked through our garbage. Trucks with satellite dishes were parked up and down the street in front of our house. She saw the whole thing as humiliating; a front-row seat on how my profession had turned on me. She said it was all my fault, which it was, but I didn't need to hear it from her.

On the phone, we went back and forth like that until all the scabs were torn off our fraught relationship. Then she got down to why she really called: Our divorce will be final next month. Her wedding is scheduled for the end of August.

I knew about the divorce, but not about the wedding. Not that it mattered. I was living in a flea-bag apartment house, trying to pay the bills selling stories to the scum of the earth and my wife called to tell me her wedding plans. Not knowing what I should do, I just wished her luck and quickly hung up.

The image of what life had been with Christine and the reality of a three-room apartment sent me out the door again to get lost in the city. When I reached Tom McCall Waterfront Park, I stood along the Willamette River watching the cigarette butts, syringes and other trash wash up against the seawall. The dinner ship *Spirit of Portland* went by, churning dark water as it headed upstream with another wedding or retirement party on board. The sleek, white-and-green ship was well beyond the Marquam Bridge before I left to walk past the colorful tents going up for yet another festival celebrating either beer, wine, food or all three.

I followed SW Morrison Street into the heart of downtown again. At Pioneer Square, the street preachers were bringing a small group of disinterested shoppers up to date on the latest from heaven and hell. I grabbed an empty table in front of Starbucks. It felt good to be lost in a crowd, to know that none of the women walking by with packages containing new shoes or a new blouse cared who I was or what I'd done. I wondered how many of them would have done the same thing as Christine. Too many, I decided, then walked home. Somewhere along the way, I lost Christine again. This time for good.

At nine that night I thought again about calling Jasmine to ask if she could tell me where Krychek's parents lived. Instead, I decided that another trip to Delaney College was in order the next day to see if I could learn more about Krychek's research. At the same time, I would see if Jasmine was free for lunch. My hand was inches from the phone when it rang.

It was her. She apologized for calling so late, but she'd received something in the mail that I needed to see. It was from Ivan Krychek. It was a manuscript. The first draft of his doctoral dissertation. She repeated that I needed to see it.

Something in her voice bothered me. She sounded strained and tense, not at all what I expected from someone I'd just spent the night with. The sympathetic tone she shared with me at the tavern was gone. I didn't know her or her moods that well, so I let it pass. I waited to see if she was going to invite me to her house to pick up where we left off, which is exactly what she did … sort of.

I asked about the manuscript. She didn't want to tell me what it said. It was too complicated to discuss over the phone. I needed to read it for myself. Since it involved Krychek, I asked if she'd called the police. She said no. Why did he send it to you? She didn't know. I remember her next words: "Please come over. We can look at it together then decide what to do." She gave me her address and some vague directions.

Despite her odd tone, I got ready for what I was sure would be a repeat of the previous night. I showered, put on clean pants and a shirt and grabbed what I thought was a good bottle of wine off the shelf at the deli across the street. I drove across town convinced that the call from Jasmine so soon after hearing from Christine was another sign that life was turning around.

Her house was in a northeast Portland neighborhood that was a collection of two-and-three-story homes built in the early 1900s and remodeled as part of the gentrification of the inner city. Volvos,

Subarus, and other SUVs were parked in driveways and along tree-lined streets. Jasmine's house was a one-story bungalow with baskets of fuchsias hanging from the large, foursquare porch. Her Volvo sat in the driveway on the left side of the house. I parked at the curb and walked up toward the house. I remember a lamp from the living room throwing narrow squares of dim light onto the porch and the front lawn. A concrete walk led across the lawn and up to the porch. The front door was open, but the screen pulled closed. Classical music—Ravel, I thought—drifted out into the night. My breath shortened. There had been some clumsy moments the night before. There would be none tonight. I was sure of it.

I knocked on the screen door, expecting to see her appear at any second, barefoot and dressed in a flowered skirt and tie-dye top. Her face eager. Her smile suggestive. When no one answered, I knocked a little louder. Still nothing other than the music. I took a few steps to the left to peer in the front window at an orderly living room with knick-knacks on shelves, comfortable furniture, and colorful rugs. Yellow light from a floor lamp set between an easy chair and an overstuffed couch reflected off bookcases that lined the far wall. Art fair posters and little Chinese paintings in ornate frames decorated the off-white walls. The music came from a small black box on a shelf near a gas fireplace. Sonos, maybe, or something like it. Beyond the wall with the bookcases was the dining room. Behind that an archway that I assumed led to the kitchen. The only sign of Jasmine Grant was a coffee cup on a low table next to an easy chair and a faint scent of gardenias.

I know I keep saying this, Harry, but once again I got that feeling that something wasn't right. Call it a sixth sense. Call it what you like. I just couldn't shake it. She should be expecting me. She should be eager to give me a hug. Whisper something suggestive in my ear. Instead, there was only silence. I opened the screen door and stepped inside. The hallway in front of me led to the back of the house. A sitting room to the right had been turned into an office with a chair, laptop, and a printer, all sitting on a modular desk unit. The shelves on one wall were stuffed with books and three-ring binders.

On the left was the living room. I walked through it to the dining room with its round glass-topped table, four spindle-backed chairs and a sideboard. Beyond was a large, brightly lit kitchen. Expensive gourmet cookware hung from a chef's rack over a waist-high butcher's block. The refrigerator door was covered with little magnets that held up recipes, photos and a picture postcard that read, "Des Moines ... a Special Place."

Even after exploring Jasmine's body, it felt odd roaming around alone in her house. Everything was neat, clean and in its place compared to the disarray of my apartment. I put the bottle of wine on the counter, hoping that it wasn't cluttering things up too much. The only thing missing was Jasmine herself.

The house was still. It was as if the air had been compressed to mute the sounds of a humming refrigerator or creaking floorboards. A fruity aroma came from a potpourri on the gas range. I pushed open the door on the far side. It led back into the main hallway, the front door at the far end to the right. To the left a screened back door and small porch with neatly arranged recycling bins.

Where was she? I thought that maybe the invitation was part of a plan or a game. Maybe she was waiting on her bed covered with rose petals. Champagne chilling in an ice bucket on the nightstand. Good by me, I thought. The door on the other side of the hall was ajar. It had to be her bedroom. She had to be there, waiting. I gently pushed it open and peered inside, heart beating a little faster.

Harry, what came next was the most horrifying thing I'd ever seen. It still haunts me. Not a day goes by that I don't remember every detail. Jasmine Grant was in bed all right, but her arms were tied to the headboard, crucifixion style, a piano wire noose around her neck. Blood from where it cut into her flesh ran down her chest and soaked the flowered sheets a sickly black. More blood splattered on the wall behind her like a macabre halo. Her eyes were open. Her tongue grotesque. The swampy smell of blood, urine and feces filled the room. All I could think was no, no, no. This couldn't be happening. Not to her. The body on the bed was a parody of the woman I'd been with the night before. Blood covered the breasts where I'd laid my head and listened to her heart. At first, I wanted to throw up, then I wanted to hold her, but couldn't bring myself to do it. Would her skin be cold yet? It didn't matter. That wasn't the way I wanted to remember the last time I touched her.

19

Playa la Ropa, Zihuatanejo

Harrison Grimes stared across the table at Standard. The stunned look on his face said he was just as horrified by what he'd heard as Standard. He'd come to Mexico to learn about one death only to come face to face with two more.

"Jesus, John," he said. "I never saw that coming. I'm so sorry. I don't know what to say."

It was getting on toward noon. Standard tried to erase the memory of finding Jasmine Grant's body by looking out at the bay and the ocean beyond. He knew it wouldn't happen. Just telling Grimes about it made the picture of that night come back in all its horror. The usual passers-by plus a few new ones were wandering up and down the beach, playing tag with the weak waves. When he looked down at The Tortuga's line of empty cabanas, he saw the small group of expats who played Scrabble every day. Ranger Bob, the group's ringleader and a retired Texas Ranger, had moved to Mexico hoping that his pension would go further than in Dallas. Bob waved at Standard while patting his backpack to indicate he was still armed. It was his way of renewing their running joke about having friends who drink and carry weapons. Standard waved back then, his emotions controlled as much as they would ever be, turned his attention to the still-stunned Grimes.

"The way in which Jasmine Grant died was Ivan Krychek all over again. Right down to the piano wire," Standard explained. "The only difference was that she lived in a world of tea bags, term papers, and tie-dye. You'd think that kind of violence would never creep into her world and destroy her. But it had. My first thought was that my curiosity about Ivan Krychek and his research made me somehow responsible for her death. It was enough to drive me crazy."

The look on Grimes' face was a mixture of sympathy for Standard and confusion over what to say next. All he could manage was to mutter another "I'm so sorry." Standard said thanks then looked around for Pablo the waiter. It was time for a drink.

"What did you do?" Grimes asked just to fill the silence.

"I backed out of the door and across the hallway into the kitchen. I leaned over the sink thinking I was going to throw up. I turned on the faucet and splashed enough cold water on my face to keep the bile down. I remember thinking that maybe it wasn't her; that it was all a mistake and I'd walked into the wrong house. But no. It was her. I just didn't understand why anyone would kill her, especially in that way."

Grimes got a pained look on his face. "I sense another Daryl Butcher encounter coming up."

"You guessed it," Standard said, shaking his head then explaining that calling the police made the most sense. "The downside was Butcher and what he would think about finding me at another murder scene. I thought about leaving, but what if someone had seen me or could identify my car? It wouldn't be the first time that had happened. Not only that, it would give Butcher all the motive he needed."

Grimes shifted in his seat, looking and feeling uncomfortable. What Standard had experienced was beyond anything he could imagine. He searched for words. "What about the manuscript?" he finally asked. "The one she told you about over the phone."

"Given what happened, I'd forgotten all about it, but remembered just as I reached for the phone. On my drive to her house I thought that maybe there was no manuscript, only a ruse to get me to come over. Now, after seeing her body, I wasn't so sure."

After Pablo delivered two bottles of Corona and a plate of fresh-cut limes, they drank in silence before paying the bill and walking up the beach to another restaurant for lunch. At a place called Paty's, they got a table overlooking the beach. Standard suggested they order ceviche then had to explain what it was. Grimes grimaced, saying he'd rather have something that was cooked. When Standard said tacos al pastor and described what that was, Grimes gave an enthusiastic nod. He did the same when Standard told the waiter to also bring two margaritas. The icy drink would cut through the heat that was just starting to build up. If it helped either of them erase the image of Jasmine Grant, so much the better.

"So you didn't call the police right away?" Grimes said, seemingly eager to hear what happened next.

"No. That's when I remembered the manuscript. If there was one. After looking around at the kitchen countertops, I moved through the dining room and living room, backtracking toward the front door. I saw nothing that looked like a manuscript. In the office next to the computer I found a large manila envelope addressed to Jasmine. The postmark was the previous Friday. The return address was the house on Baltusrol Way. The envelope was empty. Careful not to leave fingerprints, I poked around in the drawers and along the bookshelves looking for anything that might resemble a manuscript. Finding nothing, I thought about going back into her room, but that would mean seeing her again. No way. If the manuscript was in there then let the police find it.

"So you called the police?"

Standard explained that he called Alfie Gitchell at home rather than using 911. Within minutes came the far-off howl of sirens. Soon the street was filled with squad cars. The next two hours were pretty much what anyone would expect, he said. Red and white lights reflecting off houses and cars. Squawking police radios. Crime lab vans. Yellow tape strung between trees. Gawking neighbors in bathrobes. People wearing latex gloves scurrying in and out of Jasmine's house. Jasmine herself, reduced to an indistinguishable shape in a black body bag. And, of course, Daryl Butcher.

"The first uniform to show up immediately hustled me into the garage. The image of Jasmine's body still haunted me. Visions of what her last moments must've been like made me want to run outside and suck in lungs full of cool night air, but the officer blocked the door. I tried to recall what she looked like across the table at lunch or lying next to me, but her face seemed distant, like looking at her backward through binoculars. Thinking about what we had been doing just twenty-four hours earlier only made things worse. I replayed our brief time together, concentrating hard on the way she talked and the inflections in her voice then compared it to the way she sounded on the telephone more than an hour earlier. The difference was too great. She should've been excited about being together, her voice eager, playful, and full of promise. When she left that morning, she happily waved back at me through the sunroof of her car. We were like little kids. But there was none of that when she called to tell me about the manuscript. Then it hit me. Jasmine Grant hadn't been alone when she called. Someone had been with her. Someone who made her call me, maybe even coached her. Someone who wanted two thing— the manuscript and to frame me for her murder."

Finished with lunch, they ordered another round of margaritas that went down way too easily. The tables around them filled up with newly arrived tourists, some still pale, others a bright pink from trying to get a tan in one day. Some struggled with the extensive menu. Others were content with beer and chips.

"Is this where Butcher comes in again?" Grimes said.

"In living color."

20
Portland

Butcher showed up with a blue swizzle stick in the shape of a pirate sword in the corner of his mouth and a smug look on his face. I wasn't surprised, but just seeing him made me feel like any hope of finding the killer or killers of Jasmine Grant and Ivan Krychek was lost.

"I don't have to remind you that there had been two murders and you've shown up at both," he said. He took out a small notebook and waited for me to explain.

"I'll keep this short and talk slowly," I said. "We had a date. I showed up. She was already dead. Did you get all that?"

Butcher's laugh was a kind of snort. He asked about the wine on the kitchen counter. I said it was mine. Then, in pure Daryl Butcher style, he asked, "How long you been fuckin' her?"

Burying a fist in Butcher's face wouldn't help my cause, but I was already at the point of not caring. It wasn't just Jasmine's murder, but everything that had happened. During dinner at Angelina's, Jasmine had compared me to a character in a Greek tragedy. I considered myself more like a figure out of Greek mythology, forced into performing endless deeds by the bored and meddlesome gods of Olympus. In other words, my life was already suddenly out of control again, and now Butcher wanted to push it one step farther. I fought back the anger rather than give Butcher the satisfaction of watching me lose my grip. I desperately searched the garage for something to focus on that would help make dealing with him bearable. A half-empty bag of steer manure did the trick. I sucked it up and told him that I had met her a couple of days ago at Delaney College. We had dinner that night and lunch the next day. We hit it off and I came down here tonight to see her again.

Butcher sneered and flipped the swizzle stick to the other side of his mouth. He rattled off some theory about how me, Krychek and Grant were into a kinky, three-way thing that got out of hand. I was just about to explain to him that ignorance was invincible when the rumpled and cranky Alfie Gitchell showed up. He had a cigarette wedged in the corner of his mouth. Baggy jeans, grass-stained tennis shoes, and sun-bleached golf shirt made him look like he might have a life outside the police department, just not much of one.

Gitchell nodded at me then took Butcher out into the driveway. Through the garage door I could see the suddenly subservient Butcher reading his notes and looking back into the garage. Gitchell listened as Butcher used his swizzle stick to point in my direction. When Gitchell finally nodded, Butcher headed down the driveway toward the street.

Gitchell walked back to the garage to tell me what I already knew: Butcher wanted to arrest me for murder. When I started to protest, he told me to calm down then pulled the last cigarette out of a rumpled pack. "There's more to homicide investigations than circumstantial evidence," he told me. "You're as much a suspect as anyone else who happened to be at two murder scenes."

I didn't find that comforting.

After eyeing each other for a few seconds, I blinked first, telling Gitchell everything—or almost everything. For reasons I wasn't sure about, I left out anything to do with Krychek's manuscript. Telling Gitchell about the document might give the police a plausible motive for Jasmine's death. It might even get me off the hook, not that I should be on one anyway, and send Butcher charging rhino-like after someone or something else. Still, I didn't do it. It would be safer to know what was in the manuscript before telling Gitchell or Butcher that it even existed.

Gitchell nodded, apparently accepting my story that Jasmine had invited me to her house for a sleep-over and when I got there, she was dead. He asked about fingerprints. I said he'd find mine, but not anywhere they shouldn't be. After that, the only thing we agreed on was that between when she called me and when I got there someone just happened to break into her house and kill her, using piano wire just like Ivan Krychek. I had my own theory. It began and ended with Krychek's missing manuscript and what it said. It was the only reason I could think of for killing her.

Gitchell glanced out the door. Butcher stood at the end of the driveway talking to a woman in a terry-cloth robe and fuzzy slippers. Large curlers bounced as she gestured toward my car then at Jasmine's house. Standing in the background were three other women, all looking ready for bed, nodding their collective heads. Gitchell gave me a skeptical look then warned me once again not to play games.

"I don't know what's going on here," he said, "but whatever it is you're in over your head. If you know something you're not telling me, you'd better be damn careful. Whoever did this doesn't dance, John. He's one sick son of a bitch."

After another warning that I'd better be telling the truth, he reminded me that it was still Butcher's case and it wasn't going to take much to convince him that a killer wouldn't hang around and call the police. Gitchell said it while we both watched the ambulance drive away with Jasmine's body.

"You did the right thing," he said. "Now, wait here."

He walked down the driveway to where Butcher was still questioning the neighbors. They talked for a few minutes. When he came back, he said I was free to go. I walked toward the street. The crowd watched me and whispered to each other, but at least nobody yelled "Killer." When I got to my car, Butcher was leaning against the front fender. I ignored him and got behind the wheel. The engine had just started when the detective leaned in the driver's side window.

If Gitchell thought I was innocent, Butcher wasn't convinced. "I think you're a killer, word man," he said. "I can't prove it yet, but I will and when I do not even your buddy Gitchell is going to save your sorry ass." I rolled up the window, backed out of the driveway and drove through the crowd of people.

After that I just drove aimlessly around the eastside of Portland trying to sort things out. I had known Jasmine Grant for a little less than thirty-six hours but felt like I'd lost a limb. I had hoped that she would represent a turning point in my string of bad luck. Instead, she was another tragic chapter in the pathetic saga that had become my life.

After an hour, I found myself looking for the kind of dive bar that fit my mood. A sports pub on a busy intersection looked like it would work. It was empty except for two men at the bar. The décor was a half-dozen television sets turned to six different channels and an equal number of video poker machines. I ordered a beer from the bartender and took it out to an empty patio surrounded by a wooden fence that did little to mute the noise of passing cars and trucks. Body blows of anger and disappointment kept pounding at me. The beer sat untouched while I tried to remember every moment with Jasmine, every touch, every word, the look on her face. How she said that if anything ever happened to her, I would be the first person she'd turn to.

Despite the late hour, traffic swooshed by a few feet on the other side of the fence. Headlights flickering through the gaps sent fingers of light dancing across the cracked concrete. The bartender poked his head outside, noticed my beer was still full and disappeared back into the dark bar. Sipping the now-warm beer, I told myself to get a grip. At one point I said it loud enough that I had to look around to make sure I was alone.

Finding Jasmine's killer was the only option. I owed her that much. Hell, I owed myself that much. Knowing who killed her and why wouldn't bring her back any more than a jury's verdict would bring back two dead girls. All I could hope for was that it would chase away the demons and square me with the world.

The key was the Krychek manuscript. If there was such a thing then the odds were that Jasmine had died for it, so its contents must be worth at least one life and probably two, if Krychek counted. Why had he sent it to Jasmine? Did he know someone was after it? If he did, what other precautions would he take? Where would a graduate student keep a document as important as a doctoral dissertation? As important to kill for?

I ran through the possibilities then stopped on the one that was last on the list. I stood up and looked out over the top of the fence. The spire on Mayfield Hall jutted upward from the campus of Delaney College four blocks away. I drained the last of the warm beer and left.

I've had some bad luck, Harry, but they weren't the result of bad decisions. That was about to change. I had reached a point where what was going to happen couldn't be any worse than what had already happened. Even if it landed me in jail, would a cell be any worse than my apartment? Only one way to find out.

After leaving the tavern, I got in my car and drove around until I found the store with the things I needed. By two a.m. I was parked in the visitor's lot of Delaney College, staring out at the late-night calm. The campus looked different at night. The tree-lined paths crisscrossing the green lawns were empty of students. The scattered lights in the windows of the dormitories made the buildings look like half-finished bingo cards. Despite the quiet, I felt reluctant to move out of the small grove of Madrone trees. The fifty yards to the front steps of the building that housed the Political Science Department looked more like a mile.

After being accused of two murders, breaking and entering didn't seem all that serious. At least that's how I rationalized it after leaving the tavern, finding an all-night drug store, and buying a roll of masking tape and a box of rubber gloves, a pair of which were tucked inside my pants pocket. As incriminating as the purchases were, the woman behind the counter barely looked up as I stuffed all of it in my backpack.

My goal was to find Krychek's manuscript. That wasn't going to happen hanging around my apartment or in a bar. I had to take Jasmine at her word that Ivan Krychek had mailed her a draft of his doctoral dissertation. It must have been a copy. There were no original manuscripts anymore. Everything existed on computer hard drives, thumb drives or in the Cloud. There was no laptop or desktop in Krychek's house, at least none that I saw, so there had to be one in his office at the college. I guessed that Krychek had to have been a laptop guy, taking it with him wherever he went, working on his dissertation in cafes and coffee shops or at home. But not while he was patrolling the state fairgrounds. The best place was his office.

I didn't have a plan. My hope was that the doors to the building were unlocked, that the tiny cubicle that passed for Krychek's office was open and that a clearly labeled manuscript was sitting on the desk waiting to be picked up. I could just step in, grab it and leave. In and out in a matter of a few seconds. Not likely, which was why I had my car's tire iron in my backpack.

Another option would be to come back the next day with a simple request to see Krychek's office. At least then I might find out if Krychek even had a computer. That wouldn't work, though. No one would leave me alone in the office. There had to be a laptop. Simple as that. I just needed time to see if it was there.

I pulled a baseball cap down tight on my head while staring at the darkened building. The large, ornate windows were hidden in shadows. The ivy clinging to the rock walls reminded me of fingers stretching from the ground toward the back-lit spire that crowned the old building. After a deep breath, I walked out of the stand of Madrones and moved casually across the lawn toward the front steps of Mayfield Hall, trying my best to look like someone who belonged there, even at that hour.

I walked out into a circle of light cast from a nearby streetlamp. The few steps from the trees to the stairs seemed to take minutes instead of seconds. When I reached the steep steps up to the front door, I moved around to the left side of the staircase. I knew from my first visit to the building that there had to be an outside stairwell with steps that led down to the basement level. I was right. It was narrow, damp and hidden behind the bushes. Finding the top step, I groped along the wall for the handrail then carefully worked down a dozen steps that felt slick and mossy. Reaching the bottom, I put on the rubber gloves, felt around for the doorknob and turned it slowly. Locked. I put my face to the glass, looking for lights inside. Seeing none, I pulled the masking tape from my backpack. The window in the door was divided into six separate panes of glass, each about the size of a sheet of typing paper. Covering the one closest to the doorknob with the tape, I smashed the glass with my elbow. The tape kept all but a few small pieces of glass from crashing to the floor. I reached inside and opened the old, bolt-action lock.

So far, so good. I had violated the laws against breaking-and-entering without setting off any alarms. At least none I could hear. Fireworks and sirens might be going off at the police department or at some security company, but all I felt or heard was peace and quiet. I knew all along that the best thing to do was get this over with as fast as possible. I pulled the tire iron out of my backpack, held it in a sweaty hand and went inside.

My brazenness surprised even me, Harry. The reluctance I felt standing in the shadows of the Madrones disappeared. In its place was a sense that a line had been crossed. This time intentionally. The shattered glass far exceeded the reality that came with the buying of gloves and tape at a drugstore.

Not hearing the sound of sirens, my heartbeat slowed a bit and my breathing returned to normal, no more short gasps. My squeaking shoes on the linoleum floor sounded like gunshots. Before the sound died, I darted into an alcove near a porcelain water fountain. Reckless didn't mean stupid, Harry, so I stood in the dark listening for any sound that told me I wasn't alone. The only sounds were the faint ticks and creaks of the aging building. I stepped back into the hallway and walked another thirty feet. At the entry to the stairs leading up to the main floor, I crossed to the other side of the hall and felt my way past each door. One door. Two. Three. In the dim light, I could just make out the name "Ivan Krychek" on the white card in the thin, brass frame on the fourth door. The police crime tape was gone. The door was locked. I slipped the tire iron in between the lock and the jamb. With a quick push, the door popped open with only minimal damage. The light switch was inside on the wall to the right.

The office was little more than a closet with floor-to-ceiling shelves filled with a jumble of books, magazines, and three-ring binders with colorful spines. Of the dozens of binders, any one of them could be the manuscript. On one wall was a cluttered metal desk piled high with papers that nearly covered the laptop. I started on the shelves immediately to the right, running a finger along the books, stopping at each binder to read the title. Ten minutes of searching turned up nothing but a deeper understanding of the kind of material aspiring political science professors were required to read. There was no book, binder or anything that resembled a dissertation, let alone a title related to the polarization of American politics.

I sat down at the desk and turned on the laptop. The hard drive whirred and buzzed until it asked for a password. I stared at the screen then pawed through the desk drawers looking for a password or anything that might give me a clue to how to get into Krychek's computer. I scanned the yellow sticky notes on the shelf above the desk. Nothing. Finally, I just unplugged the laptop, gathered up a few cords and stuck it all in my backpack. I'd figure out later how to get into it.

Turning out the light, I waited for my eyes to adjust to the dark. Then I opened the door and began retracing my steps down the hallway. The alcove with the water fountain was just a few feet away when I heard the noise. It came from behind me, back down the hall toward Krychek's office. It resembled the faint squeak of new basketball shoes on a hardwood floor. There was only one sound. Nothing before. Nothing after. It didn't matter. I knew I was no longer alone. I could sense it.

I ducked into the alcove and peered back toward Krychek's office. As if on cue, the figure of a man appeared at the bottom of the stairs. He had no features, everything was black from head to foot, a shadow against the dark gray background. He was large, both in height and weight, but moved with a certain quickness. His head moved back and forth in swift glances in both directions. He moved away from the far end of the hall then stopped at Krychek's office. Without testing the doorknob or noticing what little damage I had done to the jamb, he moved back a step and smashed the door open with a short, violent kick. When he disappeared inside that was my chance. Before the office light came on, I ran down the last thirty feet of the hallway and out the basement door.

Standing in the stairwell, I fought the urge to run like hell. I had what I came for and I had no idea who the other guy was. I remember a dim light shining through the bushes, lattice patterns on the wall, water dripping from a leaky faucet near the top step. Think, I thought. Who was the man in Krychek's office? Why was he there? Was it for the same reason I was? If it was, he was too late. It wouldn't take him long to figure that out. Then what would he do?

I moved two steps closer to the top of the stairs before deciding to stay. Don't ask me why, Harry. I was in so deep at that point it was worth playing out the string. I knew the man was there. He knew nothing about me. It was time to change that.

I took a deep breath then went back down the dark stairwell. The light in Krychek's office was still shining across the hallway's linoleum floor. I watched for a few more seconds then grabbed the basement door. That was the moment of truth, Harry. No turning back. I opened the door as wide as possible then slammed it shut with enough force that the glass from the broken window shattered. Hundreds of small pieces flew across the waxed floor. The light in the office at the end of the hall went out the same time the sound died away.

Sprinting up the stairs, I set the backpack on the ground, pulled the tire iron out and ducked behind the rock wall that sat atop the descending stairwell, parallel to the front of the building. It was three-feet high and hidden from the open area in front of Mayfield Hall by a dense laurel hedge. There was just enough room to see both the steep stairs to the main entrance above and the basement door below. Either way, I was good regardless of which exit the man used.

I waited. The dampness of dead leaves soaked through the knees of my pants. I swatted at cobwebs. Something flew past my face. A car drove by on the street adjacent to the building, the vehicle's head and taillights visible through a line of trees. As if knowing something was about to happen, the car pulled away just as the basement door slowly opened. I tried concentrating on breathing normally and waiting. I didn't have to wait long.

First came the crunch of footsteps on broken glass. Then came the sound of shoes on the wet moss that covered the steps. The man in black was probably less than two feet away, separated only by the thickness of the rock wall. I tightened my grip on the tire iron and I listened for two more steps. One. Two. I stood up, hoping my timing was perfect. I gripped the tire iron a little harder.

The man's head appeared on the other side of the wall at the same moment I stood up. He was looking straight ahead, the same direction as the large knife in his right hand. In one swift motion, I brought the tire iron down across his forearm. I heard a crunch followed by a scream cut short when I backhanded the metal bar into his hooded face. The knife rattled on the steps. The man in black let out a groan then tumbled down the stairs into a heap at the bottom. I jumped the wall and ran down the steps. I stood over the dark figure, ready with the tire iron if he tried to get up. There was no need. The man lay motionless except for the gentle rise and fall of his chest. One arm lay bent at an odd angle. The black mask looked damp and sticky. I reached down and snatched off the hood. It slid off easily to let Buck Mather's shaved head drop back to the concrete with a soft thud.

21

Playa la Ropa, Zihuatanejo

"Mather," Harrison Grimes said. "I knew it."

Standard held up his hand, telling the lawyer to slow down. "Looking at Mather unconscious at the bottom of the stairs, things sort of fell into place. What tied everything together was Krychek and his manuscript. Krychek wrote it and he was dead. Jasmine Grant had it, now she was dead. But what did Mather want with the draft of a doctoral dissertation? He seemed more like a *Guns & Ammo* type to me. All I could figure is that Mather was after all copies of the manuscript. Maybe Krychek told him he sent one to Jasmine. Maybe he got lucky finding one at her house. Maybe he figured out the same thing I did and went to Krychek's office."

A look of concern crossed Grimes' face. "Two people died because of that manuscript and now you have it," he said.

"Exactly."

After Grimes paid the bill, they walked up the hill to his hotel. They agreed to pick things up again in the morning over another breakfast at The Tortuga. After Grimes left to go up to his room, Standard called Arturo then waited in the hotel lobby for the taxi to show up.

"Mango's," Standard said, climbing in the back seat. On the way, he called Special Ed and told him where he was headed.

"I'm at the marina," Ed said. "I'll be there in twenty minutes."

~*~

By most estimations, Ed was the richest man in Zihuatanejo, American or Mexican. He'd made a fortune during the dot com bubble of the late nineties, sold out before it burst and moved to Mexico. He started a charter fishing business with a boat called *Tuna Warrior* and tricked it out with the same electronics that made him rich. He'd earned the name Special Ed because most people thought he was just another burned out surfer roaming the beaches looking for customers. Standard and Ed had forged a friendship over a few questionable adventures and a lot of beer.

After Arturo dropped him at Mango's, Standard got a seat at the bar as far from the crowd of regulars as possible. He was halfway through a bottle of Corona when Ed arrived.

"What's up?" Ed asked after getting a Corona of his own plus a shot of Don Julio. "You sounded on the phone like you've got something on your mind. This isn't going to be another one of those crazy …"

"No. I just need your advice."

Ed had spent the summer at a house he owned on Orcas Island in the State of Washington. Now that the rainy season was over, he had returned to Zihuatanejo and back in uniform—baggy red shorts, T-shirt with the image of a leaping marlin on the pocket, a patch over his left eye and a do-rag on his head.

Standard filled him in on Harrison Grimes, his search for what happened to a wealthy tech giant and how he was drawing the story out as long as he could until he found out what Grimes was really up to.

"Who's this dead guy he wants to know about?" Ed asked.

"Proctor Scofield."

Ed barked out a laugh. "You're shitting me."

"You knew him?"

"Of course. Everyone in my business knew him. A real piece of work. Back in the mid-nineties he tried to buy my company and everybody else's best I could tell. I didn't like the guy, so I told him no, even when he kept sweetening the offer. When I saw the dot-com era coming to an end, I sold out to one of his competitors. Scofield called me up and yelled at me until I finally hung up. Turns out that four years later he bought out his competitor and ended up with my company in the deal, paying a hell of a lot more than what he offered to pay me."

"So there was a reason they called him the Prince of Snakes?"

"I guess. Couldn't prove it by me."

After ordering another round, Ed asked if he thought Grimes was on the level.

"Good question," Standard said. "I can't seem to get any answers about what he or his firm are going to get out of this. This drug smuggler they're representing claims to have inside information about how Scofield died. But I've read his deposition. He doesn't know much."

"But I take it you do."

Standard nodded.

"Are you going to tell me about it?"

"Let's just say there are only two people who know the truth."

"You and who else?"

"Sorry, Ed, but I've made promises."

"Fair enough," Ed said, "but in the meantime let me tell you something. In all my years of doing business I learned one thing about lawyers—they do everything for a reason and the reason is usually money. Not those guys who take the short money to be prosecutors or public defenders. I'm talking about the corporate lawyers. The pin-striped, country club crowd."

Standard had already guessed that Grimes and his firm were representing Nico the Drug Smuggler for reasons other than out of the goodness of their hearts. He just didn't know what it was. It was time to find out.

"How about we arrange a little ocean voyage for Grimes?" Standard suggested. "Give you a chance to meet him and tell me what you think."

Ed thought for a minute. "The *Tuna Warrior* is not ready for fishing yet, but good enough for a little outing. How about Playa Manzanillo?"

Standard smiled. "Perfect. Tomorrow work?"

"I'll set it up. City pier at noon."

They sealed the deal with a second round.

~*~

Standard got to The Tortuga early the next morning. Ranger Bob and his posse were already there, huddled around the Scrabble board while trading opinions about the sad state of the American political system from the relative safety of a Mexican beach. The group included Tan Man, the rotund Massachusetts furniture salesman dedicated to achieving the perfect tan by spending endless hours in the sun; Señora Lora, a retired librarian from eastern Idaho with skinny legs, a muffin top and shoulder-length gray hair; Nigel, the pale, toupee-topped Canadian who came to town one month a year to escape his mother and visit his gay lover; and the always entertaining Fall-Down Phil, the gangly electrician from western Montana, who got his name from the numerous times he'd fallen down and knocked himself out. Bert Bert and Hilda Hilda, from Walla Walla, rounded out the group. Standard stopped by their table to say hello and welcome them back for another season.

"When did you get in?" Bert asked.

When Standard said he never left it generated blank stares followed by a collective chorus of "Really?"

Standard dropped his backpack at his usual table, ordered breakfast from Pablo then took off on a jog along the half-mile of Playa la Ropa. By the time he returned, his breakfast was on the table along with a day-old *USA Today*. Grimes got there thirty minutes later. He sat down and ordered breakfast as soon as Pablo showed up with more coffee.

"Last night I kept thinking about what you did to Buck Mather," Grimes said. "That took a lot of nerve. Not sure how smart it was, though."

"It was actually pretty stupid, Harry, but what did I have to lose? I was already a suspect in two murders and had just committed my first B and E followed by my first theft. Adding assault and battery to the list didn't seem like that big of a deal."

The look on Grimes' face showed he clearly didn't agree, but let it go. "So, now you have Krychek's laptop. What did you do with it?"

22

The Oregon Coast

I did what any self-respecting criminal would do, Harry—I hightailed it out of town.

The decision to head for the coast was instinctive. Any direction would have worked—east into the Cascade Mountains or south toward California. Staying in Portland or going back to my apartment were never options. I only wanted to disappear for a while, to distance myself from images of Buck Mather and Jasmine Grant.

The hard part was not jumping to conclusions about Mather and whether he'd killed Jasmine. But if Mather wasn't the killer, then what was he doing in Krychek's office and who sent him there? Somehow Krychek's manuscript was involved. I knew it. Felt it. But how?

Outside of Portland, I stopped at an all-night grocery store for gas and something to eat, settling for chips, jerky and two cans of beer then ate and drank while waiting for the tank to fill. Ten miles down the road I popped the second can of beer and settled back, nursing it while driving through the darkness. The car moved from fog bank to fog bank. The thick patches of gray provided brief moments of safety before bursting into the open again. I rolled up the window to keep the dampness out then down again, over and over.

Driving at night used to offer rare moments of solitude. Riding along in anonymity behind headlights, the radio tuned to a jazz station, alone with thoughts and feelings. But in the months following the accident, I'd done everything possible to avoid it. Even at dusk, I tried to get home before the streetlights came on. I'd creep along below the posted speed limit, paying more attention to the sidewalks and curbs than what was on the street ahead. Rear-ending someone seemed preferable to running over them. Eventually, the necessity of moving around prevailed, but even now, a year later, I could remember how quickly things happened and what might be ahead around the next bend. Maybe it was someone walking along the side of the road, someone in the wrong place at the wrong time, someone who would send my life careening off again into some new, detestable direction. I slowed the car another five miles an hour and turned up the radio to make sure I stayed awake.

I toyed with the idea of calling Alfie Gitchell about what happened at the college but wasn't sure what to say. First, Mather wasn't exactly the political science type, which meant someone must have sent him to Krychek's office. Second, assuming Mather was the killer, why commit two murders over a manuscript by a graduate student at a backwater college? Must be a hell of a manuscript, I thought. So, it was time to find out. I looked over at my backpack on the passenger seat, wondering what mysteries, if any, the laptop inside would solve.

As I crossed the summit of the Coast Range and started down the other side, the curves became sharper, the road winding through the rain forest along the Salmon River. Fog banks became thicker, but less frequent. I felt like a feral cat, invisible to anything posing a threat. Lincoln City was a ghost town at four in the morning; Highway 101 a darkened bowling alley. At the north end of the city, I turned off the highway and followed a wide residential street into an area known as Roads End. It's an artsy enclave wedged in between Lincoln City and a rocky point of land that stuck like a finger into the Pacific Ocean. Just past a seafood restaurant favored by tourists was a small state park with a few parking spots, a restroom, and access to a sandy beach that fronted Roads End's modest-looking, but high-priced homes. Parking a few spots away from two slumbering motor homes, I turned off the engine and sat with the window down listening to waves crashing onto the sand. Instead of crawling into the back to sleep, I sat immobile, smoking cigarettes, and watching thin clouds drift past a million stars.

There was every reason to be paranoid, to believe that somehow, I had been followed and that there would be a price to pay for what happened at Mayfield Hall. Instead, I didn't care who found me or why. Eventually, sleep came with the sound of the ocean and the smell of a salty breeze. It was the sleep of the dead. A sleep for the dead.

The next morning started with the rumble of the diesel engine of one of the motor homes. I jerked awake to the smell and noise. An old man in baggy cargo shorts, sandals and a golf shirt fussed around the outside of a huge Winnebago. When the RV finally drove away, I walked across the parking lot to the restrooms to wash up, letting the roughness of the paper towels erase the last bits of sleep.

Back on Highway 101, I drove south until spotting a small café in a nondescript strip mall. I found an empty booth in the back, ordered coffee and toast from a tired-looking waitress and pulled Krychek's laptop out of the backpack. I fired it up and got as far as the password barrier before calling Benny Orlando for help.

"I usually don't help anyone before ten o'clock," he said.

I asked him to humor me then described the laptop, but not how I got it. He said he needed a few minutes and put me on hold. When he came back on the line he asked for the maker of the laptop and the model number. After I gave him both he put me on hold again for ten minutes then spent another twenty walking me through a series of commands I'd never heard of that opened screens I'd never seen before. Magically, the computer came to life with a screen full of familiar Microsoft icons. I thanked Benny and hung up.

I clicked on the word processing application. At the top of the list was "DOCTORATE." I double clicked and opened a document titled: "The Right versus The Left: A Study of the Polarization of Politics in America." Bingo. I'd found it, but what was it?

The unfinished document was forty-five pages and fifteen-thousand words. I ordered more coffee and started reading.

It didn't take long to figure out that Ivan Krychek had a firm grasp of the obvious. A thousand words in and I realized that I could have learned much of the same stuff by watching a couple of hours of CNN. That didn't seem to bother Krychek. He relied on statistics, charts and graphs about election results and voter preferences to demonstrate how most Americans held moderate political views but were faced more often than not with a choice between two evils. It was all familiar stuff, Harry. Right versus left. Conservative versus liberal. Truth versus lies. Opinion replacing facts. Partisan cable news. The political pendulum swinging back and forth between the two extremes. Political and policy gridlock. The rise of more conspiracy theories such as child-sex rings, staged school shootings, and false-flag demonstrations. Rants about wedge issues such as immigration and global warming. The result, he predicted, was an erosion of faith in institutions such as elections, the criminal justice system, the courts, a free press, even the postal service. A decline in voter participation as a result of apathy and voter-suppression laws.

I could go on, but I think you get the point, Harry. I knew I was. Krychek's apocalyptic view of the future of the country made for interesting reading but, best I could tell, nothing worth getting killed over. Krychek was either a visionary or a crackpot. Maybe neither—just a student trying to produce a paper worthy of a doctorate. In the end, Jasmine had been right: The zealousness of Krychek's opinions far outweighed his supporting evidence.

That's when things careened off in a direction I didn't see coming. Krychek started speculating about a future in which the political process would be left open to manipulation by anyone with the money and foresight to recognize the depth of the polarization and take advantage of it. This person or persons, Krychek wrote, would more than likely hold an apolitical viewpoint. In other words, they wouldn't care which side won, because they had feet in both camps. To bolster his argument, Krychek delved into the background of the two candidates he felt best demonstrated the polarization of politics, at least in Oregon, which he conveniently deemed a microcosm of the national political stage. Guess who it was, Harry? Brad Roark and Kingsley Landis.

The tale that emerged in the next ten pages was of two men totally ill-equipped and unprepared for their roles as the poster children for their divergent political philosophies. Yet both stood on the verge of careers that would make one of them governor and probably more. In Krychek's ivory-tower world, Roark and Landis were the Romulus and Remus of evil. What he didn't know or at least didn't write about was the identity of the she-wolf who raised them.

According to Krychek, Roark and Landis met on the first day of classes at the University of Oregon. They were freshmen drawn together by their similar upbringings, their overwhelming passion for the social side of college life and their disdain for anything that smacked of why they were there—an education. Roark had grown up in a wealthy suburb on Portland's west side, the youngest son of a successful car dealer, who used his money to keep his children in expensive automobiles and out of scrapes with the law. Landis fared almost as well by his indulgent father, a corporate lawyer from the up-scale Portland suburb of Lake Oswego, who bought him an expensive condominium two blocks off campus.

Citing other students at the time as sources, Krychek claimed the first known meeting of Roark and Landis came at a fraternity kegger on the weekend before classes started. Neither had any intention of joining a fraternity or going to classes on Monday morning. Instead, they spent the weekend exploring parties and coeds, finding plenty of both for the taking. By Sunday night, they had made an arrangement. Roark would live rent-free with Landis in his condo in exchange for unlimited use of his Corvette. By early October, Roark and Landis were the best known freshmen on campus by everyone except the faculty.

Despite their loyalty to the party life, the pair managed to scrape by their first year. They maintained grade points high enough to avoid flunking out, but low enough to guarantee them little to brag about should they ever graduate. Krychek cited rumors that they paid other students to take exams and write papers for them. At no time during their first year in college did either of them show the slightest interest in politics.

What came next, Harry, was a turning point in this whole story. After this, things would never be the same.

Krychek claimed that the genesis of the transformation that was to come appeared to be an allegation by a freshman girl who attended a party at the start of Roark's and Landis's second year of college. She told police of being drugged and repeatedly raped by the two men. When she began screaming, Landis and Roark threw her, naked and hysterical, out the door and refused to let her back in. Her screams woke the rest of the condo residents, who stood on their balconies laughing at the naked, frightened girl in the middle of the parking lot. The police arrived to find her in a fetal position on the asphalt, covered in liquor and urine that had rained down on her from the floors above. Landis and Roark were arrested the next day on rape, sodomy, and kidnapping charges. Three days later, the victim dropped the charges. Two weeks later she jumped off a freeway overpass into the path of an oncoming eighteen-wheeler.

At that point, Harry, I had to step outside for some fresh air. I hadn't read all the news coverage of Roark and Landis, so there was no way I would have missed something as significant as allegations of rape. We live in an era where there were no secrets when it came to people in the public eye. Roark and Landis appeared to be the exception. At least so far. But was this what got Krychek killed or Jasmine?

Krychek wrote that immediately following the girl's death the pair disappeared totally from the school's social scene and re-emerged as model students. They were in class every day and home studying every night. They entered campus politics, eventually mounting successful campaigns for student body president. Landis was elected first and Roark succeeded him, each acting as the other's campaign manager. They espoused political philosophies that were right for the times. They were likable and shrewd office holders, even though they shunned most opportunities to speak publicly. Three years later, they graduated in the top ten percent of their class and were accepted at different law schools in the Midwest. Their law school years, according to Krychek, were unremarkable, marked neither by trouble nor stellar grades. Both graduated at the same time, returned to Oregon, and passed the bar the following summer.

Their political careers began after three years of obscurity in blue-blood Portland law firms. Roark's employer specialized in personal injury cases, priding itself in doing pro bono work for environmental groups. Landis went to work at a conservative button-down firm that defended large corporations in product liability cases. Both took on the politics of their respective firms. Roark began showing up at fund-raisers to stop the fighting in Nicaragua and boycott bananas. Landis, while less visible, became deeply involved in conservative causes, such as banning abortion and reducing government regulations on business.

At almost exactly the same time, both left Oregon for Washington, DC. Roark became chief of staff for a California Democrat noted for his fiery diatribes against Pentagon spending and industrial polluters. Landis popped up in a similar position with a Florida Republican known as a champion of corporate welfare and never meeting a weapons system he didn't like. Throughout their capital years, the two kept in close contact with politicians, staffers, and lobbyists from Oregon. Their mutual desire to one day return home and seek elective office was an open secret among those who cared about such things.

Five years later they did just that. Citing various news accounts and property records, Krychek wrote that they bought homes in legislative districts that were ready and waiting for their respective political philosophies. Within eighteen months, both were freshmen members of the Oregon Legislature. Somewhere along the way, Krychek offered, "they picked up wives and the appropriate number of well-behaved children." Their time in the legislature included high-profile involvement in carefully selected issues. They quickly attracted the attention of the state's political reporters and quietly encouraged speculation about higher office. The seeds of that speculation bore fruit earlier in the year when Governor Martin Sloane announced he would not seek a second term because of health problems. Both Landis and Roark popped up immediately on the short list of likely successors.

That's when the dissertation took yet another turn toward the weird, Harry. The last few pages speculated that the two rising political stars were the product of a carefully orchestrated effort going back to their college days. According to Krychek, the transformation of Roark and Landis from party monsters to bookworms was the result of a deal struck between the boys' parents and the family of the girl they were accused of raping. The dissertation said nothing about who the girl's parents were or the nature of the deal. It contained only her name, Amanda Bishop.

At that point, Krychek's dissertation came to an abrupt halt. It was clearly a work in progress, but toward what? Why would he send an unfinished doctoral dissertation to Jasmine Grant, particularly one that may have gotten her killed?

I paid my bill, put the laptop in my backpack and left for Portland. I was out of Lincoln City and near the small community of Neskowin before I could stop thinking about Ivan Krychek's manuscript. Other than a dystopian view of modern-day politics, it had given me two things—insight into the untidy past of Brad Roark and Kingsley Landis and the name of Amanda Bishop.

I know what you're thinking, Harry—Proctor Scofield. I had the same thought but refused to get too far ahead of myself. I didn't want to engage in the same kind of speculation as Krychek until I knew more. Roark and Landis might be nothing more than receptacles into which an over-zealous college student seeking a doctorate had poured a conspiracy theory grown out of a cynical view of politics. But were they murderers? And if they were, where did Buck Mather fit in?

The highway turned inland past the dairy farms near Cloverdale and Hebo. I stopped at a gas station in the small town of Beaver to get rid of the gallon of coffee I'd had that morning and to call Benny Orlando again. He agreed to check my apartment to make sure everything was all right. When he asked what was going on, I told him I'd explain later.

I was ten miles farther up Highway 101 when Benny called back. He said the apartment was fine, followed by a short critique of my suspect housekeeping skills. I thanked him and breathed a sigh of relief. If Buck Mather had figured out that it was me who had cold-cocked him and why, then he hadn't had time to do anything about it, such as search my apartment for the laptop or anything else. Most likely he was in the emergency room getting his face stitched up and his arm in a cast.

When Highway 101 reached Tillamook, I turned east onto Highway 6 toward Portland and spent the next hour lost in thoughts about Amanda Bishop. Exposing what happened to her would ruin the political aspirations of Roark and Landis. Maybe that was what made the manuscript so important. Nothing kills a political career faster than rape allegations in the me-too era, no matter how old they were. But if the revelations in Krychek's dissertation were true, wouldn't they have come out eventually anyway once the two of them announced their candidacies for governor? There were no secrets anymore. The Internet made sure of that. I found it hard to believe that even Oregon's dwindling political press could overlook something as obvious as a potential governor's involvement in the rape, degradation, and suicide of a co-ed.

The path circled back again to why Krychek and Jasmine were murdered and by whom. Mather was the likely candidate, but Roark and Landis had a motive. Maybe they used Mather as a weapon, but the pair just didn't strike me as the murder-for-hire types. So what was the connection? I thought about going to Alfie Gitchell or Daryl Butcher, but showing up with a bag full of conspiracy theories was a non-starter. It would mean telling them about the manuscript and how I got it. I wasn't ready to do that. Not yet. If ever. Besides, Butcher would sneer then trot out accusations of some wild tale I'd concocted to save my own ass.

When I got to Portland, I parked, walked five blocks to my building and went straight to Benny's apartment. When he opened the door, I handed him the laptop and asked him to keep it in a safe place. I told him it belonged to Ivan Krychek. He gave me a look that asked what's going on.

"The kind of story that any reporter would kill for," I said. "Well, maybe not kill, just badly wound."

When I got to my apartment, I cautiously checked each room. Not that Benny couldn't be believed, but I wanted to make sure that everything was safe. If Buck Mather was smart enough to figure out that Krychek's manuscript might be stored on a computer at Delaney College then maybe he could figure out other things as well. I showered until the hot water ran out then crawled into bed. In the middle of a dream about Jasmine Grant and a piano, the telephone rang. The female voice at the other end was sultry and quickly recognizable, even to a man who'd been asleep for six hours.

It was Anna Krychek. She apologized for bothering me at home but wanted to make a confession. I didn't answer. I just wanted to see how this was going to play out.

She said she hadn't been totally honest with me the day I came to her house. Then she paused for a few seconds before saying that she knew more about Ivan's death than she told me. Then came the punchline: She and Buck Mather had been talking.

Anna Krychek and Buck Mather talking. A new twist on the odd couple. I told her she needed to explain a little more.

"Mr. Mather and I have talked about Ivan's research," she said. "We would like to talk to you about it. Maybe it will help find Ivan's killer."

I asked if they'd gone to the police. She said no, but they will have the three of us talk.

My first reaction was that Anna Krychek was delivering lines again, only this time they were less polished than the ones from a few days earlier. I played along, curious where this was headed.

"Would you be willing to meet us at Mr. Mather's house later tonight, around ten?" she said.

I checked my watch. Six p.m. I said sure and she gave me the address.

I hung up and stared at the phone. The story of Roark, Landis, and Amanda Bishop could wait. This was impossible to pass up. If there were two people in all of this who couldn't be trusted it was Anna Krychek and Buck Mather. Best that I get to Mather's place a little early. I got dressed, grabbed something to eat at a food cart near Portland State University then left.

It turned out that Buck Mather lived on a road called Packer Lane in an unincorporated area of Clackamas County southeast of Portland. It was a part of the metropolitan area where the last few acres of prime farmland were gradually giving way to urban sprawl. It was a forty-minute drive across the river, south to Oregon City then east. I slowed near a vacant building that looked like it once housed a small mom-and-pop grocery, almost missing the small, mud-spattered Packer Lane sign engulfed in a huge blackberry bramble that paralleled one side of the two-lane road. I doused the headlights and turned in.

Packer Lane wasn't much of a lane at all—more of a gravel track with barbed-wire fences on either side. Mather's small, two-story, ramshackle affair resembled an abandoned bait shack. It stood about a hundred yards to the right. The windows were dark. A plume of smoke curling out the chimney into the night sky the only sign of life. The front porch sagged at one end. Shingles missing from the roof looked like gaps in an old man's dentures. Beyond the house, a dilapidated barn sat beside what remained of a corral. A driveway leading down to the gravel road skirted along the far side of the property. Parked in the gravel between the house and the barn was Mather's white van.

I slowly backed the car out through the overhanging vines and onto pavement. A turnout fifty yards up the road provided an unobstructed view of the entrance to Packer Lane. It started to rain, a gentle sprinkle at first, but distant thunder promised hard drops were on the way. I checked the time. Nine p.m. An hour early. Perfect. I dug my raincoat out of the back of the car then waited in the dark to see what Anna Krychek and Buck Mather were up to.

The car that showed up twenty minutes later looked out of place in the bramble-infested back roads of Clackamas County. When it turned left and disappeared up Packer Lane, I got out and followed on foot. By the time I could see Mather's house again, the car had parked behind the white van. Its lights were on, the motor idling, exhaust pumping from the tailpipe. I vaulted the barbed-wire fence into the pasture. Keeping close to the huge blackberry bramble, I sprinted the entire left edge of the soggy field then worked my way to the side of the house opposite the driveway. Harsh lights lit up the gravel parking area, backlighting the house and casting deep shadows as I moved toward the porch.

Thirty feet from the house the skies cut loose. Rain came straight down with a deafening roar. I ran to the porch, ducking underneath and leaning against the concrete foundation. The storm lasted about ten minutes then ended as soon as it began. Angry voices from inside the house replaced the sound of rain. Sitting amid the drips and dirt, I heard the words "money" and "manuscript."

After a short pause, the old house shook as someone wearing heavy boots walked across the floor inside. The footsteps clomped overhead, stopped then moved away. A chair scraped across the floor, followed by a muffled pop. A door slammed. Gravel crunched.

Down the full length of the front porch, I could see the last few feet of the driveway. An engine accelerated. Loose pebbles clattered against metal. Headlights fanned across the pasture followed by taillights headed down the driveway. A few seconds later, I watched as the dark Lincoln that was parked behind Mather's van turned onto Packer Lane and disappeared into the gap between the blackberry bushes.

23

Playa Manzanillo

Harrison Grimes' triumphant yell was loud enough to disturb the Scrabble players at the other end of the restaurant. Then he held his arms up as if signaling a touchdown.

"Penroy's car, right?" he said. "The same one that was parked in the underground garage at the capitol. Penroy! Scofield Industries. Proctor Scofield. Now we're getting somewhere."

"Remember those dots we talked about? Well, they were starting to connect. I kept ticking the names off in my head. Mather. Penroy. Roark. Landis. Scofield was still a shadow, but I could feel him, sense him."

"So …?" Grimes said, eager to hear the next installment.

When Standard suggested they take a break, Grimes looked disappointed. He perked up when Standard told him he had a little adventure planned. They left The Tortuga and walked to the turnaround where Arturo and his taxi were waiting. Standard said, "City pier." Grimes started to ask what was up, but Standard told him to be patient.

Twenty minutes later they were walking along the massive concrete pier that jutted out into the bay. The *Tuna Warrior,* engines idling, was tied up and waiting, Special Ed sitting on the back deck with a beer in one hand and a cigarette in the other.

"Harrison Grimes, meet Ed," Standard said. "He's the owner and skipper of the best charter boat on the west coast of Mexico. He also knew Proctor Scofield."

Grimes climbed aboard and shook Ed's hand, a surprised look on his face. "You knew Scofield? How?"

"I'll explain later," Ed said, "but first things first. You get seasick, Mr. Grimes?"

When Grimes admitted to having problems once on a salmon fishing trip, Ed said not to worry about it. Things won't get too bad and they weren't going that far. Standard untied the bow and stern ropes. Ed maneuvered the sleek boat through the small fleet of anchored pangas and, fifteen minutes later, out the mouth of the bay and into the ocean.

"Care to tell me where we're going?" Grimes asked, looking nervous and unsure if he was totally on board with a sea voyage. The ocean was rougher than Ed made it sound. Adding to that were the exhaust fumes from the boat's engines.

"Lunch," Standard said. "We'll be there in a few minutes."

Ed steered the *Tuna Warrior* south, keeping well out to sea. To the left were the rocks off *Caleta de Chon*, the short headland topped with an ancient lighthouse. When Ed slowed the boat to let it ride up and down on the heavy swells, Standard knew he was trying to make Grimes as uncomfortable as possible. It appeared to be working. The queasy-looking Grimes was doing his best to keep his eyes on the horizon while staying close to the side of the boat and away from the exhaust fumes.

After another few miles, Ed turned the boat into a narrow inlet. At the far end was a small, sandy U-shaped beach in the shade of towering palm trees. Pulled up on the beach was a blue-and-white panga with an outboard motor and small cabin. Two men stood at the water's edge, watching as Ed slowed the engines and turned the *Tuna Warrior* around until they were stern first and ten yards offshore.

"Welcome to Playa Manzanillo, Mr. Grimes," Ed said, climbing down from the flying bridge. "Let's eat."

A relieved-looking Grimes gave Ed a weak nod.

The three of them jumped overboard into three feet of water and waded ashore. They shook hands with the two men waiting for them, who motioned to a line of lounge chairs set up in the shade of a half-dozen palm trees. Ed introduced them as Felipe and his son, Fidel.

"They'll be fixing lunch for us. Beer anyone?" Ed opened a cooler full of Corona neck deep in ice.

When Felipe and his son headed for the make-shift barbeque hidden in the trees, the three men settled into their lounge chairs. Standard and Ed looked like they belonged there. Grimes looked like he wanted to be.

"This is like paradise," he said, looking out at the pale blue water and the lush hills on either side of the inlet. Wood smoke from the barbeque brought the smell of grilled fish and roasted vegetables.

Ed nodded. "You're damn right, Harry. You should take a swim. I have some shorts on the boat but, to be honest, you don't need them here. You're among friends."

Grimes passed on a swim, but eagerly asked Ed how he knew Scofield. They shared a beer while Ed described how Scofield had once tried to buy his company.

"He eventually got it," Ed said. "Just not from me."

"How much do you know about him, other than he's dead?" Grimes asked. "His personal life, I mean."

Ed looked confused for a second. "Nothing. I never met the man. Only talked to him on the phone. That was enough for me."

"So there were no rumors about him floating around the industry at the time?"

"Rumors? Why would you ask that?"

"No reason," Grimes said with a shrug. "I'm just trying to learn as much about him as possible."

When Ed was about to ask why, Standard gave him a look that said enough. "How about we eat? I'm starved."

Lunch of grilled Mahi Mahi, fried plantains, and fresh fruit showed up minutes later. They ate and had another beer. When Ed fell asleep, Grimes gave Standard an expectant look that said he was ready to hear what came next.

"I told you earlier, Harry, that things were going to get weird. What happened next turned it up a few notches."

24

Clackamas County, Oregon

Watching the Lincoln disappear down Packer Lane I realized that Proctor Scofield was in play. Only because his lobbyist's car had just driven away from Buck Mather's house. Talk about both ends of the evolutionary scale. The questions started piling up. I wasn't going to get answers hiding under a porch.

When the rain stopped everything went quiet except the drips coming off the roof. I started getting that feeling again that something was wrong. There were no footsteps, no voices, no music. Nothing.

I crawled out from under the porch. Wiping mud from my jacket and pants, I moved along the end of the house toward a weed-infested backyard. A path of broken concrete blocks ran along the rear of the house. At the far end I could see a small porch with a screen door, more like a mud room. Beyond that, the barn and adjacent corral.

I rounded the corner and looked in the first of three windows. Inside was a living room with a flat-screen television, a threadbare couch, a couple of worn-out easy chairs and a coffee table covered in beer cans. Three scrawny cats hunched over a plate eating what could have been cat food but might be something else. They stopped long enough to look out the window at me then went back to their mystery meat. I moved down the path to the next window. It was a dining room in pretty much the same condition as the front room, but with more beer cans and fewer cats.

The house had a kind of mausoleum feeling. Where was Mather? Why wasn't he moving around inside getting a beer, watching porn, or assembling mail bombs? Only one way to find out. I moved down the path and stopped directly under the last window, which turned out to be the kitchen. The old-fashioned wood frame window—the kind with pulleys and a half-moon latch—was all the way open. Maybe Mather left it that way to make it easier for the cats, rodents, and flies to come and go. Slowly, I stood up then immediately dropped to the ground. A man was sitting just inside the window, his shirt collar soaked from rainwater that dripped off the sill. Afraid to even breathe, I hugged the ground, feeling trapped and waiting for the man to get up. Another thunder shower started with the same quickness as the earlier one. I stood up a second time. The man hadn't moved, and for good reason: There was a huge hole in the back of his head.

I walked to the small back porch and opened the screen door. Inside were shelves lined with canned goods, toilet paper and two cases of bottled water. A plastic garbage can filled with empty beer cans and liquor bottles had a place of honor in the corner. Through the porch and to the right was a small, galley-like kitchen with washed-out Formica counters, greasy cupboards and a sink filled with dirty dishes. More fingerprints covered a squat, fifties-style refrigerator. Flies buzzed around a long-handled pot on the gas range.

Buck Mather's body was held upright by the low arms of a chair that looked like it once belonged to a cheap dining room set. The cigarette in his left hand had burned close enough to the knuckle to produce a faint whiff of burnt flesh. The other arm, encased in a cast, stretched out in front of him on the table, the hand wrapped around a can of beer. A series of butterfly bandages covered stitches under one eye. The left side of his face was a mix of purple and black. The bullet hole in the middle of his forehead looked clean, surgical and the size of a dime. If not for the larger, more vivid exit wound in the back of his head, it might have been some kind of gag, like fake dog vomit on a carpet. I sagged into the chair across the table from him, trying to gin up some feelings of sorrow. Couldn't do it. In my mind he was suspect number one in who killed Jasmine Rice. All I could say was, "It looks like the Buck stops here," then hated myself for such a cheap shot at a corpse.

I checked the time. Quarter to ten. Now I knew what Anna Krychek was up to. She told me to be here at ten. I got there early. I guessed that the rest of her plan called for having the police show up at precisely the same time to find me standing over Mather's body. Instead, I called 911 myself, giving the operator the address as I walked back to the road to get my car. I drove into Mather's driveway, got out and took a seat on a stool inside the back porch. I listened to the rain fall on the roof while waiting for the first black and white to show up. I tried not to laugh at what Gitchell and Butcher would say if they knew Mather's killer drove away in a car owned by the lobbyist for one of the wealthiest and most reclusive men in the world. That, of course, assumed I was going to tell them.

I thought about looking around Mather's house before the police showed up but decided not to. The risk of leaving behind some tell-tale evidence was too great. I chose instead to wait, greet the cops like the host at Christmas dinner and hope to learn from them what they found in the house.

The first police car showed up fifteen minutes later. Gitchell and Butcher were five minutes behind. They hustled me off the porch and into the barn. Within a few minutes, the pasture and trees surrounding Mather's house were filled with flashing red and white lights. It was the scene outside Jasmine's house all over again only with barns and corrals. Intermittent pops from the police photographer's strobe lit up the house's streaked windows from the inside. The lights and sirens attracted a half dozen gawking neighbors, who stood at the end of the driveway under striped golf umbrellas.

"That's homicide number three," Butcher said, taking a swizzle stick out of his mouth. "You're not getting away with this one."

When I told him to fuck off, Gitchell dragged me farther back into the barn to give me another speech about how Butcher was just doing his job. I told him to save it.

"Let me guess what happened tonight," I told him. "You got two calls about this. Dead man on Packer Lane. One from me and the other anonymous. I got that right?"

He used one Camel straight to light another then broke into a coughing spasm. Somewhere in there was a nod. I took the pack from Gitchell and lit one for myself. He stopped hacking long enough to tell me that I wasn't under arrest … yet. Then he reminded me that I had been popping up in some embarrassing places lately. I waited in the barn until a uniform came in to take my statement.

An hour or so later, two technicians from the medical examiner's office wheeled Mather's body out the door to the ambulance. Butcher walked into the barn carrying a brown paper sack, saying he'd found it in the corner next to the refrigerator. He handed it to Gitchell, who opened the top, peered inside then used his pen to carefully lift out a spool of piano wire.

My thoughts turned to Jasmine Grant then to the night in the stairwell at Delaney College. I felt both disappointment and relief that I hadn't done more damage to Mather when I had the chance. Turns out it didn't matter. Mather got everything he deserved.

Butcher glared at me. The look of disappointment in his face came straight from the heart. "You're not out of the woods, word man," he said. "You could have planted the wire before we got here."

We were still glaring at each other when another uniform walked up carrying a plastic evidence bag that he handed to Gitchell. Inside was the torn corner of a piece of typing paper. Gitchell turned it over in his hands a few times. In the faint light, I could just make out what it said.

1/Krychek/Dissertation/Right v.

I knew right away what it was but kept quiet. The police didn't know about the manuscript taken from Jasmine's house the night she was killed. I didn't tell them then. I wasn't going to tell them now.

Butcher walked away without looking at the torn piece of paper. Gitchell folded the bag in half and slipped it into the pocket of his raincoat.

He looked at me and said something like, "Okay smart guy, if you didn't kill Mather who did?" It was the right question at the wrong time. I kept my string of withholding information from the police intact by deciding not to tell him about Penroy and his dark Lincoln Town Car.

"Beats me," I said, telling him that if the piano wire checks out it proves that Mather killed Jasmine Grant and Ivan Krychek. I added that whoever killed Mather was now my new BFF. Gitchell asked why I was there.

While waiting for the police I had made up a story about just trying to make a living. Krychek worked for Mather. I'd already talked to him but had a few follow-up questions. When I got there, he was dead and I called 911. Then I asked if I could leave.

Gitchell nodded but asked me to stop showing up at murder scenes. He was running out of excuses for keeping Butcher off my trail. I told him I'd do my best then left after stern reminders from both Gitchell and Butcher to be at the state police office first thing in the morning to sign a statement. Thirty minutes later, I was back on McLoughlin Boulevard heading north to Portland and doing my best to blend into traffic and not think about another night with another dead body.

Back at my apartment, I nursed the last two beers in the refrigerator. When Vanessa came home, she put on a shorter show than usual, skipped her nightly shower, and went to bed looking the way I felt. With the beer gone, I hooked down two fingers of cheap scotch and sat there thinking about murdered security guards and political science professors, dark Lincolns, and the connection with Scofield Industries. I stayed awake most of the night trying to erase the images of dead people and deciding what to do next. I was clearly on to something, just not sure what. One thing was certain—watching that Lincoln drive away from Mather's house meant that I was getting closer to something.

Before going to bed I had come up with a plan that made me eager to get a start on the day and leave the night behind. So, I left the apartment around eight-thirty the next morning. What little sleep I got was ruined by intermittent dreams that left a sense of doom. The feeling followed me up the street to where the car was parked and on the drive out of town.

I headed west out of the city on Highway 26 toward Beaverton. I slipped into a line of cars headed out of town, probably to the hi-tech firms in Washington County. It made for slow going. That was okay. I was in no hurry.

The streets of Anna Krychek's neighborhood were in full suburban bustle. Children on rollerblades and skateboards. Teams of Hispanics armed with lawn mowers, leaf blowers, and hedge trimmers descended on the more expensive homes. It all went on against the backdrop of roaring power washers. I pulled into her driveway hoping to have a frank conversation over steaming cups of freshly brewed espresso about why she tried to frame me for Buck Mather's murder and maybe her husband's and Jasmine's while she was at it. An added bonus would be finding out who helped her. When no one answered the door after three rings, I followed the brick path around the side of the house to peek in the French doors on the brick patio. The leather furniture, teak tables, and everything else were gone. All that was left were the indentations in the carpet where the furniture had been.

The door was locked. I considered kicking it in or at least breaking a window to get inside and look around for some clue to where she might have gone. Instead, I walked up the street, stopping at several houses to talk to babysitters, teenagers, and kids on tricycles. No one had done anything other than wave occasionally at the two people who lived in the house at 2852 Baltusrol Way. More surprising, no one had seen a moving van. All I learned was the obvious: Not only was the furniture gone, but so was Anna Krychek.

I drove out to Highway 217 then south to Interstate 5 toward Salem. I spent most of the next forty-five-minutes wondering what happened to the widow Krychek. It didn't seem her style to abandon a nice house because she found it too painful to live there without her beloved Ee-vahn. On the other hand, pretty much everything she'd told me had been a lie or close to it.

The freeway exit at the north end of Salem led into the center of town. Just south of the downtown business district, I turned east toward the state capital and found a parking spot on the street a half block from the state police office. When the clerk at the front desk said Daryl Butcher wasn't in yet, I asked for Alfie Gitchell. She pointed toward a glass cubicle in the far corner. Gitchell sat at his desk with an unlit cigarette between his fingers, looking like he longed for the days when smoking indoors didn't carry a jail sentence. The detective's red eyes were surrounded by dark circles set in an off-white face. The spittle on his chin told the tale of another coughing fit.

I joked that he should stick to donuts and give up cigarettes. He only nodded, too winded to speak, then handed over typed versions of my statements the previous night and on the night Jasmine Grant was killed. I signed them only after making sure there was nothing in them that said I killed somebody.

"Since there were several words here with more than three syllables, I assume Butcher didn't write it," I said.

Instead of laughing Gitchell said that if the statements were accurate and true reflections of what I told him and Butcher then I should sign them.

I scribbled my name on the statements, tossed them back on Gitchell's cluttered desk and got up to leave. Before I was out the door, Gitchell said something I already knew.

"Butcher still thinks you're guilty," he said. "Maybe not in Mather's death, but there are still two other unsolved homicides."

I thanked him for the vote of confidence then started to leave again. Gitchell wouldn't let it go. He reminded me again that the murders were still Butcher's cases. Gitchell said he had interfered enough already. He told me to remember that Butcher equated lying with guilt, so I'd better be telling the truth—all of it.

Remaining Butcher's target made me think again about leveling with Gitchell. I didn't but remained unsure why. It probably had something to do with wanting to believe the world could still be a safe place for people like Jasmine Grant. Simply letting the likes of Daryl Butcher take over while sitting on the sidelines watching wasn't good enough. The revenge and redemption gnawed at me. There would be other times to tell Gitchell everything.

We walked outside together so Gitchell could have the cigarette he'd been craving. Between drags and coughs, I told him that he could do a lot better than Butcher. He had three murders on his hands and no suspects. Time for an upgrade, I said.

He reluctantly agreed before pointing out that cops are no different than everyone else. There's good ones and bad, happy and sad, smart and dumb, honest and corrupt. "When you live in shit all day it's hard not to smell bad," he said. I suggested he use that on his headstone.

Gitchell fought back a smile. Then he turned philosophical, telling me that there are no real criminals anymore. Just punks who think rebellion means ignoring crosswalk signs. They rage against the establishment by spray painting their names on the sides of buildings in the middle of the night and calling it art. Maybe they steal someone's identity so they can buy more Mountain Dew and Cheetos. Maybe they hide behind legitimate protests so they can break store windows with their skateboards. When none of that works, they beat up somebody who's different from them. Maybe they go to a school and gun down some students because they can't get a blow job from some girl who doesn't know the difference between sex and breakfast at Denny's. Then they can't believe it when they're sent to prison for the rest of their miserable lives. They act tough in court like it means nothing to them then cry for their mommies when the doors are locked behind them.

It was a nice speech, but he was wrong. There were real criminals out there and one of them was behind at least three murders. Maybe whoever it was didn't do the killing, but that doesn't make them any less responsible. I was losing faith in Gitchell's and Butcher's ability to solve any of the deaths—especially Gitchell. He was burned out, ready for retirement.

I asked him if it was time to call it quits—give up crime fighting for fly fishing, golf, or river trips through Europe. "I'm not dead yet," was his only answer.

We talked for a few more minutes about where the investigation went next. He either didn't know or wasn't about to tell me. What he did say was that there was a killer out there somewhere and to be careful.

I walked away after telling him that I'm just a guy trying to earn a living and get square with the world. No one had any reason to kill me. I hoped I was right.

25

Sticky Fingers II, *Zihuatanejo*

When the sun was twenty degrees above the western horizon, Ed announced it was time to head back. Felipe and his son had already packed up and left, leaving behind enough beer for the trip back to Zihuatanejo.

Once out to sea, Grimes sat by himself on the back deck, fighting seasickness while muttering something about three dead bodies and still knowing nothing about the one death he wanted most to hear about—Proctor Scofield. Standard sat down and reassured him that he was getting closer to what he came to Mexico to find out.

"This is a hell of a story, John," Grimes said. "When you said I had to listen to the whole thing in order to get what I wanted, I probably should have pushed back a bit. To be honest, I didn't think it would take this long."

"And there's still a way to go," Standard said.

Grimes shook his head. "I underestimated you. After all you went through you were still willing to fight the good fight. Why?"

"Because I had nothing to lose."

When the *Tuna Warrior* reached the city pier, Grimes said the ocean trip had made him a little queasy. He wanted to catch a taxi back to his hotel. Standard said he understood then walked with him up the pier to the city square.

"What's Ed's story?" Grimes asked as they waited for a taxi to drive by.

"Made a fortune in the dot com boom and got out before it went bust. He paid his taxes, moved down here then started the charter business."

"And his eye?"

"Right after he got here he had a run in with a local slime ball peddling under-age girls. Ed tried to rescue one of them. It cost him an eye."

"What happened to the slime ball?"

"He's dead. Someone shot him. No great loss."

When a taxi showed up, they promised to meet at Grimes' hotel in the morning. After that, Standard went back to talk to Ed.

"I need something more than beer," Ed said. "Mango's?"

Standard nodded and ten minutes later they were at the bar drinking shots of Patron Anejo with beer backs.

"You get anything out of all that?" Standard asked. "Or did you sleep through the whole thing?"

"I caught enough. He's definitely a lawyer. He has that air of superiority that comes with every law degree. Other than that, not much. Sort of an enigmatic guy. After seeing him and listening to the two of you, all I can say is that Grimes didn't come all the way down here to spend day after day listening to your little story."

"Unless?"

"Unless there was something bigger than just what happened to Proctor Scofield."

"Money?"

"You're learning," Ed said then downed his second shot. "Why not cut to the chase, tell him what you know about Scofield and get him out of your hair."

"Not until I know what he's up to."

Ed gave him a sideways glance. "There's something else going on here, isn't there? That question he asked me about Scofield's personal life. I don't think he was just making conversation. He's after something other than how Scofield died."

"Let me see if he'll tell me and then I'll tell you about it."

"Aye aye, sir."

Standard took a taxi home, hung around the house for a few hours then made a call. He explained what he wanted.

"Can you take care of that?" he asked.

"Of course, Señor Juan. Anything for you."

"Great. We'll be there in a couple of hours." Standard hung up then called Grimes.

"How are you feeling?" he asked.

"Much better. A nap and some tonic water helped."

"Good enough for a little late-night outing. Nothing too strenuous. All on dry land."

Grimes hesitated long enough for Standard to jump in. "Great. I'll be there around nine. Meet me in front of your hotel."

When Standard arrived in a taxi, Grimes was standing in the hotel driveway dressed in a golf shirt, slacks, and penny loafers. "I didn't know where we're going, so I didn't know what to wear. Hope this works."

"You're fine," Standard said as the taxi pulled away from the hotel and onto the road into town. At a little after nine p.m., traffic was light. Standard had already told the driver where they were going.

"Care to tell me where we're headed," Grimes said.

"Sure, but I need to swear you to secrecy."

Grimes thought for a moment. "Fair enough. Give me a dollar as a retainer and you can be my client. Attorney-client privilege."

They sat in silence as the taxi negotiated its way through the city and out to *Ruta* 200, the main highway along the coast. At the north end of the city limits, the taxi pulled into a half-vacant parking lot next to a two-story building painted a garish purple with lime-green trim. On the front was a neon logo from The Rolling Stones album, *Sticky Fingers.* Standard turned to face Grimes.

"In Mexico, this place is known as a show bar," he said. "In the states it would be a strip club … among other things."

Grimes gave him the look anyone unfamiliar with Mexico would give—abject terror. "John, I don't think …"

"It's okay. I sort of own the place. I'll explain when we get inside."

The gorilla-like bouncer at the front entrance greeted Standard with a handshake and a man hug then opened the door.

"That's the new bouncer," Standard said. "The last one was shot in the head a few months ago." When Grimes looked ready to bolt back to the car. "Don't worry. Things are fine now. The shooters are dead. Car accident."

The room inside was about the size of half a basketball court with tuck-and-roll leather booths around the outside. A dozen small tables with chairs surrounded a sunken stage with a brass pole in the middle. Clinging to it was a dancer wearing fuck-me pumps, too much makeup and a sultry smile. Overhead a disco ball spun slowly, sending out beams of light that danced off the mirrored walls and ceiling. Standard counted eight beer-drinking customers and four dancers waiting their turn on the brass pole. Mexican pop music blared from speakers hanging on the walls.

Two steps inside and they were greeted by a man the size of a draft horse. He wore a Panama hat, a T-shirt that could double as a bed sheet, and white linen pants. He was leaning heavily on a metal cane.

"Señor Juan, it is good to see you. Welcome to Sticky Fingers Dos."

"The place looks great," Standard said.

"I have you to thank, Señor Juan."

Standard introduced Harry. "This is Tony, the owner."

"*Mucho gusto*, Señor Grimes," Tony said. "Any friend of Señor Juan's is welcome at Sticky Fingers Dos. Everything is on the house." He pointed toward a booth filled with four dancers with eager faces. "Everything."

"Hot, fast, cheap, and easy," Standard said with a wink and a nod. "That's our motto."

Grimes gave Standard a squeamish smile. "Thanks, but I think I'll just have a beer."

Tony led them to a booth in the far corner of the room and ordered three Coronas from a waiter. Grimes gave Standard a look that said he had some explaining to do.

"This place is called Sticky Fingers Two because last spring three men from a drug cartel shot up the original Sticky Fingers," Standard said. "They killed five people that night, including the bouncer and two of the dancers and wounded about a dozen more, including Tony. They shot him in the knee. He'll walk with a cane for the rest of his life."

Grimes looked at Tony. "Señor Juan gave me some of the money I needed to rebuild. We opened two weeks ago. Now, he and I are business partners."

"Just don't tell anyone," Standard said, looking at Grimes. "Especially Emma … if you're still here when she gets back."

They drank while watching a few more customers come in and another dancer swinging clumsily around the pole while shedding pieces of a sequined costume.

"Excuse us for a few minutes," Standard told Grimes. "Tony and I need to talk a little business. Have another beer. We won't be long."

"Everything is being taken care of right now, Señor Juan," Tony said when they reached his small office at the end of a dark hallway. "I will text you the results as soon as I have them."

They shared a quick shot of tequila, clinking glasses to celebrate their burgeoning partnership then headed back to the booth. When they got there, an uncomfortable looking Grimes was sandwiched between two of Tony's bar girls. They were proudly displaying their bare breasts to the gawking lawyer while running their hands through his thin hair. Tony said something in rapid Spanish to one of the girls, who nodded. She looked at the other girl and they slid out of the booth.

"Are you ready to go?" Standard asked Grimes. "Or do you want to stick around a while."

Grimes was out of the booth and halfway to the front door before Standard could thank Tony.

~*~

The next morning Standard met Grimes at his hotel and they walked down the hill to Paty's for breakfast. The beach was busier than usual, another sign that more and more tourists had shown up and still more on the way. They found a table at the front overlooking the beach and ordered *huevos rancheros* and fresh orange juice.

"That was quite an experience last night," Grimes said. "Can't say I've ever been in a place like that. Are you really a silent partner? How does that work?"

"I earned some extra money last spring helping the DEA. That's a story for another time. Americans owning businesses down here is a little dicey. I felt partly responsible for what happened to Tony, so I helped him out. My name doesn't appear on any papers. It's easier to trust Tony to do the right thing. He insists on paying me back, but I told him it wasn't necessary. Tony is a proud man. We'll see what happens."

They spent a few more minutes talking about the realities of Americans investing in Mexican businesses, especially ones like Tony's, before Standard got around to what he really wanted to talk about.

"Why don't you tell me why you're really here, Harry?" Standard asked, thinking that Grimes would be surprised by the question. Instead, he was just the opposite. "I'm not sure if I buy this Nico Adams thing. The deposition you gave me was pretty thin."

Grimes wiped his mouth with a napkin and leaned back in his chair. "I guess I owe you that much, given how much time you've spent showing me around and walking me through your little journey of murder and mayhem."

"And it's not over."

"I didn't think it was, but I assume we're getting closer to what I came here to find out."

"More or less," Standard said, "but there might be an easier way out of this. Why don't you pack it in? Go back to Seattle, tell your partners and your client that I'm an arrogant blowhard who doesn't know shit from fat meat."

Grimes laughed. "What? You mean lay awake all night trying to figure out how it all ends? No way." He paused for a few moments. "Tell you what. I'm going to hang in there for the next installment. After that I'll fill you in on the method to our madness. That fair?"

When Standard's phone beeped, he picked it up and looked at the text message from Tony. Attached was a photo of a bemused Grimes flanked by the two of Sticky Fingers' naked dancers and sitting under a sign that read: "Lap Dances 200 Pesos."

"More than fair," Standard said with a smile, closing the text message and setting down the phone. "More coffee?"

26

Eugene, Oregon

I left Alfie Gitchell with his third cigarette and fourth coughing fit. It was early afternoon when I got back to Portland and pulled into the parking lot in front of the registrar's office at Delaney College. Being summer term, the office was empty except for a few workers behind the counter. The twenty-something woman at the front desk had blue fingernail polish, streaks of green in her red hair and a Goth-like complexion. I explained what I needed.

I held her attention long enough for her to tell me that there was no one named Anna Krychek enrolled at the school. I explained that she had been married late in the previous school year and that she might have been registered under her maiden name, which I didn't know. She gave me a patient smile and said she would see what she could do. She left for a computer terminal on a desk near the back of the room. I found a chair in the waiting area and thumbed through a year-old copy of *Smithsonian*. The meeting with Gitchell had left me uneasy. That someone might want to kill me because of my connection to Ivan Krychek, Jasmine Grant, and Buck Mather made sense on some level. We all had some connection to the manuscript. Own it and you die. But why? The truth about Roark, Landis, and Amanda Bishop would come out eventually. I'd make sure of that. Since the manuscript was a draft, all I could figure was that there was more to come. Something worth killing people over.

I will say, Harry, the bright side was that in a matter of hours I had gone from murder suspect to possible murder victim.

The registrar clerk came back to tell me that Delaney College had eleven students named Anna registered last spring, all of which have re-registered for fall term under the same names. She guessed that the Anna I was looking for was never a student at the school.

I thanked her and walked over to the Political Science Department, following the same path I'd taken a few nights earlier. Bits of glass glistened in the dirt at the bottom of the steps. The broken window had been replaced with a small piece of plywood. Inside, harsh overhead lights lit up the drab hallway. The office of the acting department head was two doors down from Krychek's. The little white card on the door identified him as Professor Gerald Miller. I found him sitting at his desk puffing on an unlit pipe while peering suspiciously at me over the top of tortoise-shell readers. After introducing myself and telling him why I was there, I asked how the faculty was coping with the two murders. He said some better than others. After that I gave him a quick description of Anna Krychek. He listened while I explained that she claimed to have met Ivan during a political science seminar earlier in the year. Then I described her: tall, beautiful, with an Eastern European accent. "Sort of hard to miss," I said.

Miller answered after a slight nod. He remembered her but was pretty sure she was never a student. Besides, the school had never held a seminar on Russian meddling in U.S. elections, although he thought it was a good idea. All he could tell me was that she showed up in the building one day. The next thing he knew, she and Ivan were married. He never saw her again and never talked to Ivan about her, other than to congratulate him on his marriage.

When I asked if he'd explained all this to the police, he said yes then fumbled around in his desk for a business card. He showed it to me. Daryl Butcher. I thanked him and left.

From Delaney, I drove west to the Washington County Courthouse and the Office of the County Clerk. It took a while before learning that the house on Baltusrol Way had been purchased by Anna Marie Carson for eight-hundred thousand dollars from Trask Properties, a local development company. I called the registrar's office at Delaney just to confirm that Anna Carson had not been a student there. The answer was the same. I Googled Trask Properties, dialed the number and explained to the receptionist that I had an unusual request. She passed me off to a salesman who, of course, had the idea that I wanted to buy a house. When I told him what I wanted, he put me on hold for a few minutes. When he came back on the line, he said they didn't have a listing for any property on that street, but there was one with the same floor plan three blocks away. I tried to sound interested enough to keep him on the phone. I asked who owned the house. The sound of shuffling papers came over the phone.

He'd sold it to Anna Carson for cash, which was why he remembered her. He didn't get that many cash deals. He gave me another sales pitch then suggested we get together "to do a little noodling." I thanked him and quickly hung up.

Directory assistance had no listing for Anna Carson. The story was the same at the state Department of Motor Vehicles. I even bluffed my way past the public affairs person at the Department of Revenue to learn that no one by the name of Anna Krychek or Anna Carson had filed tax returns in Oregon in the last five years.

Whatever or whoever Anna Carson Krychek was, she knew how to make herself invisible. It was time to try something else.

Tired of the freeway and needing time to think, I headed west, picking up Highway 99W to cruise through McMinnville, Monmouth, and Corvallis. I got comfortably lost amid the vineyards, grass seed fields and orchards that flanked the two-lane highway. I knew I was getting closer to why Jasmine Grant and Ivan Krychek were killed. The feeling wasn't based on anything concrete, just a sense that what I was doing was making someone nervous. So far that someone was Mather and Anna Krychek. If not, why try to frame me? Then there was always that dark blue Lincoln. Too many questions. There was no other choice but to keep going. Jasmine would have expected it. I expected it.

During our lunch together, Jasmine had asked why I didn't leave Oregon, go someplace where I wasn't known, and start over again. I didn't say it at the time, but finding a quiet job somewhere writing thumbsuckers about county fair princesses or record-breaking pumpkins had a certain appeal. Move to a town with guys named Garth and Earl, who married their high school sweethearts and had kids named Little Garth and Little Earl. Maybe buy a house in the woods and learn to grow organic vegetables or raise prize heifers. Not that I knew anything about either one. Interesting ideas, but they were never going to happen. Instead, I was an unemployed, discredited reporter chasing one of the masters of the universe in a twelve-year-old Honda Civic.

By the time I reached Eugene, I had shaken off thoughts of fading into the woodwork. But I still had questions about what happened at the University of Oregon twenty-three years earlier. Hopefully, the man I was going to see had some answers.

I drove along Franklin Boulevard that bordered the north side of the campus then turned right on Agate Street then another right onto 13th Street. After plugging the meter, I walked into the heart of the campus. At that time, the student population was a fraction of what it was during the school year. Those who were there moved at a slow pace along the sidewalks or sat cross-legged in the shade of old elms and Douglas firs. A kiosk that once may have held handbills announcing concerts by The Grateful Dead and speeches by Abbie Hoffman was now covered in flyers promoting weekend seminars on how to improve LSAT scores. The journalism school was housed in a brick building at the end of a cul-de-sac. My footsteps echoed on the empty stairwell to the third floor then along a barren hallway.

I'd met Professor Marcus Towne six years earlier when we shared the podium at a weekend conference on journalistic ethics. I considered the phrase an oxymoron, arguing that all ethics went out the window as soon as one news organization gained an edge over another. Privately Towne agreed, but publicly espoused restraint and responsibility by both television and newspaper reporters to stick to a strict set of ethical standards. That night, our friendship grew over dinner, drinks, and an animated conversation about the future of journalism that lasted until closing time. Afterwards, I had been a frequent visitor to Towne's show-and-tell days for freshmen eager to be the reporters who would someday unearth more ground-shaking scandals about NSA abuses, the deep state, and Donald Trump's taxes.

Walking into Towne's office, I thought the old professor was asleep. An unlit pipe jutted out from under a gray, walrus mustache stained a dim yellow from years of tobacco smoke. Thin gray hair lay like cotton candy across a shiny pate head. His typical dress of white shirt, bow tie, suspenders and baggy slacks was complimented by a clothespin dangling from one ear lobe.

He looked both surprised and happy when I knocked on his door and walked in. He came around the desk to shake my hand, give me a hug then offer a seat at the small conference table wedged into the corner of the office. I had to ask about the clothespin.

He looked surprised for a second then pulled it off his ear. He'd been having a toothache, but no time to get to the dentist. The pain from the clothespin took his mind off it. Fair enough, I told myself. We exchanged small talk before he said that he had tried to call me after hearing about the accident. He'd left a message that maybe I didn't get. I had gotten it but felt too embarrassed and ashamed to return it. Towne would've offered well-intentioned advice on how to handle the aftermath of the accident when all I had wanted was to crawl in a hole and pretend to be someone else. I had always looked up to Towne as someone who still viewed journalism as a noble profession rooted in the

First Amendment and John Peter Zenger. I felt that I tarnished that image and let down my profession and my old friend. It was easier to avoid him. Until now. I apologized for not returning his call, blaming myself and the circumstances then told him I needed his help.

Over the next half-hour I laid out the entire story, starting with Ivan Krychek in the portable toilet and ending with the disappearance of Anna Krychek. Towne looked concerned and surprised when I described finding Jasmine Grant's body. He frowned about how I withheld information from the police and my temporary status as a murder suspect. The night at Mather's farmhouse turned Towne's already pale complexion another shade of white.

The good news was that sharing the whole story for the first time with someone I trusted made me feel twenty pounds lighter. He could tell I had feelings for Jasmine Grant and how finding her killer would close some doors for me. I nodded in agreement because there was nothing to add. The perceptive Towne had things pretty much figured out.

Towne leaned over to open the bottom drawer of his oak desk and pull out a bottle of Teachers and two smudged glasses. While pouring two shots, he described my story as "quite a tale" and fodder for the school's class on journalistic ethics.

We clinked glasses and Towne finished off his shot with the effortless motion of someone who wasted little or no time with beer, wine, or mixers. I followed suit with a less practiced move then reached across the desk to pour each of us a second shot. It was time to talk about why I was there: Krychek's draft doctoral dissertation and its revelations about Brad Roark, Kingsley Landis, and Amanda Bishop.

I asked if he knew them. He nodded, sipped his drink, and stared out the small, grimy window behind his desk. Huge fir trees blocked the light and kept the little office in perpetual gloom. The old man's eyes sunk back in his head as if he were reeling in the years, bringing long-forgotten images back into focus. I remember every word after that.

"I've been on this campus for more than fifty years," he said. "I came here as a freshman, graduated from here, got my master's then my Ph.D. I'll retire next year when I turn seventy. I can't even guess how many students have been through the school during those years. Several hundred thousand for sure. Maybe even a million. Most of them I never knew, or even saw for that matter. But I've heard all the stories—good, bad, and otherwise. Everything that had gone on in this country since the 1960s—assassinations, man on the moon, Vietnam, the computer, September Eleventh, Donald Trump, George Floyd. They all acted out on this campus in one way or another. Sometimes in joy. Sometimes anger."

Then he paused for a while. His face went dark, his eyes needlessly focused on the shelves behind me and all the books by and about the greats of journalism.

"In all those years," he finally said. "After all those students, and all those stories, I have never seen anything like what happened with Roark, Landis, and Amanda Bishop."

I knew Towne well enough to know that he wasn't prone to exaggerations. Years of beating news writing into the heads of aspiring reporters left him with an acute ability to say what he meant in as few words as possible. What he had said about Roark and Landis left no room for doubt. The three students from two decades ago had left an indelible mark on him.

The old man's voice turned into a heavy whisper as he explained that the changes in Roark and Landis were like night and day. One week the two of them were losers taking up space that rightfully belonged to those less fortunate, but with a greater desire to learn. The next week, they were model students. The kind every professor yearned for, eager to learn, to advance, to make something of themselves and of the world around them. It was hard not to be a little suspicious, he said, adding that the world was less cynical and more forgiving in those days. Everyone gave them the benefit of the doubt. Within a few weeks it was clear that they were serious about turning their lives around. Months of partying had suddenly been rechanneled into education and politics.

I watched as Towne slowly shook his head, still amazed by the turn around despite the passage of time.

"And Amanda Bishop?" I asked.

Towne nodded. She introduced herself to him during a freshmen orientation session. He remembered her as looking and acting so shy and vulnerable that it seemed like torture to walk up to him and say hello. She was doll-like with porcelain skin, little pink circles of rouge on her cheeks, tiny red lips, and curly blonde hair with ribbons in it. She had the kind of personality that made him want to put his arm around her and protect her from the world. She enrolled in a journalism class. He didn't teach it but ran into her several times in the hallway. When he heard what happened and that she had committed suicide, he went to the president of the university and demanded that Landis and Roark be expelled. It was no use. Their parents were generous financial supporters of the school. Expel them and a million dollars in athletic scholarships and academic endowments walked out the door at the same time. His voice trailed off when he described hearing that no charges had been filed against the two.

Towne turned in his chair to stare again out the dingy window. When he finally spoke, there was awe in his voice like someone reliving a mystical event.

"Looking back," he said, "it was as if Amanda Bishop had been reborn in the two of them. They became what she would've been, should have been. It was as if three people died and two completely different people lived on."

It was a stunning admission coming from someone as hard-sided as Marcus Towne. We stared at each other. The secret of one had been passed to another. Towne appeared relieved at ridding himself of what he'd held inside for so long. I, on the other hand, felt burdened. I came seeking answers, but only found more questions.

After a short silence, the old professor looked at me with pleading eyes. He placed a gnarled hand on my knee and squeezed. I could see it in his face. His words are unforgettable: "Roark and Landis didn't change because they wanted to. I believe they did it because they had to because … their lives depended on it."

We sat in silence for a few moments. Towne started to pour two more drinks then stopped to simply stare at the bottle as if it held answers to what had happened so long ago. I broke the silence by offering to drive him home, maybe stop somewhere for a late lunch or early dinner. He said no. He had a faculty meeting soon and he needed to get ready for fall term. It would be his last at the school. I got the hint, thanked him, and said I needed to go. He didn't get up, only waved and mumbled something about keeping in touch.

I left to meander around the campus, Marcus Towne's words still ringing in my head. Even the leg where the old man touched me itched like poison oak. I walked past Deady Hall, the granite building with its tall, church-like spire that reminded me of Mayfield Hall at Delaney College and of Jasmine Grant. Nearing the library brought images of Amanda Bishop walking along the same paths that crisscrossed the block-long lawn known as The Walks. She would've been wearing a bright yellow slicker with the pointed hood pulled over her head to keep the rain off. The University of Oregon Fighting Ducks might have had a home game at Autzen Stadium that weekend, so there'd be a large "Go Ducks" button on her raincoat. An army surplus backpack would be slung over one shoulder. Inside would be the *History of Western Civilization* or *The Norton Anthology of English Literature.* She would've been young, bright-eyed, and eager to learn. Instead, it had all been taken away from her. I wondered what she would say if she knew that one of the men who raped her, humiliated her, and drove her to suicide would be Oregon's next governor.

The words "Ye shall know the truth" were carved over the entrance to the Knight Library. I passed underneath then wandered the halls for several minutes before asking the woman at the front desk where to find old University of Oregon yearbooks. She was young with large, black rimmed glasses and a nose ring. I told her I was looking for photos of the student government from twenty-three years ago. She wrote a website address on a sticky note and pointed to a line of computer terminals on the wall across the room. I thanked her and took the note.

A few minutes later I was looking at a series of photos of something called the Panhellenic Council and the ASUO: Associated Students of the University of Oregon. At the center of the first photo stood a youthful Brad Roark with the same rumpled Dockers-and-Polo look as that day on the floor of the state senate. To his left stood Kingsley Landis, his blond hair long and cut in bangs. He wore a dark, three-piece suit with a conservative tie and a striped dress shirt.

Roark, Landis, and the others wore the same serious looks required of those who assumed they represented the next generation of national leaders. Future congressmen and women, senators, ambassadors, captains of industry. With one exception. The figure at the far right hand side of the photo was shorter than the others. His expression was more intent and defiant. Jet black hair matched his shirt, pants, and shoes. Kind of a Johnny Cash look. A drooping mustache curled around a down-turned mouth. Dark glasses with small, round lenses hid his eyes.

I ran a finger along the caption beneath the photo. It identified Roark as president and Landis as secretary-treasurer. I skipped the others and went to the name that corresponded with the somber, darkly dressed student at the far right: Mitchell James Penroy.

I searched for a few more photos. Roark and Landis appeared again and again as student body officers. Same with Penroy. Always standing at the far end with the same defiant look on his face. The caption on the photo described him as "administrative assistant." His hair got longer with each photo. By the time I reached the last one he had added a full beard to go with the droopy mustache. The clothes were still dark. Same with the demeanor and the glasses with the small, round lenses. I got the feeling I was looking at a puppet master, or at least one in the making. I could also be looking at a potential murderer.

I tried not to jump to conclusions, Harry. Oregon's population in those days was small, so there was nothing unusual about three people involved in campus politics showing up years later involved in state politics. Still, coincidences bothered me as much as small, purposeful-looking people with vague titles, who grew up to drive dark Lincolns, represent large corporations, and perhaps kill people.

I made copies of the photos and thanked the woman behind the desk before retracing my steps back to 13th Street then down to the Office of the Registrar in Oregon Hall. There were no lines for Academic Records and Graduation. I told the work-study student behind the counter that I was a reporter for *Inside Oregon*. She acted unimpressed but seemed eager to help. I told I was looking for any information the school might have about someone who had been a student there twenty-three years earlier. I gave the name Amanda Bishop and asked if I could see her records.

That earned me a blank look followed by "Do you have her permission?" I told her Bishop was dead. When that earned me a second blank look, I asked if I could talk to her supervisor, who it turned out, of course, wasn't available. Apparently, it didn't matter. It was school policy not to give out information about students to just anyone. Dead or alive. I tried another approach: Could she tell me who Amanda Bishop had put down to notify in case of an emergency?

"A little late for that, isn't it?"

This was turning into one of those conversations that divide generations. I did my best not to act impatient when she handed me an information request card. I filled it out, pushed it back across the counter. She took it and disappeared behind a computer on the other side of the room. She came back ten minutes later with a one-page printout.

She ran her finger down the long sheet of paper. "It says here that in the case of an emergency the school was to contact her stepfather," she said.

"Who would that be?" I asked.

She squinted at the form again, ran her finger farther down the page. "Proctor Scofield."

27

Playa la Ropa, Zihuatanejo

A stunned Harrison Grimes flagged down a waiter. "Tequila," he said. "Two glasses and leave the bottle." He was clearly at a loss for words beyond ordering more liquor. Standard sympathized. He'd felt the same way at the time.

"Roark and Landis raped the stepdaughter of Proctor Scofield," Grimes said. "Pretty hard to believe, John."

"No kidding. I don't know where it fit into everything else that had happened. What I did know was that I had one hell of a story on my hands."

The waiter showed up with the tequila, poured two shots, and left the bottle. Grimes downed his and poured another, all the time staring out at the bay as if it would give him a glimpse of things to come.

"If I want to hear what happens next then I guess I better let you in on more than what I've already told you."

"Fire away," Standard said.

"I need to ask you something first. Did the local news pick up on any of these murders or how they were connected? It seems to me that would be a pretty big story in a state like Oregon."

"Not really," Standard said. "Krychek's bizarre murder earned a few seconds on a couple of the local TV stations. Same with Jasmine Grant's. Mather not so much. That was fine with me. I needed more time."

"I see," Grimes said, nodding in agreement. "So, where to begin?" He took a deep breath and leaned forward, arms on the table. "Do you know how many high-tech workers there are in the United States, John? Somewhere north of ten million and more all the time. Very few of those workers, or any for that matter, are unionized. Some of the unions my firm represents have been trying for years to get their foot in the door with little or no success. The companies won't let us in and the workers are too busy to be all that interested. The closest anyone got was a vote to unionize an Amazon warehouse in Alabama. It failed, but at least the union got a vote. Anyway, our clients keep trying, always looking for an opportunity."

"Let me guess," Standard said. "Nico Adams, the drug smuggler."

Grimes nodded. "It was dumb luck, really. If Adams had been broke, he would have ended up with a public defender or some store-front firm with little chance of staying out of prison. Instead, thanks to his past smuggling activities as well as more legitimate work, he was flush with cash. As soon as he told us his story, we saw a chance to use it as leverage against Scofield Industries."

Standard downed his shot and smiled to himself. He knew the legal fees involved in negotiating a union contract with a company the size of Scofield Industries would be enormous. The payoff for whatever union got its foot in the door would be even greater. Still, he had a hard time believing this was just about unionizing high-tech workers. It had to be something more sinister to bring a high-priced lawyer like Grimes all the way to Zihuatanejo on what could be nothing more than a snipe hunt. He could afford to be patient. The photo on his cellphone assured him of that.

"Yesterday you asked Ed if he knew anything about Scofield's private life," Standard said. "Care to tell me what that was all about?"

Grimes shrugged off the question. "Just fishing. Doing due diligence."

"Are you sure you don't know something about him that you're not telling me?"

"Not really," Grimes said, but with a lack of conviction that made Standard even more suspicious.

When Grimes started to pour more drinks, Standard waved him off. "What if I told you that the way this ends is not going to give you the leverage you're looking for?"

"That's for me to decide. I just want to hear the rest of it."

"And what happens to Nico Adams in all of this?" Standard asked.

"Adams is guilty. Caught red-handed. He knows it. We know it. We'll negotiate a plea deal with the feds and he'll spend a few years in a federal prison. Maybe even get off with probation. He does have a family and a good war record. That might help. We'll see."

"And Scofield Industries when the truth comes out?"

"That depends on what the truth is. If they don't want the truth to come out then we're in a strong negotiating position. If it turns out they don't care one way or the other then our firm and our clients will try something else."

"How much is at stake?"

"Millions, tens of millions if you throw in health benefits and pensions."

"For your firm, I mean."

"I'm talking about my firm." An evil smile crossed his face as he reached for the bottle of tequila. "Now, back to your story. Things just keep getting more and more interesting."

28

Portland

I left the registrar's office in a daze. There was no room in my mind to think about driving or about the miles of farmland along the interstate north to Portland. I passed a couple of dozen slower cars and trucks and let an equal number of faster ones pass me. Either way, they were little more than colorful blurs against the gray pavement. With each overpass came the vision of Amanda Bishop flying down into the windshield.

The same names ran through my head over and over again. Roark. Landis. Penroy. Mather. Krychek. Bishop. Then there was the new name—Proctor Scofield. Not that it was all that new, but it did close the circle and connect some of those dots we talked about. What I knew was that it all seemed too good to be true. Politics, money, sex, and violence all wrapped up in one tidy package starring a reclusive billionaire and the two rising political stars who had raped his step-daughter. You can't make this stuff up, Harry.

When I got to Portland, I parked two blocks from the apartment and sat in the car, watching the rush-hour traffic go by. The last few people on the street scurried into car parks and emerged minutes later in their German-made sedans and sport utility vehicles. Slowly, the homeless came out, pushing shopping carts and checking the trash cans and Dumpsters for cans, bottles, or lunch. That I existed somewhere in between didn't seem to matter anymore. I left the car and walked home, feeling excited and afraid. The feelings were familiar, but never at the same time.

That night, I drifted in and out of sleep, marking each hour by glancing at the clock next to the bed. At six a.m. I showered, dressed, and walked across the Park Blocks to become the first customer at the neighborhood Starbucks. With a latte and a cranberry-cinnamon muffin, I sat at a table outside reading the paper while SW Columbia Street filled with morning commuters. At seven-thirty, I walked back to my apartment, watched Savannah Guthrie and Martha Stewart make crepes with raspberry sauce. Right after eight a.m. I called the office of State

Senator Brad Roark. When a friendly female voice answered, I identified myself as a writer for *Inside Oregon* and asked to speak to Senator Roark. She put me on hold. I waited expecting to be transferred to Roark. Instead, I got a nasally press aide with the inflated sense of importance that comes with getting involved in politics at too early an age. He played dumb by asking me what news organization I was with. I bit my tongue. If I wanted to talk to Roark, pissing off some staffer wasn't going to get it done. I took a deep breath and asked again to speak to Roark. He told me that the senator was out of the office at the moment and asked if he could help me.

I wondered how the aide would react to wanting a comment from the senator about drugging and raping the stepdaughter of one of the richest men in the world. Instead, I said probably not, that I was working on a story that required that I talk to him right away.

"What are the chances of having Senator Roark call me?" I asked.

"Not good without knowing what this is about," he said.

I'd had enough. I gave him my name and phone number and hung up.

Kingsley Landis came next. After making a few calls, I quickly learned that Landis really didn't work at the law offices of Morgan, Grodin, and Dean, as it said in his legislative biography. He merely maintained an office there so his name could appear as one of several associates who handled the firm's corporate clients. Landis's real profession was politics, and any success he had in that field was supposed to rub off on the entire firm. So would his shortcomings, I thought, imagining the reaction of the stodgy firm's gin-soaked partners when they learned that Landis was a college rapist and party monster. It might even mean something as drastic as an extra martini at the Arlington Club. I called the law offices anyway, identifying myself to the overly polite receptionist as a reporter who would like to talk to Senator Landis.

When she asked what I would like to talk to him about, I decided to take a different tact that would hopefully get some sort of reaction. "Tell him it concerns Amanda Bishop. He'll know what that means."

I spent the rest of the day in the apartment waiting for the phone to ring. After a wrong number and two attempts to sell me season tickets to the Portland Opera, I was ready to start chewing on the wallpaper. Then Roark called. His tone came off cold and impatient. That changed after I told him that I had some questions regarding an incident twenty-three years ago that might be related to a story I was working on. It would be better if we talked about it face to face. When Roark didn't answer I told him it was about Amanda Bishop. The silence returned, only this time it was longer.

"I see," he said, "but I'm afraid I don't have anything to say about that matter."

I explained to him what was going to happen. I would write about what he and Landis did to Bishop. He would be quoted as having no comment, something that never goes over well with readers … or voters. In that case, he said, he could make time for me the first thing next week. When I told him that wouldn't work; I needed to talk to him that day. He mumbled something about being tied up in hearings until after six p.m. and after that a mandatory appearance at a party fundraiser. He apologized, said next week was the best he could do and to call his office on Monday. Then he hung up.

Not to be put off, I called the Democratic Party of Oregon, told another polite receptionist that I was planning to attend tonight's fundraiser but had misplaced my invitation. She told me the event was at The Woolen Mill Museum in Salem and it started at seven p.m. I looked at my watch. Three hours. Plenty of time.

I arrived about seven-thirty and fell in behind a group of men dressed in Democratic uniforms: Dockers, Rockports, and tweed sport coats with thread-bare elbows. I followed them across the parking lot, through the gate in the black wrought-iron fence and down the asphalt drive that led to the mill itself. Small groups gathered on the brick-and-concrete patio, drinking donated beer out of white plastic cups.

Not seeing Roark, I went inside and took the elevator up to the party on the third floor. The doors opened on to a long, wide room with open rafters and floor-to-ceiling windows along each side. A display outside the elevator door included grainy, black-and-white photographs of tired-looking young women standing next to huge looms. They wore long dresses, wire-rimmed glasses and hair piled up Gibson Girl style. The several hundred people stood gathered in groups, talking and laughing above the din created by a band playing ditties by Jim Croce and Creedence Clearwater Revival. I hoped to find Roark before the band broke into a medley of Cat Stevens tunes. A woman at the buffet line told me Roark had not arrived yet, but said he was expected any minute. She added an unsolicited endorsement of Roark's candidacy for governor that appeared to be based solely on his good looks. She would probably fall face first into her plate of celery sticks and ranch dressing if I told her he had also raped the daughter of the state's largest political donor.

Instead, I thanked her then grabbed a half dozen meatballs and a handful of chips from the buffet. After pouring a beer from the keg in the corner, I rode the elevator back to the ground floor and headed toward the front gate. An empty picnic table near the information kiosk gave me a good view of the entrance and a place to eat the bland finger food.

By eight o'clock my food and beer were gone. When a cool breeze came up, I glanced around for a warmer place to wait. The sign on the large building adjacent to the wrought-iron gate identified it as the Wool Warehouse. It looked warm but closed. Behind me a mill race rumbled down a spillway and under a wooden footbridge, eventually disappearing beneath the main mill building itself. To the right, were three clapboard buildings that dated back to the mid-1800s. Two of them had served as homes. The third was a Methodist parsonage.

Determined to stay patient, I watched as more people arrived in groups of three and four. Most ignored me, but some came over to shake hands and introduce themselves as if we were veterans of some long-forgotten political battles. I played along, smiling and nodding while keeping an eye on the entrance.

Roark arrived a little before nine, followed by two young aides. Predictably, one of them whipped out a cell phone and began talking. I moved quickly across the asphalt to fall in step beside Roark. I introduced myself and reminded him that we talked that afternoon. Roark frowned, angrily muttered something about not having time for an interview and suggested that he might have a position paper that would help with what I needed.

Slick, I thought, even for a Democrat.

I walked faster to get ahead of Roark then turned to face him. Roark stopped. The aide put away his cell phone and started acting like he was some kind of security guard. When I said, "Back off," the aide stopped in his tracks.

"I'm here to talk about Amanda Bishop," I told Roark.

His face turned pale. His shoulders slumped. We stared at each other until Roark motioned for the aides to go ahead, telling them everything was fine and he would be there in a few minutes. He looked around then motioned me to follow him.

A narrow path led along the spillway to a small, one-story building huddled under a gnarled oak tree. It had a wooden porch with a set of stairs at each end. The weathered sign stuck in the middle of a flower bed identified it as "The Pleasant Grove Presbyterian Church, 1858." Roark tried one of the double doors. The first was locked, but the second opened. We slipped inside where a dozen wooden pews faced a simple altar that favored no particular religion. A switch next to the door turned on two dim lamps on antique tables along the back wall. Roark pointed to one of the pews at the rear of the chapel. He took a deep breath and rubbed the bridge of his nose with his thumb and forefinger. He didn't wait for me to ask a question. Instead, he launched immediately into an explanation that started with an admission that sooner or later the story of Amanda Bishop would come out. He was sitting with his back against the end of the pew. The anger gone, his tone seemed suddenly equal portions of sadness, contrition, and resignation appropriate to the setting.

"I guess it's too much to ask these days not to have events from the past enter into the political debates of the present," he said.

I stood in the aisle staring down the length of the pew at Roark and laughed. "Seriously!" I said.

Roark held up both hands in submission then began complaining about how the sins of the past should remain in the past and I, of all people, should know that. This wasn't about me, I told him. "You and your buddy raped Amanda Bishop. Did you really think no one would find out?"

He kept both hands in the air then started offering excuses that began with "I'm not the same person I was twenty years ago." Both he and Landis knew the story would come out eventually. They even talked about it before getting into politics. There was never any intention of denying what happened or downplaying its significance.

I told him to save it for the editorial boards and that I couldn't care less whether the story of Amanda Bishop helped or hurt anyone's chances of being governor. When Roark looked confused, I leaned forward and put my hands on the end of the pew. He listened while I explained that what happened years ago was somehow related to three murders that occurred over the last few days. I believe he and Landis knew something about those murders. They may or may not be involved, but there's a pretty good chance they knew who was and why those people were killed. I ran through the list of dead people: Ivan Krychek, Jasmine Grant, Buck Mather.

He answered the first two names with a shake of his head but admitted to knowing Mather as "the security guy at the capital." He knew Mather was dead, called it a terrible thing, but didn't understand what I was driving at. He couldn't believe that I thought he was in any way involved in these deaths or what happened to them was in some way related to Amanda Bishop. He was back into full whine with an added dose of indignation.

I could have told him that was exactly what I thought but knew it would be a waste of time. No way was he going to admit that the murders were somehow connected to a doctoral dissertation on politics or that the dissertation contained information about him, Landis, and Amanda Bishop. Still, it was worth a try for no other reason than to get him on the record.

He insisted again that he had no idea what I was talking about or that he knew anything about a doctoral dissertation. After that he fell back on what sounded like well-rehearsed talking points—What happened to Amanda Bishop was a life-changing tragedy; Landis will say the same thing; their reputation during their early college days has been grossly exaggerated; what happened made both of them better people.

Ya-dah. Ya-dah. Ya-dah. I sat back and listened to what I had come to believe were canned excuses worked out over the years. Obviously, the kind of transformation Marcus Towne had described didn't sound the same coming from Roark. Towne made it sound miraculous. Roark made it sound like he'd gotten a flu shot.

I asked about Penroy and Scofield. He said they met in college. Penroy went to work for Scofield right after graduate school. They stayed in touch. Penroy had become a friend and adviser to both of them.

"Did Penroy broker the peace agreement between you and Scofield over what happened to his stepdaughter?"

He gave a reluctant nod. The four of them hadn't talked about it in years. They had all moved past it. Now, they agree on some issues and disagree on others. Scofield has given money to his campaign and he lets him know where he stands on issues before the legislature of which there are not that many. Scofield Industries was worldwide with very few holdings in Oregon.

Roark looked around as if just realizing where he was and that there was nothing wrong with talking about rape in a church. Having apparently run out of rehearsed responses, he asked if I was going to publish something. When I didn't answer, he issued the kind of warning any reporter worth the title had heard dozens of times before: "Listen carefully, Mr. Standard. I accept full responsibility for everything that happened to Amanda Bishop, but to suggest that I was involved in any other deaths would be a reckless disregard for the truth."

You're a lawyer, Harry. You know as well as I do what he was saying. "Print it and I'll see you in court."

I thanked Roark for his time and left him sitting in the pew, gazing at the small altar, and moving in his lips as if in prayer.

Kingsley Landis called the next morning just as I was fixing coffee and munching on what could either be a fresh bagel or a week-old doughnut. Before I could even get to what I wanted to talk to him about he told me that Roark had called. He had nothing to add beyond what Roark had told me. They had made a terrible mistake then dedicated their lives to rectifying it. His tone was casual and collegial, out of place for someone whose dirty laundry was about to become part of the public domain.

I asked how Proctor Scofield felt and about what happened and if he had apologized to him. That changed his tone. Any conversations he's had with Scofield were none of my business, he said. Like Roark he wrote off my questions about the murders of Krychek, Grant, and Mather as a "snipe hunt." Same with asking him if he knew about Krychek's dissertation and what it said. He closed with accusing me of engaging in the kind of journalism people in public life have come to expect. His advice to me was to be very careful about printing anything beyond what happened more than two decades ago.

29

Playa la Ropa, Zihuatanejo

After downing three more shots of tequila, Grimes said he'd had enough and asked the waiter for coffee. Standard did the same then asked Grimes if he knew Roark and Landis or knew of them since, like him, they were lawyers.

"We have a small office in Portland," he said. "I can ask the associates we have there, but my guess is they've heard of the firms where they worked, but not them. At least not until four years ago when their names started being mentioned as candidates for governor."

"I thought the legal community was pretty tight," Standard said.

"It was at one time. I was told that the only things there are more of in Portland than lawyers are coffee shops," he said. "I can check when I get back about how good of lawyers they were, but it sounds to me like these two wanted a career in politics and getting law degrees was more about resume building."

It might have been the tequila, but Standard sensed that Grimes was both stunned at the direction the story was taking and disappointed. He came to Mexico looking for quick answers that might offer some leverage on Scofield Industries. Instead, he was getting way more than he bargained for and still didn't know who killed Proctor Scofield or why. If he was going to get to the truth, he'd have to wait a little longer. Mostly because Standard wasn't sure yet how much of the story he wanted to reveal. Parts of it were sacred. Very sacred. He had every intention of keeping it that way.

"I'm confused," Grimes said. "Why kill people over something that was part of the public record anyway? There were police reports and eyewitness accounts. Whatever other evidence Krychek cited in this thesis. And this is the age of the Internet. There are no secrets."

"Don't forget they both admitted it. To me. On the record."

"Well, there is that."

"Remember," Standard said. "Krychek's manuscript was unfinished. Jasmine Grant told me over the phone the night she was killed that what she got in the mail was a draft."

"And the people who wanted the draft didn't know that."

"That's my guess. Once they read it the killings stopped."

"Only you still weren't sure who 'they' were?"

"Right, but I was getting closer. Scofield was just out of reach. Except I didn't know it at the time. What I did know was that the story I was going to write would rattle his cage. If he didn't know who I was before, he would very soon. Roark and Landis had prepared for the truth to come out. The question I had was whether Scofield was prepared."

"Tell me about it."

30

Portland

After talking to Roark and Landis, it was time to go to work. I didn't leave the apartment for three days other than to dart across the street to the deli for an occasional sandwich and a carton of potato salad. The rest of the time was spent hunched over the computer or on the phone, lost in a search to piece together the story of Amanda Bishop, Brad Roark, Kingsley Landis, and, of course, Proctor Scofield.

A reluctant clerk at the Eugene Police Department agreed to find the original report filed the night of the attack on Amanda Bishop and email it to me. I had less luck with officials at Lane County, which had gone through five district attorneys since then, so no one had any idea why the charges against Roark and Landis were dropped or showed any interest in finding out. I finally tracked down Charles Morse, who was police chief at the time. He'd retired five years earlier to the sun and cheap golf of Thousand Palms, California. Morse was gruff and direct, even over the phone. "You have to remember that Scofield was not a big deal then like he is now. I had never heard of him. So, he got no special treatment, at least not from me. He sat in my office demanding that we drop the charges. Most parents would come in demanding we castrate guys like that. Scofield was just the opposite. He said in simple terms about wanting to save the girl the embarrassment of having to testify against those two assholes. I didn't want to do it so I passed the buck. Told him to go talk to the DA. The next thing I knew the whole thing just went away."

Morse said he wrote it all off as some emotional co-ed distraught over losing her virginity to the wrong guy. He had never personally interviewed Bishop but read the transcript and talked to the female investigator who did. He came away thinking that Bishop was handling the whole thing pretty well. "I guess she kept it all inside," he said. "Maybe that's why she killed herself."

A cooperative clerk at the Oregon State Police had little trouble locating the report on Amanda Bishop's suicide. It included the name of the driver of the truck that killed her. Barney Alweather lived in Elko,

Nevada, at the time of the accident. I found him through directory assistance, still living at the same address.

I called twice but got no answer. The third time was the charm. It didn't take long for him to remember the accident because he never forgot it: "I was twenty-nine when that happened and had been driving a truck about four years. I'm fifty-two now and still behind the wheel. I figure I've driven a few million miles in all these years and probably under a couple of hundred thousand overpasses. Never passed a one that I don't think about what happened, about seeing that girl draped over the front of my truck, her body impaled by the hood ornament, one of her arms reaching toward the windshield, toward me. Hell of a thing."

It took several more calls to the Eugene Police Department and the University of Oregon Registrar's Office to track down a witness from the condominium complex. Leslie Post, by then a nurse in Seattle, was reluctant to talk on the record, but willing to verify everything contained in the police report: "I got there about the same time as the police. There were at least fifty people standing on the balconies throwing things. This girl was curled up in a ball on the ground with her hands over her head. No one tried to help her until the manager showed up. It was horrible. I'd never seen anything like it and hope I never do again."

I asked how the girl looked. How she acted.

"She wasn't crying. Instead, there was this blank look on her face, like what just happened to her wasn't real. I remember thinking how odd that was. If it had been me, I would have been hysterical."

She didn't recognize the names Brad Roark or Kingsley Landis and knew nothing about a rape. She didn't find out until later that the girl in the parking lot was Amanda Bishop.

With more help from the registrar's office, I located Mary Franco, Amanda's roommate from the dormitory. She was a schoolteacher in Oakland, California. Amanda, she said, was like a ceramic angel that would break if you handled it too much. On the inside, though, she was different. "I can't explain it other than Amanda seemed to have a kind of inner strength, like she knew more than anyone else and had seen and done things no one else had, and not all of them good things. She was never very outgoing or demonstrative, but after that night it was like her mind just erased the entire event. I never saw her cry or even mention what happened. I tried once or twice to talk to her about how she was dealing with it and if there was anything I could do. All she gave me were reassurances that she didn't remember enough of what happened to have affected her and that I shouldn't worry about her."

When I asked if she had any last thoughts, she paused for a moment. She slowly, almost reluctantly, told me how Amanda kept little dresses and petticoats in her closet along with a pair of patent leather shoes. She would sometimes take them with her when she left to stay with friends. At least that's where she said she was going.

Franco said Amanda didn't date anyone that she knew of and seemed uninterested in boys or the social side of college. When the rest of the girls in the dorm would talk about men and sex, Amanda would sink into the back of the room and wait for the subject to change. "That's what made it all so strange," she said. "Going off with two guys just didn't fit."

I was writing furiously, taking notes on my laptop, scribbling thoughts on a notepad. I was starting to get a clearer picture of Amanda Bishop. When I asked about the night Amanda died, Franco said Amanda had a new Ford Mustang that she'd take out at night by herself. Sometimes she wouldn't come back until morning. So when she didn't show up that night or the next day, she didn't think too much about it. Then a woman from the president's office showed up and told everyone in the dorm what had happened. A few days later some men arrived and packed up all her things. That was the last she heard.

Mary Franco never met Amanda's parents, but recognized Proctor Scofield's name when I mentioned it. She didn't know he was Amanda's stepfather. She had no insights into why the two men accused of raping Amanda were never charged. She had never even learned their names.

I had less success with the parents of Roark and Landis. James and Barbara Roark refused to discuss the incident. Wilbert Landis had died two years earlier and his widow, Carol, burst into tears over the telephone at the mention of Amanda's name.

No luck talking to Proctor Scofield either. All I got from the Scofield Industries PR department was an email with a statement. "Mr. Scofield is well aware of the painful events twenty-three years go. He also recognizes that senators Roark and Landis have turned their lives around to become dedicated public servants. Mr. Scofield considers the incident closed."

What was odd about the statement, Harry, was that it made no mention of Amanda Bishop. I let it go because I knew that it was all I could get.

Confident that I had all I needed, I called Eldon Mock at *Inside Oregon*. A brief description of what I had learned and Mock was all in. I told him I needed three times the usual rate. When he quickly agreed I felt I should have asked for more.

After that, the story wrote itself. When it was finished, I sat in Eldon Mock's office watching him and the paper's lawyer go over the story line by line. Mock yelled at the lawyer, calling him a "bed wetter" when he raised concerns or expressed doubts about the wisdom of publishing it at all. Mock's disdain for politicians was legendary. He considered them the lowest form of life on earth and insisted he had the right to say anything he wanted about them. His mantra was, "They don't care as long as I spell their names right."

I guess, Harry, if I tell you something about Mock it might put things in perspective. He was in his early fifties, a wiry New Yorker with an attitude and a booming voice to match. He grew up in Brooklyn. Went to NYU. His first job was at *The Village Voice.* Thick hair pulled back into a tight ponytail made his nose and ears look too large for his small head. He wore a plaid shirt, striped tie, and baggy khakis. When he yelled, he had to take out his upper plate of false teeth so he wouldn't spit them into someone's face.

His lawyer couldn't be more different—a Berkeley graduate named Clausen, a junior associate in a large firm that specialized in libel law. He was two years out of law school and wore a heavily starched shirt with gold cuff links and a dark double-breasted suit. The electric beach tan went well with his tall, trim body and blond hair stylishly cut to hide an expanding bald spot. A tightly knotted tie made him look like he was choking on something other than Mock's stubbornness.

When Clausen tried explaining his positions, Mock would cut him off, accusing him of covering his ass and protecting his right to say I told you so when someone sued the paper. Clausen finally gave up when Mock shouted, "Fuck 'em. Let 'em sue."

I sat on an ancient leather couch in the corner watching the two men argue, content to be a disinterested observer in the fate of my hard work. I'd been in this kind of meeting before with worse editors than Mock and better lawyers than Clausen. They all came out the same. Sooner or later Mock would brush aside the lawyer's concerns by declaring he'd print what he wanted. It would be Clausen's job to figure out later how to defend it.

When a disgusted Clausen packed up his briefcase and left, Mock turned gleeful. He slapped me on the back, pulled a bottle of whiskey out of his desk and announced that I was going to be famous. I was going to be back on top again once the other editors in town saw my byline.

I knew that was coming and held up my hand. No, I told him. Putting my name on that story would only dredge up a lot of old stuff I'd just as soon forget. Roark and Landis were the story. I didn't want to give anyone an opening to discredit the story because of my past. I said he could put his name on it, leave the byline off altogether or use something like "Staff Reports." Mock wouldn't hear it. He couldn't understand why I didn't want my name on something that would make my old employer sit up and take notice and maybe get my old job back. I conceded the point with a shrug, but in the end stuck with the demand to remain anonymous. I had no intention of writing any follow-up stories about Roark and Landis. This was one story that someone else could chase. Mock had plenty of other reporters to ferret out reactions and whatever fallout there was. I was done. It was time to focus on the personal business of who killed Jasmine Grant and why.

After another half hour of back and forth, Mock agreed to run the story without a byline.

I left the offices of *Inside Oregon* wondering what Proctor Scofield would think about having the backstory of his daughter's death finally made public. I was sure that Roark and Landis had told Penroy that I had talked to them. Penroy would have undoubtedly passed it on to Scofield. I imagined Scofield reading the story online or having his limo driver find a copy of *Inside Oregon* as soon as it came out. No matter how he read it, he would have to decide how to break it to his wife. I could only guess at the steps Scofield had taken to insulate her from the past. Would reliving what happened bring them closer together or drive them apart? Did she even know about Scofield's demand that Roark and Landis not be prosecuted? If she did, how would she react? For that matter, was she still alive?

It was the first time I'd thought about Scofield's wife, Harry. It wouldn't be the last.

Not that any of this mattered much to me at the time. I had given Scofield and his corporation a chance to respond. All I got was a bland statement. I'd done my job. I could walk away with a feeling of accomplishment. Let others try to coax an explanation out of Scofield or his company. Let others keep the company in the news, hoping to force a more detailed response. Good luck with that was all I could say.

I could now turn my attention to what the story didn't say. I had purposefully avoided any mention or implication that what happened to Amanda Bishop was somehow connected to three unsolved murders. I wasn't in the speculation business. Same with Krychek's manuscript. The less said about that the better until I found out why it was so important.

The Amanda Bishop story appeared the next day under a headline that was pure Eldon Mock.

THE NIGHTMARE PAST OF THE DREAM CANDIDATES.

The stepdaughter of billionaire Proctor Scofield committed suicide twenty-three years ago after being raped by Brad Roark and Kingsley Landis.

The story generated a predictable response. The media frenzy produced by television, newspaper, and radio reporters trying to play catch up was in journalism's best tradition. Mock had released the story to the Associated Press right after the late-night news. By the time *Inside Oregon* hit the streets, the story was already a major topic on local television and radio stations, all of them carefully citing *Inside Oregon* as the source. The morning dailies, including my overly cautious and resentful former employer, could do little more than run the wire-service story. Talk radio hosts were practically lactating. Bloggers filled websites and chat rooms.

Reactions from the Roark and Landis camps had all the markings of a public relations strategy two decades in the making. Crisis management at its best. In a packed joint news conference called to get their spin on the story as soon as possible, the pair admitted everything while repeating verbatim the quotes they had given me and which I had included in the article. Their responses to questions were candid and contrite. They came off genuinely regretful. What happened to Amanda Bishop, they said, was the catalyst that redirected their lives into a commitment to public service. On cue, the two politicians' aides handed reporters separate fact sheets describing the accomplishments both men had achieved since Amanda's death.

I watched the whole thing live on the television in my apartment. It was a virtuoso performance by both men, especially Landis, who looked directly in the camera and, with emotion in his voice and tears in his eyes, said, "In many ways, what we've done with our lives over the last twenty plus years is dedicated to the memory of Amanda Bishop." It became the sound bite used that night by every local television station and nationally on CNN.

From the news conference, the two men made separate rounds of key editorial boards around the state. They and their surrogates eagerly accepted requests for interviews from TV news anchors and radio talk show hosts. By the end of the day they were off to shore up relations with key constituents and well-heeled interest groups.

The strategy was clear: Unlike others caught up in the Me Too Movement, they admitted everything, asked forgiveness, and pointed to how they had turned their lives around. Honest and contrite apologies left no room for confusion. It didn't take long for the political reporters to take over the story. Soon, what happened to Amanda Bishop became lost amid speculation about what would happen to Roark and Landis. Were they damaged goods? Had they lost the respect of voters? Were they electable? Did this open the door for other candidates to enter the race? The political handicappers, partisan pollsters and spinmeisters stepped in with enough speed to suck the political press in behind them. The temptation to treat political campaigns like horse races prevailed.

The evening news became little more than a parade of dull analysts, usually political scientists from obscure departments in equally obscure colleges. They offered conflicting opinions about the future of both candidates but were always careful to hedge their bets. The pollsters were the worst, gleaning deep insights into the minds and attitudes of voters, assuming they were paying attention.

Finally came the press secretaries, public relations experts, and party hacks eager to put the best face possible on the rape and suicide of a long-forgotten co-ed. Try as they might, they were hamstrung by the fact that both men admitted to doing the same thing. That made it hard for one camp to criticize the other. They were left with nothing to do or say except follow the talking points issued by both sides. Those who expressed outrage that one of two rapists might become governor were shunted to the fringes of the debate. Those who carried signs reading

"Remember Amanda" were treated as sideshows and given short shrift by the political press and only seconds on the nightly news. Within a few days after the story broke, the conventional wisdom had been established: Voters had short attention spans and the whole thing would be forgotten by primary election season next spring. The name Amanda Bishop faded away. More and more frequently she was reduced to "the stepdaughter of reclusive billionaire Proctor Scofield."

The story was two days old when my lawyer called to say the papers officially ending my marriage were ready to sign. I found it oddly satisfying to sit in his plush, high-rise office, thumb through the documents and put my signature or initials on pages fixed with little red stickers in the shape of arrows that read: "Sign here." The decree gave me half the proceeds of the sale of our house, which, whenever it sold, would cover the rest of my legal bills and still leave enough to find a better place to live. Everything else went to Christine. Fair enough. Most of it belonged to her anyway. Unfair as it was, I really didn't care. It was over. Nothing else mattered. I thanked the lawyer then rode down in the elevator promising myself to never get married again.

The late afternoon sky was a hazy blue, the temperature hovering in the high eighties again. Shirt stuck to my back, I walked up SW Columbia Street toward home. The sudden sense of freedom left me oblivious to both the heat and the long walk. One by one, the bonds of my old life were cut, leaving me to float away and forget what had been. It also left me free to find out what role, if any, Proctor Scofield played in the death of Jasmine Grant.

No arrest had been made in the murder of Buck Mather, which meant I would probably being hearing from Daryl Butcher again. He had called once asking why my fingerprints were all over Jasmine Grant's kitchen. I explained again what I did when I walked in her house. It didn't wash with him, but then nothing I said was going to make any difference. I considered once again whether to tell Butcher about the dark Lincoln but cringed at the thought of having to explain why I didn't tell him about it in the first place.

All I knew for sure was that Krychek's murder had set off a series of events that had grown into an intricate web of crisscrossing lines that masked almost everything. Through the cracks, I could see three things: Ivan Krychek sitting in a portable toilet, Jasmine Grant tied to her bed, and a car racing down Packer Lane.

Even if Mitch Penroy wasn't driving the Lincoln that night, the lobbyist must know something about the murder. If Penroy knew then it followed that Scofield did as well. There were too many coincidences not to believe that somehow Scofield Industries wasn't involved right up to its hard drives in trying to keep secret the contents of Krychek's dissertation.

The night before I had sat in the leather chair, scribbling notes and questions about the motives and actions behind the murders. Vanessa was across the way fine-tuning a new act. It had a military theme involving a camouflage costume, a combat helmet, and a field rifle. Watching her rehearse in front of the bedroom mirror, I thought about going down the hall, knocking on her door and asking why would the rich and powerful hang out with the scum of the earth? What is it that ties two ends of the evolutionary scale—Proctor Scofield and Buck Mather—together? Is Penroy the missing link? Someone in her profession must have gained some insight into what motivates men to do what they do. Or was she too removed? Did she shut her mind off, do her routine, never see the men on the other side of the stage lights and go home at night no wiser for the experience? The questions kept coming, lingering like a bad jingle until another came along. One ear worm replacing another.

Rather than go home, I walked down SW Fifth Avenue into the heart of the city then up Burnside past Powell's Books, The RingSide Steakhouse, and Providence Park. It took more than an hour to reach Papa Haydn's on NW 23rd Avenue. I sat at the same table where I'd had lunch with Jasmine, ordered the same food and drank the same wine. Finished, I walked up to the Knob Hill Bar and Grill, found the table we'd shared and ordered a beer. Through it all, nothing about my five years with Christine crossed my mind. Only the few hours I'd spent with Jasmine Grant.

After two beers, I caught the trolley back downtown then walked up SW Park Avenue to the apartment. Back in the leather chair, staring at Vanessa's empty apartment, I ran the names through my head again trying to find a way to get to Proctor Scofield. After nine that night the heat and growing frustration of what to do next drove me out of the stifling apartment and into the streets again.

The outdoor tables in front of the restaurants along SW Broadway were filled with people with the same desire to escape the heat. I walked around the corner to a pizza place on SW Alder Street to nurse a beer and read the early edition of the local daily. It had been three days since the revelations in *Inside Oregon* and already the stories about Roark, Landis, and Amanda Bishop had been shunted off the front page and on to "airplane pages," B12 and F15. The strategy of admitting everything and asking forgiveness appeared to be paying off—for now. The story would come up again during the primary next spring, but for now it was slowly dissipating.

I gave up the table at around ten-thirty, but still didn't feel like going home. To kill time, I walked down Broadway and into Old Town. The homeless were eating up the night. Sleeping, smoking, or urinating along the dark streets of what had once been a thriving Chinatown. Doorways had become tombs with a view.

I caught the MAX at First and Davis and headed back downtown. After getting off at Pioneer Square, I trudged up Broadway past the Heathman Hotel, the Arlene Schnitzer Concert Hall, and around the corner by the Oregon History Center before cutting over on SW Jefferson Street to the South Park Blocks. The key was almost in the door of the apartment building when the man appeared on the sidewalk.

He was tall and thin with a pale complexion, a round head and a neatly trimmed black mustache. Early fifties maybe, but it was hard to tell in the dark. Despite the heat, he wore a black suit, white shirt, bow tie and expensive leather gloves. The cap on his head resembled a Greek sailor's hat. I slowly nodded when he asked if I was John Standard.

"Would you mind coming with me for a moment," he said. "My employer would like to speak to you."

"Who would that be?" I asked.

"All in good time, Mr. Standard," he said, then let me know that his employer was waiting in a car nearby. "I promise you won't be gone long."

When I hesitated, the man took a business card from the breast pocket of his coat and handed it to me. It came with his guarantee that I was not in any danger. One glance at the card was all I needed.

I followed the man around the corner and up a block to the Safeway store at SW Tenth and Jefferson. In a dark corner of a nearby parking lot and away from the other cars lurked a black limousine with its parking lights on. The man opened the rear door and stood at attention. I looked inside. A woman's voice laced with a hint of Georgia invited me to get in and have a seat. She said it with a tone both gentle and direct. It was the voice of someone comfortable with giving orders and having them obeyed.

The inside of the limo was red leather, polished mahogany, and thick black carpet. A crystal decanter with four matching glasses sat in special holders on a console above the small television set built into a side panel. The interior lights were turned low, making the woman sitting on the far side of the rear seat little more than shadow.

The chauffeur closed the door, leaving me to ramble around inside before finally sitting down at the far end of a J-shaped seat, my back to the front of the car. I was facing an elegant woman who looked to be in her late sixties with thick gray hair, elegantly cut to curl softly behind small ears with large diamond studs. Glasses with dark red frames rested on high cheek bones. A discreet color of lipstick. A hint of eye shadow. Under her full-length coat was a black dress with a high collar, large white buttons and a hem line that resembled an inverted tulip. The style was newer than the body it covered, but she made it work. In one hand sat a crystal glass half full of what looked like scotch. Everything about her spoke of privilege and elegance. She didn't just sit in a limo, she owned it in more ways than one.

"I'm Margaret Scofield," she said. The voice that thanked me for taking time to see her was soft and tired.

I fingered the business card the chauffeur had given me then dumbly asked if Proctor Scofield was her husband. "Just to be sure," I said.

She confirmed it with a slight nod of her head.

"Then you're Amanda Bishop's mother?"

She answered again with the same slight nod then pushed the hair on one side of her face back behind her ear with a long, graceful finger. Her eyes were like sapphires that had retained their luster while everything around them slowly surrendered to age.

The glass partition behind my head was closed, so I didn't know the chauffeur had slipped behind the wheel until the limo started to move. Margaret Scofield picked up the intercom telephone, told the chauffeur to drive around for a while then hung up and looked at me. I had a sense of why I was there, but I waited until she asked if I was the person responsible for the newspaper story about her daughter's death. She said it in a tone that suggested sadness, but no anger. I said yes then asked if there was a problem?

"No," she said, "other than bringing back some painful memories. Enough memories, in fact, that I thought we should talk."

Since there was no byline on the story, I asked how she'd found me. "I am the wife of a billionaire, Mr. Standard. I have resources, including people who work for my husband but who maintain a certain loyalty to me." Her eyes darted quickly from me to the front of the limo and back again.

Having been admonished, I had no choice but to accept the explanation with a nod. I asked again if there was a problem. She waited to answer, choosing her words carefully.

"Not a problem so much as an oversight," she said.

"What did I miss?"

"I don't believe my daughter killed herself because of what those two men did to her."

The statement landed on the lush carpet like an anvil. I blurted out a weak comeback about what Roark and Landis had told me and what they admitted to in public after the story came out. Why would they take total responsibility for something they didn't do?

Margaret Scofield reached into her purse and pulled out a wrinkled envelope. She handed it to me while staring directly into my eyes. I took it out of her hand and opened it. Inside was a type-written note on plain white paper.

"That's Amanda's suicide note," she said then turned away to stare out the window at the passing streetlights and do some damage to the scotch.

I read the note. It was short and enigmatic, I guess, not that I've ever read a suicide note. After reading it, I folded it and slipped into the envelope. All I could think of to tell her was, "I don't know what to say." I handed the envelope back to her. "To be honest, Mrs. Scofield, it seems pretty clear to me. Sad, but clear."

She gave a nod that said she knew exactly what I was talking about. She'd had the same reaction twenty-three years ago when she read that note the first time. It was clear, too clear. Her daughter killed herself. Then she reached into her purse again and pulled out a second envelope. "Then I found this." She handed it to me.

This note was in a small, pale blue envelope. I opened it. The note inside was much longer, undated, and hand-written instead of type-written. It was on white stationery, the kind with flowers across the top.

It started out with "To my wonderful mother." She had signed her name at the bottom with a large A.

I read the note once, paused to look at Margaret Scofield then read it a second time. After that I carefully folded it and put it back in the envelope. When I handed it back to her, she carefully put it in her purse with the first one.

She explained that she had no idea when the second note was written. Her housekeeper found it in a box of belongings that were removed from Amanda's dormitory after her death. It was there with some other letters and papers. This happened several months after her death.

She kept a composed look but reliving this in front of a stranger was taking a toll. As hard as she tried to get herself under control, there was a choke in her voice that made her stop every few minutes to gather herself. To me, she had all the appearances of someone who had been living with sorrow for far too long. I watched as she fought through it. The scotch appeared to help.

Slowly at first she said she'd been carrying both of those notes with her for twenty-three years. She had read them thousands of times: "To understand those notes, you would have to understand Amanda. I did, which is why I believe those two men … I can't even say their names … had nothing to do with her death. There was something my daughter was struggling to tell me. Something that she couldn't find the words for then died before she could."

The chauffeur had navigated the limo over to Taylor Street and west to Interstate 405. Through the smoked glass, I could see we were headed toward Interstate 5. The car seemed to float along, moving easily through traffic and through the Terwilliger curves. I asked her the obvious question: If Amanda didn't kill herself, who did and why.

She shook her head. That didn't make sense. She'd had more than twenty years to think about it. She must have some kind of theory. I said, "There's something you're not telling me."

The same graceful finger pushed the hair back behind one ear again, followed by a half-hearted apology. She went back to the scotch for a few moments: "Amanda's real father was a cruel man incapable of demonstrating any emotion that didn't involve profanity and violence. Don't ask why I married him. I don't understand it myself and it was a long time ago. All you need to know is that I left him shortly after Amanda was born to protect both her and me."

I have to tell you, Harry, that what she told me after that sounded like the plot for a novel. She and Amanda moved from South Carolina to Portland and changed their names. She struggled for years waiting tables and doing secretarial work, anything that would help give Amanda a normal life. Eventually, she earned a real estate license and was hired as an associate for a large firm specializing in high-end homes. One of her first clients was Proctor Scofield. They were married two years later. Amanda was six years old at the time.

That was the short version. The long version seemed to take all the strength she had. She put the crystal glass in its holder between the seats and opened the mahogany console. With silver tongs, she lifted three ice cubes from a bucket and dropped them in the glass, refilling it with the scotch. She leaned back into the corner of the seat. "When we met, Proctor Scofield had money. Nowhere near what he has today, but enough to give me everything I ever wanted and he doted on Amanda. There was nothing in the world he wouldn't do for her. She wore the best clothes, went to the best private schools, and had all the best things. We spent summers at the beach house that I helped him buy. Later, we traveled through Europe, Asia, and South America. When Amanda was in high school, he'd take her with him on overseas business trips. She had seen most of the world by the time she left for college."

When I asked how Amanda felt about Proctor, the question seemed to surprise her. She held the glass against her lower lip while describing how they weren't like father and daughter. Not being her real father seemed to make Proctor treat Amanda differently. After that, her voice trailed off, taking her thoughts with it. When I asked if he meant that they were more like friends, she quickly agreed. Too quickly.

The limo passed the Highway 217 exit, then settled into the far right-hand lane before turning off onto Interstate 205, which circled through the south and east sides of Portland. The big car glided through the late-night traffic. Other cars seemed to move out of its way. Drivers gawking at the dark windows. Margaret Scofield poured her third drink as the limo crossed the Willamette River at Oregon City.

Amanda, she explained, had the choice of any school in the world, but decided to go to the University of Oregon rather than back east to one of the Ivy League schools. They had the money and she had the grades. Getting into any school in the country would not be a problem and, if it were, Proctor could pull some strings. But Amanda insisted on going to Oregon. What few friends she had were going there and she wanted to be close to home. Margaret was ambivalent, but Proctor was thrilled. He would drive down to Eugene every weekend he was home to take her to dinner. He'd come back with stories about her classes. She had never seen him happier.

I wanted to know where the story was headed. Instead, it was better to be patient. The car and the story were hers. I just rode along and listened while she described how excited and eager Amanda was to make new friends and to learn: "After a football game she was invited to a party at one of the sororities. Amanda never drank in high school—at least not that I knew of. But at this party there was a keg of beer and loud music. She met one of the boys, or both, and left with them."

Watching her, Harry, was painful. I began thinking that maybe this was the first time she'd talked about the events leading up to her daughter's death. I wasn't sure why she was telling me other than wanting to unburden herself. Either that or she had no one to share it with. If that was the case then it spoke volumes about the loneliness of her life.

Margaret Scofield sought sanctuary in her scotch, finishing the drink in one gulp. I couldn't blame her. It was the kind of memory that demanded liquor and plenty of it. She reached for another drink and stopped. If she was going to exceed her limit it wasn't going to be in front of me. She leaned further back in the seat until her face faded in the shadows again: "There was no way Amanda was sexually active. I couldn't imagine anything more horrifying for her than to be assaulted. But when Proctor and I got to Eugene, Amanda seemed oddly calm. I assumed she was in shock and that sooner or later her emotions would take over. I stayed with her while Proctor talked to the police. He told me later that the matter would be taken care of and that there was no need to file charges. I was too worried about Amanda to pay much attention. Like with some other things, I trusted Proctor to take care of it."

"Did you think it was odd that no charges were ever filed?" I asked.

"Not at the time," she said, but days later it began to bother her. Amanda's death seemed incomplete without those responsible paying a price for what they'd done. When she finally asked about it, Proctor said it needed to be kept a private matter. He explained that he had the resources to take care of it personally, that those responsible would pay a price and there was no need for Amanda to go through the trauma of a trial. She believed him. Why wouldn't she? When Proctor said something was taken care of, she knew it was.

"Those responsible?" I asked.

I found it hard to believe that for all those years Margaret Scofield didn't know the names of the men who raped her daughter. If it was true then it was a tribute to Proctor Scofield's power over his family and her subservience to it. It also spoke volumes about the depth of Margaret Scofield's grief. She never questioned, not even about what he meant by "taken care of."

After the funeral, Proctor Scofield took her to Europe for several months, all the time making sure she had everything she wanted. He did his best to keep her occupied in the hope she wouldn't dwell on Amanda's death. It was hard watching her describe how in all the years they'd been married they were never closer than on that trip. It made her realize, she said, that having him as a husband was a blessing. Then, she paused while looking at the empty glass, said, "Over time, that would change."

She gave me a look that said that was all she had to say about it.

The limo took the Interstate 84 exit off 205 and headed west back into the city. She finally poured more scotch for herself and offered me a glass. I took her up on it. She still hadn't explained why she thought Roark and Landis weren't responsible for Amanda's death. When I asked her about it, she reminded me that I had read the notes. "What could Amanda have possibly done that would come between Proctor and me? Every time I read those notes, I ask myself the same question. The life the three of us had together was near perfection. I couldn't imagine what would destroy that other than her death."

Pointing toward her purse with the notes inside, I asked what her daughter had meant by saying that Proctor was a better father to her than she was a daughter to Margaret.

She leaned forward. The face that came out of the shadows looked suddenly older, more tired. "You need to understand that Proctor was nearly sixty-years old when we were married. It was his first marriage and his first experience with raising a child. There were some difficult times where things got a little tense. When I first read the note, I thought she was referring to an adjustment period then, later, I thought it was something more complicated. After reading those notes so many times, I could probably give you dozens of different meanings for each word and phrase. That is what sorrow does to you, Mr. Standard. It makes you think too much, lose perspective, see things that probably aren't there."

I sat back and waited to see what came next. She told me that her husband didn't know about the second letter. She hadn't shown it to him but cautioned me not to ask why. She just didn't know.

"You don't trust him, do you?" I asked.

She stared at me for a moment, once again choosing her words carefully. She didn't know all the details of how Proctor went from selling typewriter ribbons to being one of the richest men in the world. She didn't want to know, but when she learned that he was known in the business world as the Prince of Snakes, she wasn't surprised.

Before she leaned back into the shadows again, her eyes begged me not to press the issue. It was too late. She was giving me insights into the personal life of Proctor Scofield that no one had seen before and probably never would. If he was involved in murder, I had to know what kind of man he was.

"Are you going to make me regret that I talked to you?" she asked.

"Never," I told her.

That either satisfied her or she wanted to tell the whole story; get it all out at one time: "Proctor Scofield is like any other man. Someone capable of doing anything given the right set of circumstances. That's all I'm going to say." It wasn't a ringing endorsement, but I knew it was as far as she would go.

I changed the subject and asked about Mitch Penroy. She knew very little about him. The few times they'd met she found him polite and fiercely loyal to her husband. When I asked if she thought he was capable of murder she looked surprised then curious about why I would ask.

"A shot in the dark," I said.

The limo crossed the Willamette on the Morrison Street Bridge and drove up SW Washington Street to SW Park Avenue. It squeezed along the narrow street before stopping in front of my apartment building. We sat in an awkward silence before I asked what she wanted me to do. She reached into her purse for another envelope and handed it to me. I looked inside long enough to see that it was filled with hundred dollar bills.

"I told you that I believe Amanda didn't kill herself because of what they did to her," she said. "Find out who did and why. Find out for Amanda … and for me."

The envelope contained fifteen-thousand dollars. I pulled the money from the envelope and fanned the bills out like a deck of cards. Each one represented hours of work writing articles for airline magazines and grant proposals for school districts. With a silent sigh, I returned the money to the envelope and handed it back to her. When she began to protest, I held up my hand. Telling Margaret Scofield about two dead Hispanic girls and a murdered lover seemed a waste of time.

"It's a long story," I said.

She said she'd look forward to hearing it one day then put the money back in her purse. She was leaving for New York later that night and be back in Portland in three days. She and Proctor would be out of town after that, but would it be okay if she called me. When I nodded, she reached out to gently lay a hand on my sleeve. "All I want is that you never forget Amanda." She pressed Amanda's two notes into my hand. "Keep these. Read them as many times as I have. Maybe then you'll understand more about what happened and why."

All I remember after that, Harry, was standing in front of the apartment building watching the taillights of the limo disappear into traffic. No amount of culture and refinement could protect Margaret Scofield from the damage of two decades of grief. Losing a daughter wasn't made any easier by unlimited wealth. People die for all kinds of reasons, Harry. Most can be understood, explained, dealt with, and then forgotten given enough time. The memories of the dead appear richer and more textured to those left behind because death has a way of sifting out the bad and leaving behind a concentrated image for others to enjoy and relish. The Margaret Scofields of the world are the product of people dying for the wrong reasons and leaving behind too many unanswered questions.

After she drove away, Harry, my only thought was that I'd never met a woman so alone.

31

Playa la Ropa, Zihuatanejo

Standard and Grimes sat silently, both taking in the sad image of Margaret Scofield. Unsure why, Standard got the feeling that Grimes has been moved by the story, or at least parts of it.

"The suicide notes," Grimes said finally, acting like he was still not sure it was the right time to ask about them. "What did they say? Can you remember the exact words?"

"I can do better than that," Standard said.

They left Paty's and walked down the beach. On the other side of The Tortuga they cut through a closed, open-air restaurant to the dusty alley that led to the turnaround. After another fifty yards, Standard turned left up a narrow, cobblestone driveway that eventually turned into a set of steep concrete stairs. By the time they reached the top, Grimes was puffing, panting and in a full sweat. At the top of the steps, Standard unlocked the gate in a bamboo fence. He led Grimes up the path to the house where he plopped down in the first chair he saw. He looked around while waiting to catch his breath.

"Interesting place," he said.

The one-level house Standard shared with Emma Parrish was all open air, with a thatched roof, wooden railing around the outside and set firmly on a concrete foundation. There was a large kitchen, a comfortable front room and a terrace that looked out through the jungle to the beach. The master bedroom and bath were at one end. The spare bedroom at the other.

"It's called a palapa house," Standard said. "Emma had it built about twelve years ago. I moved in last January. There's another, smaller house in the back of the property that Emma rents out on Airbnb. She advertises it to ecotourists."

Standard pulled a bottle of water out of the small refrigerator under the kitchen counter, handed it to a grateful Grimes then went into the master bedroom. He came back holding two envelopes and handed them to Grimes.

"Read them for yourself," Standard said. "If you learn anything, let me know." He left for the kitchen to pull a bottle of Patrón off the shelf over the sink.

Grimes opened the first one and read it out loud. "Dear Mom and Dad, please forgive me and don't blame yourselves. I love both of you more than you will ever know. I did this because I can't live with what happened to me. It's so unfair. I'm sorry. Good-bye, and God bless you both."

Grimes put the note back in the envelope "Seems pretty cut and dried, but, like you, I don't have much experience with suicide notes."

Standard stood on the doorway to the kitchen, a shot glass in his hand. "Try the second note." When Grimes opened the other envelope and began reading it to himself, Standard said, "Out loud."

"Dear Mom, I must have started this letter a thousand times in the last three years. Each time, I tear it up and try again. I just can't seem to find the words to tell you that there are things that have happened that can never be changed or made right again. I have lost something that I can never regain. More importantly, I have betrayed someone I love very much, you. We are the lucky ones to have escaped a life of misery for one of comfort. You made that happen and I can never thank you enough. After what you went through with my biological father, you deserve the kind of love you've found with Proctor. What I'm afraid of is that I'll be responsible for the loss of that love. I have come to think of Proctor as my real father. He gave me everything a girl could want. We made mistakes, but I think he has been a better father to me than I have been a daughter to you. I hope that after I tell you everything, you'll forgive me and not hate me. I'll explain everything when I see you."

Grimes carefully folded the letter and put it back in the envelope. "Losing her love? Made mistakes?" he asked. "What did she need to explain?"

"All good questions, but we'll never know the answers," Standard said. "There seems to be a lot of riddles and unfinished ideas. Her secret, if she had one, is buried somewhere between the lines for someone else to understand."

"You kept these notes for four years. Why?"

"Maybe I knew that someone like you would show up one day and ask questions about how Proctor Scofield died."

"You don't really believe that, do you?" Grimes asked.

Standard shrugged. "No, but it doesn't hurt to hang onto the things that are important, things that one day might make a difference. Margaret Scofield gave them to me because she thought I could use them to learn the truth about Amanda's death."

"Did you?

"Sort of."

Standard could tell that Grimes was having second thoughts about why he came to Mexico and what he hoped to find out. Telling him about Margaret Scofield seemed to weigh on him as much as it had Standard.

"I'm not sure I want to hear the rest," he said, "but I can't walk away now."

32

Salem, Oregon

After waving goodbye to Margaret Scofield and her fifteen thousand dollars, I went back to my apartment building to talk to Benny. I pulled him away from his favorite movie, *Trapeze,* long enough to ask for his help finding what he could about Proctor Scofield. Not the usual stuff available on the Internet, but about his personal life. His likes, dislikes, habits. I was hoping that Benny and his online friends could help me out. Benny smiled and gave me an evil wink that said he would do what he could.

I left for Salem the next morning after spending the night staring at the ceiling and going over the list of questions I'd written down the night before while watching Vanessa rehearse a new act that involved a dog collar and a fake cattle prod. I decided not to waste time trying to go straight at Proctor Scofield. I'd been down that road before. It led nowhere. The only option was to attack the snake's head from the tail. That meant going back to the beginning.

Another wreck on the Terwilliger curves on Interstate 5 south of Portland brought traffic to a standstill and put me on slow simmer. By the time I arrived at the state capital building, I was working hard to remember that boiling over into a rage wasn't going to get me what I wanted. With a forced smile, I slowly worked my way through a half-dozen legislators and an equal number of hide-bound bureaucrats before learning the answer to one of my questions: How did a low-life like Buck Mather get the contract to provide security at the state capital?

It took three hours of work to learn that the contract went up for bid a year earlier as part of an on-going effort to privatize something that had always been left to retired police officers. Prestige Security was one of four bidders and came in with the lowest price. After reviewing each bid, a recommendation went to the legislative committee charged with making the final decision. Senator Brad Roark chaired the committee. One of the other six members was Senator Kingsley Landis. The committee administrator, Ellen Tillman, occupied an office that was part of a partitioned area of a large room on the third floor. She was young and serious with wash-and-go hair, sensible shoes and a mail-order suit that looked stiff and scratchy. After a few moments of staring through oblong glasses with dark frames, she apparently decided there was no choice but to help me. She pulled a buff-colored file folder from the state-issued credenza behind her chair. After shuffling through the papers for a few minutes, she said the initial recommendation was to retain the services of Four Star Security, which had the contract for the preceding two years. She politely reviewed the minutes of the committee meeting at which the contract was discussed. The debate centered on cost and some dissatisfaction with Four Star over a security issue the previous year. I declined her offer to listen to the tape of the meeting, asking instead who made the motion to hire Prestige even though I had a pretty good idea who it was. No surprise. Landis made the motion. Roark seconded it.

When she grudgingly handed over the telephone number for Four Star Security, I headed for a quiet corner of the capital and called its offices in Tigard. The owner, John Shoemaker, was a talkative ex-policeman more than happy to vent his frustration over politics, politicians, and lost earnings. He called the whole business "slimy." Accusations that his company had botched a security problem at the capital were "cooked up" and that his employees had saved people. According to him an anti-abortion activist ran amok in the senate gallery, waving a gun and kicking out a glass doors before they could get him under control and out of the building. He said Landis accused the guards of treating the man with disrespect because of his views on abortion. Shoemaker called that "total bullshit." When the contract came up before the committee, he was firmly told not to raise a stink or he'd lose more than the security contract at the capital. When I asked about the other contracts, he told me that his biggest clients were two small high-tech firms outside Portland. It was made very clear to him that if he did anything to protest the awarding of the capital contract to Prestige, he would lose those contracts as well. Turned out he lost them anyway.

I thanked Shoemaker and hung up, knowing now that all the players were on the same team. The only thing missing was what Krychek left out of his doctoral dissertation that got him and two others killed. Time to move one more link up the chain. I called Benny to ask him to work his magic and find the home address of Mitchell Penroy.

He called back twenty minutes later with an address in southeast Portland.

An hour later I was parked in front of Mitch Penroy's single-level, river-view condominium tucked away in a secluded corner of the city near a private country club. From the narrow cul-de-sac, there was little to see other than the closed garage door and a recessed front door. Facing the street were two narrow windows with vertical blinds turned shut.

There was little chance that Penroy was home at two in the afternoon, but it was worth a shot. I went to the door, rang the bell a few times and knocked as hard I could. When no one answered, I got back in the car and called Penroy's office. After being danced around the maypole a few times by Scofield Industries' automated telephone system, I hung up and drove to a convenience store on SE Tacoma Street for some rations.

With a paper sack filled with diet cola, several pieces of beef jerky, a small bag of trail mix and a couple of peanut butter cups, I returned to the cul-de-sac. Backing the Jeep into a parking space across from Penroy's garage door, I pulled a can of cola out of the sack and waited. Two hours later I was out of food and had seen nothing other than two guys walking a schnauzer.

I was searching the radio dial for some local news when a blonde in an Audi A-6 pulled into Penroy's driveway. Leaving the car's motor running, she went to the front door, unlocked it, and disappeared inside. Ten minutes later she came out, talking on a cellphone, her large sunglasses pushed up on top of her head. I watched her slide gracefully behind the wheel and back the car into the street. She wasn't who I was looking for but would do for the time being.

Heavy traffic made it easy to follow the Audi up McLoughlin Boulevard and across the Ross Island Bridge into downtown. I stayed three car-lengths behind as she drove slowly past Waterfront Park then west on SW Taylor Street. The car entered the parking structure on SW Fifth Avenue. When she parked, I pulled into a spot three spaces away. The blonde took the elevator to the street level while I hoofed it down the stairs. I got there in time to follow her up the street and watch her disappear into Nordstrom. I hung around outside, smoking a cigarette and trying to keep an eye on her through the mannequins in the window displays. When she came out and walked down the street to Pioneer Place, I stayed fifty yards behind her.

Sitting on a bench near the brass-and-glass escalator, I watched while she moved quickly through two of the more upscale stores. When she took the stairs to the lower level, I jumped on the elevator and got off just as she entered a lingerie shop. I waited a few minutes then followed her inside where she was pawing at a carousel of skimpy bras and panties.

"Is this where all the best-dressed widows shop or is it just for those who try to frame people for murder?"

Anna Krychek looked like she wanted to bolt, but I stood between her and the only exit.

"Leave me alone," she said in a harsh whisper. The look on her face reminded me of a cornered cat. "I have nothing to say to you."

Her short, blonde hair had replaced the long, dark hair that had been so mesmerizing the day we met. Other than that, everything else seemed to be intact. The comfortable clothes and shoes said that it was early drinks with a friend after an afternoon of shopping.

"How did you find me?"

"I was looking for Penroy but spotted you instead. You were too hard to pass up."

Her eyes turned from angry to vulnerable then went into a full-blown list of excuses. She'd done nothing wrong; what happened to Ivan Krychek was terrible; it wasn't her fault; it was all a mistake. It was a nice performance, but not on a par with the one she gave as Krychek's widow. When I told her we needed to talk, her protests were enough to attract the attention of a clerk, who glared at us while still trying to keep another customer's attention on a red satin teddy.

No way was I going to put up with Anna Krychek's whining. I let her know that I knew her real name—or at least what I thought was her real name. I knew where she lived. The license number of her car. I also knew a couple of homicide detectives who would love to hear the story about how she called me the night Buck Mather was murdered so I would find his body. It was pretty simple—she could talk to me or talk to them.

I leaned on the carousel, trying to talk in a tone that I hoped would keep the clerk at bay for a few more minutes. Anna looked over her shoulder. Seeing no help, she gave a resigned nod. We rode the escalator back to the main level and found a small table outside a Starbucks. She sat stiffly in the metal chair while I got two small coffees in paper cups.

"It didn't take you long to get out of the house on Baltusrol," I said. "Not even the neighbors knew you were gone."

"It was too painful to stay there after Ivan died," she said.

When a tear started rolling down one cheek, I tried not to laugh. She didn't cry the day she learned he'd been murdered, so why start now. I asked why she married Krychek in the first place, and not to insult me with more stories about nonexistent seminars and a shared affection for Czechoslovakia. She said it was true. I said it wasn't.

The pout on her face turned to terror then resignation. She said Ivan was a nice man and she was sorry he was dead, but swore she had nothing to do with it. She was only doing what she was told.

"Mitch Penroy," I said. "He wanted you to get close to Krychek and find out what you could about the research he was doing for his doctoral dissertation. I got that right?"

Her tears returned, but this time they were real and spoke the truth. She sipped the coffee, leaving perfect lipstick marks on the edge of the cup. Penroy, she said, told her he needed to know more about Krychek. He paid her to meet him, flirt a little, and then go out with him a few times. Then, out of the blue, Krychek asked her to marry him. She couldn't believe it. Later he told her he'd never even been on a date. Marrying him was never part of the plan, but when she told Mitch he laughed and said it was perfect. He took care of everything after that. A quickie wedding in Nevada, a honeymoon in Mazatlán, and a new house when they got back.

"Then Krychek was murdered."

She nodded: "Two days before Ivan died, Mitch sent me to Southern California to stay with these people he said would act as my parents. He flew me back the day after they found Ivan's body. Then he got me out of the house as fast as he could. The movers showed up in the middle of the night. That was fine with me. Murder was never part of the deal. Staying in that house would only make me look like more of an accomplice than I already was. Mitch even suggested I go to Europe for a month, but all I wanted was to get back to my own home and my old life."

When I asked about Krychek's research, she said he never told her anything specific. All she knew was that he was working on some kind of manuscript. When she told Penroy about it he started pressing her to find out more, but Ivan was too secretive. He never talked about what he was working on. He'd always said the same thing—a work in progress—then changed the subject. All she knew was that it was important or why else would Mitch pay her money to meet Krychek then make her marry him and buy them a house.

Once again, Harry, all roads lead back to Mitch Penroy, and with Penroy you got Scofield.

I asked her about the night Mather was killed. Was it Penroy's idea? Did he talk her into it? Was he with her when she called me? Did he coach her on what to say?

I got no argument from her, only more tears and more apologies. She blamed Penroy for the whole thing and said she didn't find out until later what he was trying to do. She said Penroy was livid that I got there early, found the body, and called the police. I believed her when she told me she didn't know who killed Mather.

Anna looked like she wanted to run and never stop. I didn't blame her. Penroy was using her and not just to find Krychek's manuscript. Once again, I got the feeling that there was more going on here than an innocent doctoral dissertation that was going to expose something that would become public eventually anyway.

Anna reached across the table to put her hand on mine. All she wanted was for this to be over and to be left out of it. She never thought for a second that things would turn out the way they did, with people dead. She lowered her voice when a couple at the next table turned to look at her.

I moved my chair closer to the table, leaning forward until I could smell her perfume and see the red veins in her eyes. I told her I wanted her to go back to Penroy. Tell him that I saw his car leaving Mather's house that night. Tell him I saw the whole thing. Tell him I know he killed Buck Mather.

She picked nervously at her carefully lacquered nails. "Do you really think Mitch did it?"

"What do you think?"

She refused to look at me. Through an awkward silence, we sipped coffee and watched shoppers scurry in and out of stores on the opposite side of the mall.

"I saw you leaving Penroy's condo," I said. "You and he an item?"

She nodded then looked around as if hoping Starbucks had suddenly started serving something stronger than coffee. I asked if Anna was her real name. She shook her head. "No. It's Tina. Tina Davenport. Can we go somewhere and get a drink?"

I hustled her out the door and down the street to the Red Star on SW Fifth Avenue. We got a booth in the rear. The red-eyed Tina sat with her back to the sparse lunch crowd. I ordered her a glass of red wine. I could tell from the look on her face that she was still worried about whether I would go to the police. She had nothing to worry about, but I wasn't going to tell her that. Instead, I asked why she was so willing to do everything Penroy told her to.

When she said, "You mean other than the money, right?" I felt like some gomer who only came to town to buy new boots. Turns out her answer was simple enough. Her looks were her career. "I've heard all the speeches about beauty school and opportunities in real estate, but Mitch gives me everything. Money, clothes, security. He even paid for my boob job. If it weren't for him, it would be someone just like him. I'm not someone who could live in the 'burbs with kids and a husband who sells insurance. I like what I have. What I do for Mitch and Mr. Scofield is a small price to pay."

"Other than play house with Mitch Penroy, what exactly do you do for Scofield?" I asked.

She answered by gulping down the rest of her wine and looking like she badly needed another. Catching the waitress's eye, I motioned for a refill. While we waited, she gave me a vague description about entertaining businessmen from out of town without defining entertaining except to say that it was not what it sounds like. I knew it sounded exactly like what it was but didn't say anything. It didn't seem to matter, at least not yet. When the wine came, she waited until the waitress put it down and left with the empty glass. The tears had stopped altogether. The red that rimmed her dark eyes had faded to a pale pink. Persistent sniffles were tended to by an endless supply of tissues in her purse.

We talked about Penroy and his role at Scofield Industries and his relationship with Scofield. Despite her loyalty to Penroy, what she described was someone who was little more than a stylish gofer who stepped and fetched for the boss man. In exchange for a company car, a nice home and a trophy girlfriend willing to do anything to keep living the good life. Then, of course, there was the occasional murder. I wondered how that got explained in Penroy's job description. But that wasn't what I came for. I need to know more about Scofield. What made him tick? Why all the exclusive, reclusive bullshit?

She waited so long to say anything I thought she hadn't heard me. When she finally answered it was not what I expected: "To be honest, he gives me the creeps. I'm nice to him because I'm expected to be and he's Mitch's boss. Doing what he wants is my job. It's just that there's something about him that makes me want to wash my hands each time after I see him. In all the times I've been around him he never paid any attention to me or other women, grown women I mean. He was always a gentleman. Even steering us toward other men, which seemed odd since he could have any girl he wanted. Of course he is more than eighty years old now."

When a small shiver rolled through her body, she did some damage to the wine. Since she'd brought up the issue of women, I pressed her. If not her, then who? If not other women at the parties, then who?

She got a look on her face indicating that she may have said too much. I ignored it. I needed to know more. I didn't care. Eventually, neither did she. "Maybe not women. Girls would be more like it. I thought it was just gossip at first until Mitch asked me to take one of Mr. Scofield's secretaries shopping and gave me a list of things to buy. It was mostly little girl clothes. Patent-leather shoes with little buckles, dresses with lots of petticoats and makeup that would make her face look paler. The only things I wasn't supposed to buy were panties and bras. I'd only seen his secretary once. It was the day we went shopping. She was very young with pale skin and curly hair. She didn't talk or act like any secretary I've ever met. That was several years ago. There have been others since then. They all sort of look alike.

I was starting to like Tina Davenport or at least the idea of what she was. As the dispassionate Anna Krychek, she had played a small part in a production too big for her to understand. I could overlook that, as well as her cameo appearance in the effort to frame me. After all, being told what to do by men was how she made her living. But it was how she did what she was told that intrigued me. Tina Davenport was a beautiful hooker, a bedtime companion for the rich. What was there not to be curious about? But underneath was the sadness and discontent of someone resigned to their fate. Someone who lived day to day without concern for the future. It was easy for me to be sympathetic.

It sounded to me, Harry, like Penroy either didn't know about Scofield's taste in girls or did and wanted nothing to do with it. She agreed, explaining that Penroy had been unhappy about something. She'd seen his bank account and heard him on the telephone talking about investments, so she knew he had plenty of money. Enough that one day he'd quit and they could move somewhere together where it's peaceful and warm.

It was an interesting picture, Harry, but unlikely. I could imagine Penroy hanging out in the South Pacific or the Mediterranean, but not with Tina Davenport. He didn't come across as the hold-hands-and-watch-sunsets type. As far as I was concerned, he was a killer.

I asked about Scofield's wife. It turned out I knew more about her than she did, including having seen and talked to her. In other words, Tina was no help on that front. She knew nothing about her. She considered her something of a mystery woman who still mourns her daughter's death, spends most of her time in New York or Europe and drinks a lot.

"I need to get to Scofield to talk to him. Can you help me?"

She looked at me over the top of the wine glass. It was her turn to start asking questions. It started with why do you care so much about all of this? It ended with questions about whether I was going to write something about Mitch and Mr. Scofield. After that came a plea to keep her name out of it.

"It's personal," I said. "Just tell me where Scofield is now."

She didn't know where he was at the moment but knew where he might be soon. She had been at a party the night before at Scofield's house. She overheard Penroy say that he and others were going to Scofield's beach house for the weekend. That got my attention. I asked where. "Somewhere near Cape Perpetua, south of Newport," she said. "I've been there a couple of times, but always by helicopter. Scofield lets Penroy use the place when he is out of town."

I leaned across the table toward her. I wasn't much on career counseling for professional party girls, but if she was going to help me, I could at least try to do something for her. I told her that her boyfriend and his boss were involved in something very weird and very dangerous. Probably murder and more than one. I knew some of it, but not all. Mysterious manuscripts and murders were part of it, but it's more than that. Her little fling with Ivan Krychek meant she was involved. If she hung with that crowd much longer, she'll be just as deep as they were. "Protect yourself," I said. "This isn't over. Not by any means."

She stared at me until the tears welled up again then reached for the purse and the tissues. Her face said it all: She was on the gritty edge of panic.

For her own protection, I told her it would be wise to tell Penroy that I found her and that we talked, but don't tell him everything we talked about. Tell him that all I wanted you to do was deliver a message about the night Mather was killed. Tell him I know everything and that the price for my silence was a meeting with Scofield.

I wrote my telephone number on the back of a Red Star coaster and slid it across the table. "All I need to know is the exact location of that beach house. Find out and call me."

She looked at the coaster, rolling it around in her hands with the perfect nails. "If I tell Mitch I talked to you he'll be angry. Very angry. I don't know what he'll do."

I pulled the coaster back and wrote my address next to my phone number. "Just in case you run out of options." Our eyes met for a moment then we both looked away.

She slipped the coaster into her purse then excused herself and left for the bathroom. I ordered a scotch and was halfway through it when she returned, looking good as new except for a few red lines in her eyes. The panic I'd seen earlier was gone. She was back together. All pieces and parts back in place. There was no way of telling if she understood a word I'd said about her boyfriend, his boss, and the danger she might be in.

Instead of sitting across from me, she slid into my side of the booth and let her leg rest against mine. She was playing nice, but it was unnecessary. I was past the point of caring about her role in luring me to Mather's house and I had no intention of telling the police about her. I let her apologize in a way that I wanted to believe was honest. Even if it wasn't, I had done my best. I got from her what I needed and gave her the best advice I had. The rest was up to her.

With a breathy kiss on my ear she got up and left.

33

Zihuatanejo

Standard stopped long enough to ask Grimes if he'd had a chance to see much of Zihuatanejo.

"After last night I'm not sure I want to see any more," Grimes said.

Standard laughed. "I can find something tamer than that. How about the *central mercado* in town? No visit to Zihuatanejo is complete without it."

"Done," Grimes said.

The *central mercado* took up an entire block in the center of town. It was filled with shops that sold everything from screw drivers to tomatillos. There were stalls offering fresh fish and vegetables sitting side by side with food stands that, in Standard's estimation, had some of the best food in town. Grimes looked like he wasn't so sure. He followed Standard through the narrow aisles with his hands in his pockets. He eyed the hanging meat and freshly butchered chickens with suspicion that turned to disgust when he learned there was little or no refrigeration other than ice for the fish.

Sensing Grimes' uneasiness, Standard led him to a table in a large seating area near a restaurant-lined aisle where women in food-stained aprons worked in cramped kitchens preparing *chili rellenos*, shrimp soup, and tacos with fresh tortillas. Grimes passed on the food, but quickly agreed to a cold beer.

"So," Grimes said, "all you could do was wait to hear from Tina Davenport about the location of Scofield's beach house. How could you be sure she would tell you the truth or tell you anything at all?"

"I couldn't," Standard said. "I'd done my best to scare her with threats about going to the police. I just wasn't sure she would believe it. Not that it mattered. I wasn't going to turn her in anyway. Not only that, she had the one thing I needed—Scofield's location. There was no way I could find his beach house without knowing exactly where it was. All I could do was wait. If it didn't pan out then I'd try something else."

Grimes looked across the aisle at a woman making *pico de gallo* then at another shredding pork for *carnitas*. Standard could tell that Grimes was one of those people who like to see their restaurant dishes made somewhere other than right in front of him.

"You sort of took a liking to Tina Davenport, didn't you?" Grimes asked, turning his attention back to Standard and his rapidly warming bottle of Corona.

"It was hard not to," Standard said. "It wasn't just her beauty, which was breathtaking, but she had a certain vulnerability and insecurity about her that made you want to take her home."

"And you had vulnerabilities of your own."

Standard knew he was right. Divorce and the death of Jasmine Grant had reduced his love life to little more than watching Vanessa the Undressa rehearse.

"I left Tina Davenport thinking that I had convinced her she was in trouble and that she had the option to seek refuge with me. So, I went back to hanging out, killing time with Benny Orlando, and waiting for the phone to ring."

"And find out from Benny what he'd learned about Scofield. How did that go?"

"I'll get to that later, but after what Tina told me about Scofield and his secretary, I could pretty much guess where things were going."

Grimes looked like he wanted to say more but stopped. Standard had already figured out that Grimes was after more than the true story of who killed Proctor Scofield. He had another agenda, which was fine. So did Standard.

34

Portland

Benny dove into his plate of mu shu pork as if it were the last in town. The chopsticks worked like extensions of his pudgy fingers as he shoveled the food down between swallows of Tsing Tao. All this while telling me how the Germans introduced beer to China. I half listened as he explained that sometime in the late 1800s, the Chinese started giving away land to European countries, including Germany. The first thing the Germans did was build a brewery and start making beer out of rice. The Chinese eventually threw them out but kept the brewery.

I didn't know if any of that was true and, Harry, to be honest, I didn't care. I couldn't get my mind off Tina Davenport and the feeling that Proctor Scofield was just out of reach. I poked at my plate of General Tso chicken, but didn't feel like eating. I'd sat in the oven-like apartment all day waiting for the call that would tell me where to find Scofield. When Benny came by at six to suggest dinner, I reluctantly agreed, but once there all I did was repeatedly check my cell phone. When Benny hungrily eyed my half-eaten meal, I slid the plate across the table. As he plowed through the last few bites of what had been my dinner, I told him about my meeting with Margaret Scofield and her theory that Amanda Bishop hadn't killed herself. He asked if I believed it. All I could tell him was that after what happened over the last few days, I was ready to believe pretty much anything.

When I asked what he'd found out about Scofield, he rattled off a bunch of stuff I already knew. Rags to riches. Started out selling typewriters. Forbes ranks his wealth as somewhere just south of Bill Gates and ahead of the Koch brothers. Scofield Industries ranked fifth on the Fortune 500 and had its fingers into everything and anything that has to do with computers and then some.

When I asked if he'd learned anything personal, Benny waited to answer until he'd finished his meal and mine. A little girl at the next table watched with a horrified look as he snared hunks of chicken with his chopsticks. With a mouthful of food, Benny mumbled something about Scofield not being seen in public for decades then described how he found some people who'd actually seen Scofield's private jet land in places like New York, Mumbai, Jakarta, and Rio, all of which was a testament to Benny's world-wide networks of geeks, freaks, and fellow hackers.

Apparently, Scofield's plane was hard to miss. It had a weird design on the tail. Two intertwined snakes or something like that. According to Benny, Scofield's plane lands somewhere and people get on and off. Some even bring their kids. No one ever sees Scofield. The best anyone can tell, he does all of his business right there on the plane then flies away.

Benny was a master at what newspaper editors called "burying the lead," meaning that the real news was in the eighth paragraph rather than the first where it belonged. Knowing that, I waited to hear what he'd learned about Scofield's personal life. When Benny started dithering again, I told him to speed it up.

"The word on the street is that Scofield is something of a freak, or at least he was," he said. "He's pretty much past his prime these days."

When I told him that Tina Davenport came close to describing Scofield the same way, Benny shrugged again and drained the last of his beer. As it turned out, Benny had found some obscure websites with rumors about Scofield and his personal life. Just not a lot of details. One thing was certain, he threw great parties with the best Portland has to offer. In Benny's words: "Silicone girls for silicon guys." I asked if any of the rumors had to do with young girls. Best he could tell, everything was fair game.

When the waitress brought the check, I cracked open one of the fortune cookies. It read, "All that ever stays the same is change." It was the same quotation from Lao Tse that Jasmine Grant had left on my bathroom mirror after our one night together. Without a word to Benny, I quickly slipped the small piece of paper into my shirt pocket.

I told Benny about Tina's taking one of Scofield's secretaries on a shopping spree for little-girl clothes and how one of Amanda Bishop's college roommates said Amanda kept little-girl clothes in her dorm room and would take them with her on weekends to visit friends. Benny's thick eyebrows started bouncing up and down. Before he could say something about Ivy and in defense of young girls, I asked if he found out anything about Scofield's wife. His answer was nothing that I didn't already know.

It was all pretty skimpy stuff for someone with Benny's reputation as a researcher, but I couldn't blame him. It was obvious that people either didn't know anything about Scofield or they were afraid to talk. All Benny could find were people who seemed to have a little piece of the puzzle, but not the whole picture.

"I did find out one interesting tidbit," he said. "I'll tell you in the car."

We each tossed a twenty on the table and headed for the door. Outside, Benny asked about my continuing interest in Scofield. After the *Inside Oregon* piece, why keep chasing him?

I made up a story about wanting to interview him for a profile I could sell to some business magazine. Benny called bullshit on that. We both knew that no one had talked to Scofield in years. If he's all of a sudden going to break down and give an interview, he wasn't going to give it to me. Scofield was no Bill Gates and I wasn't from *The New York Times.* Scofield didn't write books or appear on big-screen televisions to lecture the world's other CEOs on corporate responsibility. He was a classic recluse. The Howard Hughes of high-tech. I wasn't even sure if all the stuff Benny found or that Tina Davenport told me was even true. For all I knew, Scofield could be dead or just crazy.

What I found odd about Scofield was that I couldn't get a picture of him in my mind. Usually when you know something about a person, you get a sense of what they look like. The color of their hair, their eyes, their height, and weight. With Scofield, it was like he was more than just reclusive. He was invisible. He cast no shadow. A vampire in a mirror. His name evoked money and power, but no image. All I knew was that he was in his eighties and I'd only learned that from Tina Davenport. When I ran all this past Benny, he agreed. Of all the material he looked through—the newspaper and magazine articles—none had pictures of Scofield or even a description. They didn't even mention that it was impossible to find out what he looked like.

Back in the car, we rode along in silence into downtown. At an intersection near city hall, street people moved slowly along the sidewalks in the cool of the early evening. A hooker in tight, yellow shorts and a striped tube top stood in the doorway of a closed tattoo parlor, munching suggestively on a corn dog. Benny rolled down the window and yelled at her. The hooker scowled then smiled and waved back. She shook her booty at Benny and said something about not needing the corn dog if business was better. Benny laughed and rolled up the window.

I gave him a look that said who was that. She was a hooker named Sugar, who worked for a guy named Joey the Freak, aka Joseph Frecanado. He owned a tittie bar on the east side and ran a string of three or four girls on the side. Sugar called him the Italian Scallion because he smelled like onions.

I shook my head in amazement. "Is there anyone in town you don't know?"

Benny's answer surprised me. "Yeah. You." My glare demanded an explanation. He said this whole Scofield thing was showing him a new side of me. He didn't know me when I was at the top of my game but guessed that what he was seeing now—my obsession with Scofield—was pretty close. He was also sure that all this had something to do with Jasmine Grant and getting myself square with the world. In his words, mitigation for two dead girls. I went silent, reluctant to tell Benny more than the little man needed to know.

We drove up SW Taylor Street, found a parking spot near the First Congregational Church on SW Ninth Avenue and walked across the street. Benny struggled along a few steps behind me. A block from the apartment building I stopped and turned around. Benny caught up then tilted his baseball hat back in order to look up.

Listen, I told him, what I was doing was for my own reasons. I believed that I needed to take some risks or nothing was ever going to be right again. The night Jasmine died gave me an odd sense of recklessness, as if I really didn't care what happened to me because things couldn't be any worse. I'd never really lost that feeling, and the closer I got to Scofield the stronger it became. I lost Jasmine Grant, but so did everyone else. The world was a lesser place when people like her died the way she did.

After Benny unlocked the door to the apartment building and we stood waiting for the elevator, he mentioned Amanda Bishop and things she could tell if she were still alive. Then he said something that I was never able to get out of my head: If she didn't commit suicide then how did she die? What if someone threw her off that bridge?"

He was right, but it sounded pretty far-fetched. Even if that were true, the problem would be proving it.

That's when Benny remembered that he had something to tell me. "I told you that some of the people who visited Scofield on his plane sometimes brought their kids. Well, sometimes those kids didn't get off the plane. Make of it what you will. I've told you everything I know."

I was sitting in the chair in my apartment still trying to unravel Benny's news about children and Scofield's private jet when Tina Davenport called a few minutes before midnight. After some awkward small talk she told me Scofield's beach house was just south of the little town of Yachats near a turnout where Highway 101 takes a hairpin turn. She thought he was there alone but wasn't sure. Penroy was supposed to be there soon.

Reluctantly, I asked if she was going with him. She hesitated before saying it was possible, but not for sure. She asked if I was going to try finding him tonight.

Now was as good a time as any, I told her, then asked if she'd given any more thought to her future with Penroy. That brought another prolonged silence followed by a vague explanation that Penroy would probably be with Scofield for a couple of days. If he didn't ask her to go with him, she would have time to think about what to do. "If I left, I don't know where I'd go," she said.

I glanced around the apartment, trying to imagine Tina Davenport living in a place that even I could barely tolerate. A few hours in the peeled paint and stained porcelain of my adopted world would send her scurrying back to Mitch Penroy, wondering why she left in the first place. The thought made me feel stupid and confused. Instead of resenting her for trying to implicate me in a murder, I suddenly wanted to tell her that while I was no great catch, I at least cared enough not to peddle her to other men. I was almost to the point of saying she could stay with me for a while but stopped. It wasn't her I wanted. It was anybody.

Telling her to stay in touch with whatever she decided to do was as much of a goodbye as I could muster. She hung up with a thank you that was thick with what I wanted to believe was disappointment.

I went out to the kitchen to rummage through the drawers for a crumpled road map of Oregon I'd thrown in there months before. I spread it out on the kitchen table, running my finger down the red line of Highway 101 from Tillamook to Lincoln City. South of Newport, the highway ran hard up against the beach all the way to Yachats. Scofield's beach house was somewhere between Yachats and Florence, the next town twenty-five miles farther south. It was time to go, but I needed one more thing before I left. I refolded the map, called Benny then took the elevator to the second floor. When I told Benny what I wanted, he gave me one of his are-you-sure looks then walked back to his office. He returned holding a sleek Beretta 92 in a shiny, black leather holster. The gun looked huge in Benny's small hand. I took it, surprised at its weight and how comfortable it felt when I gripped the handle and pulled it out of the holster. The feeling of security and power was immediate, like the rush of a good drug.

The gun was just a precaution, I told him. I had no intention of using it.

"That's not how guns work," he said. "When you have one, they have a tendency to get used."

Putting the Beretta in my coat pocket, I left the apartment building and walked across the park to where I'd left the car. I drove out Barbur Boulevard to pick up the highway to the coast.

35

Zihuatanejo

"In law school I had a professor who hated the rich only slightly more than he hated the corporations that made them that way," Harry Grimes said. "Sort of a Bernie Sanders before there was a Bernie Sanders. His parting words when I finished his labor law class were 'never pass up a chance to tweak the cheek of the giant.' I always took his advice, but I never went anywhere with a gun."

Standard and Grimes were still sitting at the table in the *central mercado* drinking fresh-squeezed orange juice and watching local businessmen line up for lunch at a food stall called Fonda Irma. The smell of hot oil, fresh fish and raw meat mixed with the chatter of cooks and customers. Kids in dirty shorts and T-shirts worked the aisles selling bobble-head toys and Chiclets.

"The gun was an afterthought," Standard said. "Three of the people who came in contact with Krychek's manuscript were dead. I didn't want to be the fourth. Better safe than sorry. Besides, I had no idea what I was walking into."

"Really? You must have had some idea."

"How could I? All I knew was what I'd learned from Benny and Tina Davenport and what I'd surmised about Scofield's involvement in three deaths. All that did was give me a dim picture of what he might be capable of, just not who he was."

"But you went anyway?"

Thinking back on it, Standard knew he probably should have just stayed home trying to figure out a plan that made more sense than taking off in the middle of the night with a gun and a vague idea of how to find a man he'd never seen. He went anyway. Once again he had the same thought the night he broke into Krychek's office: What did he have to lose?

"I know," Standard said. "It sounds crazy now, but at the time it made sense in a weird way. Not only was I at the end of my rope, but I was convinced that Scofield was the key to everything. Nothing else made sense. Even a vague idea of where he was and no idea of how to get near him seemed better than doing nothing at all. So …"

"And you were sure that Tina Davenport had told you the truth?"

"There was only one way to find out."

36

The Oregon Coast

Twenty miles southwest of Portland the traffic had all but disappeared. The radio offered little more than the poison of conservative talk radio or rock 'n roll that was either too old or too new. I finally found a jazz station that lasted as far as the wine country around McMinnville before fading into static. What I needed was a new car with satellite radio and Pandora. Instead, I had nothing other than my twelve-year-old Honda with an engine pinging its way toward the Coast Range. I passed the time reading garish billboards advertising Indian casinos, motels, aquariums, and the other tourist traps found along coastlines everywhere.

Two hours later I was once again cruising through the dimly lit streets of Lincoln City. After getting coffee to go at a twenty-four-hour convenience store, I scanned the highway map again, trying to pinpoint the exact location of Scofield's house. Based on what Tina Davenport told me it was near where the highway took a hairpin turn around a small cove. The gas-station map didn't have the necessary detail, but I could at least narrow it down to a couple of places. Twenty-five miles farther south, Newport was as quiet as Lincoln City. The drive through town and over the Yaquina Bay Bridge took less than ten minutes instead of the usual thirty. Around Seal Rock, the night sky clouded over and the temperature dropped. Five miles later a light mist started then quickly turned into a heavy drizzle. Sort of typical Oregon coast weather for August.

I reached Yachats at four a.m. The correct pronunciation was yah-hots, but that didn't prevent visitors and some Oregonians from calling it yeah-chits. I found an all-night diner with no waitress, just a cook sitting at the end of the bar doing a crossword puzzle. A stained T-shirt stretched across an enormous belly. The tattoos on his forearms proclaimed a life-long devotion to the US Navy and someone named Delores. I made up a story about getting lost trying to find a house where I was supposed to spend the weekend and how I'd left the directions at home. I threw out the name Proctor Scofield and how the place was somewhere near an old lighthouse. Mentioning Scofield seemed to snap the cook out of his stupor.

"Three miles south on the highway," he said. "Look for the sign that says 'Lighthouse.' He added that the place I was looking for was the first driveway around the next curve. Or at least he was pretty sure. He blew his nose on a napkin. "It's not like I've been there."

I thanked him, got another coffee to go and went outside to sit in the car for a few minutes. I was close, Harry, very close. The cook was more help than he knew. What he told me matched what I heard from Tina. I needed some kind of plan. The map wasn't much help, but it gave me a vague idea of what I needed to do to find Scofield. Benny's Beretta sat on the passenger seat looking more comfortable than I felt. Picking it up, I let its weight and sleekness provide a little additional courage then put it down and drove away.

Just south of Yachats, the highway narrowed, clinging to the edge of a cliff as it followed the rugged outline of the coast. With one eye on the odometer, I ticked off the distance in tenths of a mile. Two turns and a little less than three miles later, I slowed at the small, green sign that read "Lighthouse." The parking lot immediately off the highway was vacant, but open. I parked near the "Closed" sign that hung on a chain across an asphalt path that led into the darkness. The ocean sounded like the distant rumble of cannon fire. I rummaged in the car's center console for a flashlight that came with a car kit my ex-wife had given me for Christmas several years earlier. The beam was small, but adequate.

I got out of the car, pointed the flashlight in front of me. Since there was only one path out of the parking lot it had to lead to the lighthouse and the ocean beyond. I was hoping that it would lead to a place where I could at least see Scofield's house, get a sense of what I was up against. I'd figure out what to do after that. It was another vague plan, but, like the others, it might get me closer to Scofield.

The path was lined with ancient fir trees dripping with the pre-dawn rain and salty mist. Huge ferns and low rhododendrons reached out from the dark, groping at the edges of the asphalt like hands from a grave. Large patches of emerald-green moss clung to rocks so large the path had to wind around them. The air was thick with the smell of salt and seaweed. I didn't see the abandoned lighthouse until I reached the end of the path. The short, stubby tower with a rusted metal catwalk around a conical top was fifty yards away. Next to the tower was a smaller, octagon-shaped building that probably served as a storage shed for those who maintained the facility in its heyday. Sadly, what the salt water hadn't destroyed the graffiti artists and vandals had. All the windows were broken out. Spray-painted initials and symbols covered the curved base of the tower. Still, the forty-foot lighthouse stood its ground, a ghost beacon warning ghost ships.

I stopped at the end of the trail, hanging back under the limbs of one of the ancient firs. The lighthouse stood in the center of a narrow, triangle-shaped peninsula that jutted into the ocean. To the right, a stand of more old-growth trees extended behind the lighthouse and into the darkness. To the left, on the south side, a weathered, split-rail fence stretched maybe seventy-five yards toward the ocean. The expanse of grass between the lighthouse and the fence looked ragged and patchy. During the day it would probably be a sickly brown, burned by the daily assault of sea water.

Moving across the grass toward the fence, I sensed danger before seeing it. I aimed the flashlight's narrow beam at the ground. The grass ended three feet beyond the fence at the ragged edge of a cliff. I leaned over the fence as far as I dared. Fifty feet below, a churning punchbowl of angry waves gnawed at barnacle-encrusted rocks. Dirty-white foam shone with a dim luminescence against the dark water shifting constantly into a hundred different shapes. A kaleidoscope of water-soaked logs bobbed up and down with each rise and fall of the waves. The chaotic movement of water and debris was confined to a long, narrow crevasse. An eternity of waves, pushed by the insistent ocean, threw themselves into it in a relentless contest to see which could reach the farthest inland. At the end, the waves crashed in desperation against the steep rock cliff then retreated, each time taking a fraction of the surrounding cliffs with it.

I moved along the fence line toward the ocean, careful to split the difference between the cliff on the left and the lighthouse on the right. The wind had increased, but at least the rain had stopped. Low clouds to the west parted enough to allow the faint light of a half-moon to escape. The crashing of the waves grew louder. The ocean was near. My steps slowed.

The flashlight beam flickered and went out. It didn't matter. The sky to the east was turning a faint silver. That and the moonlight was enough to keep me from stumbling over the edge into the ocean. The grass had disappeared. The sandy ground was dotted with large rocks and tufts of grass. I'd reached the end of the peninsula. Beyond lay nothing but ocean. The combination of wind and waves was deafening. The rain started again, heavier this time. It soaked through my coat and gave my pants a clammy feel. I pushed it all out of my mind.

On the other side of the crevasse was another peninsula, a mirror image of the one I was on. Looking back toward the east, I saw a large, two-level house that looked like it had been carved out of the rocks by some ancient king. In the dim light, I could see a curved bank of windows on the upper level with a deck that wrapped around three sides of the house. The lower level was more like a daylight basement with windows fronting a stone patio that cascaded down onto a wedge-shaped lawn that came to a point at a cliff overlooking the ocean. Dim lights, blurred by the rain, shone along the deck and the patio. The roof was decorated with an array of satellite dishes. Two more stood guard on small cement pads in the yard. The house looked modest for a billionaire, but capable of being the reclusive home of an international wheeler dealer and, in my mind, lethal puppet master.

A helicopter sat on a concrete pad in an open area fifty yards south of the house. The way its four blades were tied down gave it the appearance of a giant insect caught in a few strands of a spider's web. The intertwined snakes of the Scofield Industries logo on the door were just visible in the faint glow of the house lights.

I hunched down in an effort to get under the wind. I wanted a cigarette but trying to light one would be useless. Instead, I studied the house while trying to figure out the best way in. The crevasse with its raging waves prevented any access from the lighthouse side. That left little choice but to backtrack and follow the highway until I found the driveway the cook at the diner had described.

Ducking into the shelter of a large rock, I tried to come up with a third alternative. That was when I saw the figure of a man move along the deck fronting the second floor of the house. The figure disappeared around the far side then reappeared on the patio below. After standing for a few seconds under the overhanging deck, he walked out onto the grass and stood watching the ocean. He pulled up the hood of his parka, turned away and walked back toward the shelter of the patio.

I studied the figure for a few moments, muttered "damn" before slowly working my way past the lighthouse and back toward the path to the parking lot. Along the way, any doubts I had about whether it was Scofield's house disappeared.

By the time I reached the car, Harry, everything had fallen into place. Blind anger added to the resolve to confront Proctor Scofield on his own turf. Something that started out sounding like a bad idea had suddenly turned into a good one. The sense of recklessness that had never really gone away was suddenly stronger than ever.

I got the Beretta off the car's passenger seat and put it in my jacket pocket. The weight of the gun brought back an immediate sense of security. I had taken the gun more as a precaution with no intention of using it. Now, I wasn't so sure. It was hard to ignore the seductive fascination of firearms. Besides, there was at least one person at Scofield's house who needed to be shot. Maybe Benny was right: Guns do have a tendency to get used.

I walked east for about a hundred yards to where the highway did a one-eighty and headed up a slight incline to where the pavement turned south again. The tide was high. I could hear and feel the waves crashing against the rocks to my right as I walked along the gravel shoulder. I just couldn't see them. I fought back the feeling that the sea wanted to climb up the cliffs to grab me. I walked at a steady pace, never even considering turning back. The anger that came with seeing Scofield's house added to what I already felt about freak accidents and dead lovers. It had gone on too long for too many different reasons. I'd found his lair, Harry, but was the monster in it and was everything going to end that night one way or the other? Time to find out.

Instead of following the highway as it curved south again, I kept going straight into a small, gravel turnout. It looked like a place where travel trailers and motorhomes were supposed to pull over to let other cars pass, but seldom did. At the southern end of the turnout, hidden from view by a small tree-covered mound, was an opening that looked like the start of an unmarked road that disappeared down into the trees. It was nothing more than two dirt tracks running through rotting pine needles. It didn't look anything like the road to a billionaire's hideaway.

Healthy ferns and salal that had crept onto the hard surface had the same crypt-like appearance as the path to the lighthouse. Thirty yards from where the driveway left the turnout, the rotting pine needles turned to smooth asphalt. This was more like it. Another hundred feet and the driveway was blocked by brick walls and an electronic gate hung between two pillars. A sign on one pillar warned trespassers of certain prosecution. A plaque in the middle of the gate bore the entwined snakes of the Scofield Industries logo. If one didn't scare off the curious, the other would. To me it was all confirmation that I was in the right place. I barely paused before walking around the pillar, hoisting myself over a five-foot wall, and back onto the driveway on the other side. My pants and shoes, already soaked from the rain, couldn't get any worse. I ignored the cold creeping up my legs.

With each step came the greater possibility that men with guns and Rottweilers would leap out of the trees. People like Proctor Scofield didn't live without some kind of security. Even if it wasn't men and dogs, it was probably surveillance cameras monitored by people like Buck Mather. I scanned the trees, but it was still too dark to see them even if they were there. A couple of minutes beyond the gate, I heard voices followed by the high-pitched whine of a powerful engine and a slow thumping sound that quickly grew louder and faster. It took a moment to remember the helicopter sitting on the dimly lit pad. I could feel the noise as much as hear it. It came from directly ahead, which meant I was just south of Scofield's house. I moved to the far side of the driveway and followed it down in a gradual turn to the north.

When the helicopter lifted off, I stepped off the asphalt and behind a large Douglas fir. The aircraft rose over the tops of the trees, the lights on its underside flashing through the branches. Hovering above the dense foliage, it rotated gracefully in place before darting out over the ocean, gaining altitude before turning east to head inland. I stepped back onto the pavement. The screaming helicopter engine and the heavy thumping of its rotors had faded. I checked the time. Almost five a.m.

I had to be nearing the house. My hands were fists. My teeth clenched until my jaws ached. There had to be more security than the man I'd seen on the front lawn. But where? I moved closer to the brush along the side of the driveway. Ten more yards and Proctor Scofield's beach house rose from the mist and darkness. There was a three-car garage under the house. Above that was the profile of the deck and some of the wrap-around windows that looked west toward the ocean. The back of the house extended fifty feet to hug the hillside behind it. That meant there was nothing that resembled a back door. Access to the front of the house was blocked by a rock wall that extended from the garage, past the helicopter pad and ended at another cliff overlooking the ocean. A wooden gate, large enough for a car, breached the wall halfway between the house and the helicopter pad. I trotted over to the gate, all the time wondering where all the guards, motion sensors, lights, sirens, and dogs were. When I got to the gate, I pushed on it. Locked.

Moving away from the house and past the gate, I felt along the top wall for embedded glass. Finding none, I pulled myself up. Belly-down and ready to drop to the other side. Then I looked across the lawn toward the ocean. The flare of a lighter and the quick outline of a man's face just twenty feet away made me hug the wall and hold my breath.

The figure in the parka paused to take a deep drag on his cigarette then headed toward the house. As he neared the lower patio, I dropped silently to the ground and moved toward the ocean. If I wanted to see Proctor Scofield, dealing with the man smoking the cigarette would be the price of admission.

The lawn ended at a sandstone point littered with large rocks covered in a thin veneer of bird shit. I stood on top of a smaller one, pulled out the Beretta and fired a shot into the air. I jumped down and hid behind a larger rock to wait. It wasn't a particularly innovative plan, Harry, but good enough, given the circumstances. I kept the Beretta in my hand, let it hang muzzle down and leaned against the rock. The gun felt good. Too good. I peered carefully around the rock toward the house.

The man with the cigarette was standing at the edge of the lawn, his own gun out and pointed straight ahead. Slowly, he began moving forward, backlit by the dim house lights. I waited until he was on the other side of the rock then moved around behind him. With one swift motion, I pressed the Beretta to the back of his head. It took all my self-control not to pull the trigger and leave the body to the gulls and sand crabs.

"Doing a little moonlighting?" I said.

Alfie Gitchell hacked out a cough before turning his head and dropping his gun without being asked.

37

Zihuatanejo

After leaving the *central mercado,* Grimes and Standard negotiated the narrow, crowded sidewalks through the center of town and in the general direction of the waterfront. Standard was steering the stunned Grimes toward a corner bar called Cohiba. It had six stools, a small television that seemed to show nothing but soccer games, and a grizzled bartender with a ponytail. On the back bar were single bottles of gin, vodka, scotch, bourbon and twelve different brands of tequila. A hand-made wooden sign hanging over the sidewalk in front read "Cold Friggin' Beer."

They sat down and ordered two bottles of Corona. When Grimes mumbled something about eating, the bartender reached under the bar and pulled out a basket filled with the kind of pretzel packages you get flying coach. Grimes scowled then ripped one open.

"I guess that after seeing Gitchell, things sort of fell into place," Grimes said.

"Not all of it, but enough to know that I had been played."

Standard and Grimes were Cohibas only customers. The bartender was too busy cutting limes and watching the television to pay any attention to what they were talking about. When the beers were gone, two more appeared without asking. Grimes downed two more packages of pretzels then looked around to see if there were any restaurants nearby.

"Still, you must have been as disappointed as you were angry," Grimes said. "You and Gitchell were friends."

"So I thought."

In the four years since Scofield's death, there was plenty of time for Standard to think about Gitchell and his betrayal. He knew the old cop's string was running out. He was facing retirement with a pension that would probably barely make ends meet. He had two ex-wives and three feckless children. Then there was always the chance that he was dying of lung cancer. Signing on with Scofield to cover up a string of murders must have sounded like easy money.

"So, did outing Gitchell get you into see Scofield?" Grimes asked.

Standard laughed. "If Gitchell was what passed for security then I was pretty much home free. Assuming there were no other so-called guards, all I had to do was walk in the house with Gitchell as my guide and I was good to go."

"What about Butcher? Was he part of this?"

Standard shook his head. "As much as I obsessed about Butcher and his clumsy attempts to arrest me, in the end he meant nothing. After what the police pulled out of Mather's house the night he was killed, Butcher dropped out of sight. He had all the evidence he needed that Mather was behind the murders of Krychek and Jasmine Grant and had no reason to think I killed Mather. So, why continue chasing me around?"

"So, Gitchell was your ticket to see Scofield. How did that go? Anything like you planned?"

"Not even close."

38

The Oregon Coast

Had I known what was coming, I would have marched Gitchell off the end of the cliff into the ocean. Instead, I picked up his gun, tossed it into the sand near one of the large rocks then shoved him in the direction of the house. He muttered something about how I was going to die an ugly death. I reminded him that I could blow his brains out right there and introduce myself to Scofield.

It was a cheap line, but Gitchell bought it and stiffened before turning back toward the house. I stayed two paces behind him to look up at the windows. They were all dark except for a faint light at the south end of the upper level. If anyone was inside it was probably way too early for them to be up. Fine with me. There was only one person I wanted to see.

I followed Gitchell as he walked across the patio and through the sliding glass doors into the daylight basement. When I said turn on a light, Gitchell snapped on a table lamp to reveal a room decorated like something out of *Master and Commander.* Colorful pennants and framed prints of graceful wooden ships in full sail plowing through stormy seas. Starting up a spiral staircase to the upper level, I felt like Ned Land on his way to see Captain Nemo. The large room at the top of the stairs stuck with the same nautical theme, but slightly more modern. It resembled the bridge of a cruise ship with wrap-around windows looking out at the dark ocean. Two long, leather couches sat facing each other. They were perpendicular to the windows, creating a perfect place to watch the constantly changing sea. To the right in back of one of the couches was a hallway that looked like it led to the bedrooms. The kitchen was toward the rear of the house through a large archway. The place was roomy, but far from elegant or grand. In fact, it was modest when you think about the kind of money Scofield had and what he could buy with it.

"Where's Scofield?" I asked Gitchell after we were a few steps inside the living room.

He motioned toward a small room at the far end of the house. It looked like an office just off the living room. It was the same dim light I had seen from the yard. Now, though, I could make out the thin figure of a man hunched over a computer keyboard.

"Call him," I said.

"Call him yourself," Gitchell grumbled.

I kneed the little man in the crotch, sending him tumbling into a glass table that shattered under his weight. I suddenly felt better, the anger down a quarter tank.

Gitchell was still curled up amid shards of thick glass, clutching his groin and moaning between coughs when the man appeared in the doorway of the office. We stared at each other for a few moments, my gun still pointed down at the fetal Gitchell. What came next, Harry, was just another in what would be a long line of surprises that morning.

"You must be John Standard," the man said. "I'm Proctor Scofield. I've been expecting you. Would you care for some breakfast? You must be starved after that long drive from Portland."

I looked down at Gitchell then back at Scofield. He said, "Leave him and come with me. There are a lot of things we need to discuss."

Even with only a faint image of Proctor Scofield, I was still surprised at the appearance of the small, gentle-looking old man with chalky complexion and thin, wiry build. Large ears stuck straight out from a small, round head. Razor-sharp lines radiated from the corners of dark, deep-set eyes. The nose resembled a small beak perched over a down-turned mouth with thin, slightly chapped lips. The dark moles on his face looked like spatters of dried blood. A three-day growth of beard was as gray as the mussed hair that barely covered the top of his head. An oversize, terry cloth bathrobe sagged on stooped shoulders. The liver-spotted hands that poked out of the robe's floppy sleeves had the swollen knuckles and twisted fingers of an advancing case of arthritis. His left hand shook with some kind of tremor. Peeking out from the bottom of the robe were small feet encased in leather sandals that squeaked as he tottered across the room.

What I had expected, Harry, was someone vigorous and larger than life; a dapper, gracefully aging aristocrat. Maybe an over-ripe Bill Gates. Instead, I got Grampa Simpson.

I told him that breakfast sounded great then pointed down at Gitchell again. "You can take him back outside and shoot him," he said. "If not, leave him there. He'll recover. Now, about that breakfast?"

Once in the kitchen, I got a closer look at Scofield. Tina Davenport had told me he was over eighty years old. Seeing him up close I decided she was being generous. The skin on his face was pulled tight, like plastic wrap over a bowl. The same thin, brittle-looking skin stretched over his bony arthritic hands and feet. A smile revealed a set of ill-fitting dentures that gave his voice a reedy lisp. He smelled of moth balls and mouthwash.

Scofield motioned toward a large table in the expansive country kitchen. I sat down and watched as he began pulling things out of the refrigerator. He expertly diced, sautéed, poured, and stirred, eventually producing two perfect omelets with tomatoes, onions, and green peppers.

"I was nearly sixty years old before getting married," he said. "So, I learned early on to cook for myself. I still enjoy it even though most of the houses I own have cooks and other servants."

"How did you know I was coming?" I asked.

The look on his face told me I was not going to like the answer. "Tina Davenport," he said. "She called me not long after she talked to you."

I tried to hide my disappointment. Tina Davenport was a slave to her environment, another victim of Proctor Scofield, only she was still alive. At least I could put the whore-with-a-heart-of-gold image out of my mind.

Scofield gave me a sympathetic look. He told me not to be too disappointed. I wasn't the first man to fall victim to her charms and I wouldn't be the last. Turns out that Penroy met her several years earlier at a party in D.C. She was rented arm candy for some deputy assistant undersecretary of something or other. He brought her back with him to help out with some of what Scofield called his "more difficult clients." He described her as an amazing young woman who knows that he can do more for her than anyone else, including me.

He served up the omelets with fresh fruit and toast. While we ate, he filled me in on his research into my background as if I didn't know what it was. Parents died in the crash of their private plane. Younger brother a victim of AIDS. Acquitted of murder. Divorced. Living in a rundown apartment house. Scratching out a living as a freelance writer. When he said my only living relative was a great aunt in Iowa, it was news to me. I made a mental note to look her up—

assuming I ever got out of there alive. When he described Benny Orlando as a former rodeo clown, I corrected him—circus clown.

What he was getting at, Harry, in a not-so-subtle way was that if something unfortunate were to happen to me, I wouldn't be missed.

"So John," he said. "Did you come here kill me?"

It was a good question. One I'd asked myself several times on the drive from Portland. I just didn't have an answer. I wasn't ready to rule it out, but I needed to know more. What I really came for were answers, I told him. Best I could tell he'd ordered three murders. The big question was why.

"Let's finish eating first," he said, "then we'll talk some more."

While we ate, he talked about the house, its history, how he found it and the changes he'd made. He lamented not spending as much time there as he'd like when he was younger. Now he found himself staying there more and more all the time. Finished eating, Scofield cleared the table, put the dirty dishes in the sink, and poured us both more coffee. When he sat down at the table again, I could almost hear his bones creak.

"You have no family and only a former circus clown for a friend," he told me, "Which means you have little or nothing to lose by coming here. I admire that. After what you've been through, most men would have crawled in a hole and died. But not you. You want revenge at my expense. Like I said, admirable. A rare commodity these days."

Pretty sure where he was going next, I got out ahead of him and told him to save it. There was nothing of value he could offer me, so let's not even go there. I was not another Alfie Gitchell and didn't want to be insulted with something like, "We could use a man like you on our team."

A smile danced across his face. "Touché, but keep in mind that I have greater resources on my side than Alfie Gitchell."

"I would hope so," I said.

Enough small talk and feeling each other out. I asked him why he had Jasmine Grant and Ivan Krychek killed. Mather, I added, was a one off. He didn't matter. Then, just to get a reaction, I brought up the name Amanda Bishop as yet another victim.

That hit a nerve. Scofield squeezed his eyes shut and held them that way for a second or two. When he opened them, he looked out toward the windows on the front of the house and then at his watch.

"It'll be light soon," he said. "I suggest we move to the front room. I always enjoy watching the ocean come alive in the morning."

After that came this strange story about his first visit to the east coast and watching the sun come up in the east. He had grown up in Oregon watching the sun go down in the west. He made it sound as if watching the sun rise in the east was some kind of mystical experience. I tried not to laugh, Harry. I mean, where the hell did Scofield think the sun came up? I was starting to get the feeling that Scofield was well past his sell-by date; that maybe the tycoon nicknamed Prince of Snakes had lost a fang or two … or a few marbles.

When we got to the front room, Alfie Gitchell was gone, but the outline of his fat, little body remained visible in the shattered glass on the expensive carpet. We stepped around the mess and sat on one of the long couches in front of the windows. With his back to the hallway leading to the bedrooms, Scofield propped his feet on the coffee table. I sat opposite him on the other couch, watching his frail body melt back into the overstuffed cushions. Scofield stared at the lightening sea while asking me "How much do you know, John?"

I gave him the short version. Mather killed Krychek and Jasmine Grant at his request then he ordered either Penroy or Gitchell to kill Mather. All of it over a manuscript. Scofield's head bobbed in a way that said I was right and to keep going. Krychek was killed because his doctoral dissertation threatened to expose what Roark and Landis did to his stepdaughter. Jasmine died because she had the manuscript and he wanted it just to find out what it said. Mather was next because he was probably shaking him down and couldn't be trusted anyway. Either that or he was just an annoying and expendable liability.

Scofield slowly clapped his hands. "Very concise and accurate," he said. "Congratulations."

I wasn't through. I let him know that none of those people had to die. The whole story of what Roark and Landis did to his stepdaughter was going to come out anyway. So why the bloodshed? What was I missing?

Scofield ignored the questions in favor of marveling at how reporters were so good at getting right to the heart of things. Years of work, he said, decades actually, and I had narrowed it down to a few short sentences. He rocked back into cushions that seemed to make him look even smaller. "You're right, of course," he said, describing how he burned the manuscript Mather took from Jasmine Grant. After reading it he realized it was not as damning as he feared. He just didn't know that at the time.

"She's dead, Scofield." I was trying not to yell. It was hard. He'd had her killed over a manuscript that was no threat to him.

Scofield refused to look at me, staring instead at the ocean. He started blaming Tina Davenport for failing to learn more about Krychek's research and what was in his manuscript. If she had then lives could have been saved. Unfortunately, she didn't. I sat back and numbly listened while Scofield launched into a detailed description of how Alfie Gitchell started working for him a few days before Krychek was killed. How his marching orders were to keep the heat off Mather until he found the manuscript. How it had been Gitchell's idea to find a patsy then turn the investigation over to Daryl Butcher. He called me to come down to Salem to see Krychek's body then put Butcher on my tail to keep the investigation away from Mather. Given my past, it wasn't going to be hard to convince Butcher that I was his man. Gitchell knew Butcher had a hard-on for guys like me. What better way to deflect attention and avoid any connection to Scofield than call in an inept cop like Butcher? On the night Jasmine Grant was killed, Mather was there in the house with her when she called me. I conveniently showed up to find body number two.

Scofield stopped then smiled about how things had worked out up to that point. He raised his coffee cup in a mock toast to his own cunning.

"How did you find out about Krychek and his dissertation?" I asked.

"That's complicated," he said with a sigh.

"I'll try to keep up," I said.

It started with Penroy. Scofield said he was as paranoid as they come. He knew what happened twenty-three years ago and lived each day dreading how and when it would come out. Added to this was his mistrust of Roark and Landis, especially as the stakes got higher. He arranged for Mather to get the security contract for the state capital with orders to keep an eye on the two of them. Mather unwittingly hired Krychek then found him snooping around Roark's office one night. Krychek told him everything—political science major, working on a doctorate and the sordid history of Roark and Landis. He told him about the manuscript and how it was going to get him a professorship.

Unfortunately, Krychek knew nothing about the connection between Mather and Penroy. I could pretty much guess the rest.

Did Penroy hatch the idea of using Tina as bait in a honey trap? Did he think that would get him the manuscript? Only Krychek actually fell in love with her.

Scofield shrugged. "Can you blame him?" he asked.

Scofield denied any personal knowledge of Tina Davenport's skills but could imagine that they were beyond anything someone like Krychek had ever experienced or ever would. Regrettably, those skills were not good enough to find out how much Krychek knew.

And Jasmine Grant?

Process of elimination, he said. Someone had to know what he was working on. Who better than his advisor and dean of the department?

"Mather didn't have to kill her. He could have just taken the manuscript and left."

Scofield gave me a sad little nod that said he knew I was right, that Mather had gone too far. "That's why he's dead." He said it without sympathy or remorse. Fine with me. All I'd done was hit Mather with a tire iron. Scofield had gone me one better.

"So, whatever secret you're so scared of must be pretty big to cost the lives of three people," I said.

He waited a long time to say anything. When he did it was to apologize ahead of time for what was going to be a long answer to a short question: "My ability to make money and be a successful businessman are both a blessing and a curse. A blessing in the sense that I can own anything I want, anyone I want, and make people do anything I ask. The curse is that what I want is not always to my liking. I am not a vicious or mean-spirited man by nature, John. In fact, just the opposite. There are times in my life, however, when I have had to be."

I felt comfortable enough to let Scofield ramble, but not sure where he was going. Everything he'd told me so far, I already knew or guessed to be true. Turns out there was a point to all of it, just not what I expected.

Scofield slowly painted a picture that became more and more clear. He believed that politics and government in the United States were going to hell, sooner or later chaos would prevail and men like him would find a way to take over. He saw modern-day politics as the last refuge for the desperate and uninspired. He even had a name for it—

chaordic, a combination of the words chaos and order. That made it a playground for men like him, mischievous men with too much money in their pockets and too much time on their hands. To him it was all a game, but one he played with great enthusiasm while others sat, waited, and wrung their hands. I remember his words, "Politics is a gun. Money is the trigger."

If this is starting to sound familiar, Harry, it should. It was right out of Krychek's manuscript. I was ready to point that out, but Scofield showed no desire to be interrupted. He was on a roll, if not a full-blown rant. Best I waited.

Scofield got up and continued talking while pacing the room, all the time lamenting the country's poor condition and describing the people who run it as either uninspired or venal. Eventually he sat back down, out of breath and gazing out the living room windows. A dull morning sun creeping over the mountains to the east lit up the underside of clouds the color of gunmetal. The swells off the end of the point became more visible. Spray from waves hit the cliffs, creating a thin curtain that rose above the rocks. The heavy glass muted the sound of the surf, turning the scene outside into a living mural with the ocean rising and falling like a giant beast breathing in and out. After a few minutes, Scofield got up again, this time to stand at one of the plate glass windows. It was an odd scene. The frail little man in the oversized bathrobe framed against the vast sea and sky.

Sensing an opening, I told him that none of what he described explained how he ended up being the cash cow for the two men who raped his stepdaughter and caused her to kill herself. When he turned around there was a look of pride on his face: "Without me they would've gone to jail for a few years then wasted the rest of their lives squandering their fathers' meager fortunes. Instead, one of them stands on the brink of greatness, maybe both. Frankly, I don't really care which one. I'm willing to accept that the natural forces of politics may well anoint one and discard the other. Not that it matters. Should the political winds shift, as they surely will, the other will be waiting to step in. Either way I would win, eventually owning a governor or a senator and maybe even more than that."

That, Harry, was a pretty stunning revelation. Scofield was coming across as more crackpot than visionary. When I said he couldn't possibly be serious, he started to get angry then reeled himself in. He said he was deadly serious. He owned two men who had learned the craft of politics and trained in making laws. Sure they espoused certain philosophies, but who cared? It wasn't like they really believed in them. They just did what he told them to.

The more I listened, Harry, the harder time I had figuring out who was the most despicable: the puppets or the puppet master. Not that it mattered. None of them were worth looking up to.

Scofield could have let the police charge Roark and Landis for what they did to Amanda then he could have sued their families into oblivion. In fact, he said, that was his first inclination. When he'd learned what they'd done he wanted to strike them down, to use what wealth he had at the time to destroy them. When I asked why he didn't, he raised a finger, ready to impart some gem of wisdom. Instead, he described a different path, one that would destroy them in ways no one had ever heard of.

"Revenge born out of blind rage is for the ignorant," he said. "I wanted more. I wanted their souls. I wanted to own every breath, every heartbeat. I wanted them to know that they walked this earth because of my generous spirit. That I was the only one who could wash away the guilt of what they had done to her."

What came next, Harry, were words I will never forget: "I wanted to be their religion, their god."

I leaned back against the cushions until the Beretta pressed reassuringly against the small of my back. Two gulls landed on the deck outside. They waddled up to the windows, tilting their heads as if trying to get a closer look at Scofield's insanity. Because that is what it was, Harry. Proctor Scofield was fucking nuts.

The problem was, I had only heard the start of it.

All I could say was that none of it made sense. "Why would Roark and Landis or their families go along with a plan like that?" He laughed, more of a cackle really, as if he were enjoying reliving the moment. Two reasons, he said. First, because of him they were now both rich, but the kind of rich that would disappear if they reneged on the deal. Second, they knew he would have them and their families killed. They believed him because there was nothing in Scofield's past that would make them think otherwise. In fact, the eventual handling of Ivan Krychek, Jasmine Grant, and Buck Mather only served to reinforce his hold over them. He had the power to destroy them and they knew it.

Scofield smiled as he described what he believed was a "simple business proposition" that would keep Roark and Landis out of prison and their families out of poverty. After making deals with presidents, kings, and sheiks, negotiating with a car dealer and a lawyer was a piece of cake. "There's a reason they call me the Prince of Snakes."

I sat there stunned, not knowing who to be more disgusted with, Scofield for making the offer or the families for accepting it. I had a hard time imagining how Scofield got the authorities to drop the charges then went about arranging the rest of Roark's and Landis's lives. Law schools, law firms, congressional posts, legislative races. Everything. Watching Scofield and the look of accomplishment on his face only added to my belief that he was crazy. Not so crazy, though, that people weren't willing to go along with him. That says a lot about the power of wealth. It can attract a following no matter how crazy you are. I thought back over the last few days. What started with a bizarre murder of an obscure doctoral candidate ended up as a demented tale of how a reclusive billionaire turned two men into indentured servants.

"But they're rapists," I said.

"Reformed rapists," he replied, "with loving families, solid records of public service and the endorsement and financial backing of the father of the woman they raped. That gives them a certain amount of redemption. If you don't believe me just look what happened after your article in that paper. A few days of hectic coverage and then it all but disappeared. Welcome to journalism in the twenty-first century."

I couldn't let go of the idea that something was missing. Something beyond the out-of-proportion response to Krychek's dissertation. Finally, all I could ask was, what good did it all do?

Scofield's eyes wandered across the panorama of the rocky coastline and chaotic ocean before answering. When he spoke, it was slow and deliberate, as if every word had to be delivered in precisely the right way. I'll never forget the words. "What good it does is that every day of their lives Roark and Landis are reminded of what they did. How Amanda's death cost them their freedom. Don't you see? In many ways she's still alive. It was a perfect plan. If I had it to do over again, I would do everything exactly the same."

It was my turn to pace the room. I was looking out the living room windows when I felt a thumping in the air followed by the sound of a powerful engine. To the north, the helicopter with the Scofield Industries logo appeared in the sky above the lighthouse. It banked in over the ocean, moved slowly across the lawn in front of the house and gently settled onto the concrete pad. I watched as Roark and Landis popped out of the helicopter and ran, hunched over, toward the house. The blast from the craft's rotors smashed their hair down and beat at their pants legs.

39

Zihuatanejo

Standard and Grimes were still at Cohibas. A middle-aged couple with matching Green Bay Packers hats and looking fresh off the plane, had taken up seats on the other side of the L-shaped bar. When they showed off their Spanish by ordering a "beer-o with a lime-o," the bartender walked away shaking his head.

"So you really thought he was insane?" Grimes asked.

"Clinically? Who knows? I'm no psychiatrist, but I know bat-shit crazy when I see it. Use whatever metaphor you want—not playing with a full deck, off his rocker, a few ants short of a picnic—it doesn't matter. They all fit."

"What Scofield had to say about Mitch Penroy made it sound like he was the one responsible for carrying out Scofield's orders," Grimes said.

"Either that or Penroy was operating on his own, but I found that hard to believe. Scofield described Penroy as the perfect political operative. No conscience, no morals, and hated public attention. Without him, things could never have gotten as far as they did. He just said it with what sounded like a certain amount of regret, that maybe he had given Penroy too much freedom. When I called Penroy an earthworm, Scofield smiled then laughed. I was right, he said, 'but he's my earthworm.'"

They finished their beer and went in search of food. Standard figured the safest place for Grimes was back at Mango's with its tablecloths, extensive menu, and waiters who spoke English. Grimes eagerly agreed.

"So now you're a party of four," Grimes said. "You, Scofield, Roark, and Landis."

"Not exactly," Standard said. "Gitchell was still wandering around somewhere and there was another guest I didn't know about."

Standard explained that when Roark and Landis walked into the room they went straight to the bar after giving cold greetings to Scofield and bored glances at the shattered table. If they noticed Standard, they didn't show it. As if on cue, Mitch Penroy emerged from the hallway behind Scofield, looking freshly showered and wearing jeans and a golf shirt.

"Was he there all the time?" Grimes said. "Had he been listening?"

"Probably, but it didn't matter. He knew everything. There was nothing left for him to learn. Or so I thought."

When their lunch of fish tacos showed up, Grimes looked eager to hear the last of Standard's story.

"Before I tell you how all this ends," Standard said, "I need you to do something for me."

"Such as?"

"Cut the bullshit about trying to unionize Scofield Industries and tell me why you're really here."

Grimes tried to act offended, but quickly traded it in for a look of embarrassment. "How long have you known?"

"Pretty much since the first day. Unions don't need blue-blood firms like yours to organize workers. They've been at it a lot longer and are better at it than anyone else."

"Was I that obvious?"

"No, but you're a partner in a well-established law firm," Standard said. "Guys like you hang out at private country clubs playing golf or cruising Puget Sound in your yacht. Coming down here to find me would be something better left to one of your low-level associates."

Grimes smiled. "You're smart, John. Instinctive. You should have been a lawyer."

"That's what my lawyer father said. Now, what's this all about?" Standard pulled out his cellphone and set it on the table, ready to show Grimes the photo of him with the girls from *Sticky Fingers* if he balked at telling the truth.

Grimes pushed his plate of tacos to the side of the table and motioned over a waiter. "Tequila, please. The best you have and keep them coming."

The waiter looked at Standard, who nodded.

"Our client, Nico Adams, gave us more than just your name," Grimes said. "For seven years he was not only Proctor Scofield's personal helicopter pilot. He was also the co-pilot and on-board assistant on Scofield's corporate jet. For three years Adams traveled the world with Scofield. He saw and heard things. According to Adams, Scofield did a lot more than business on those overseas business trips. He told us how everything was arranged before Scofield arrived. How he'd fly in, sign a few papers, shake a few hands and then spend the rest of the time indulging his … appetites."

"Let me guess. It had something to do with young girls."

Grimes gave a slow sad nod. "Some as young as twelve. Powerful men passing around powerless children like they were boxes of chocolate."

"Men? As in plural?"

"The way Adams tells it, Scofield would pick up a child in Shanghai or Rio, maybe even buy the child from her parents. Once on board his plane, he and the child would spend the trip in his private suite in the back of the plane. When they landed in some place like Mexico City or Bangkok, he'd move the child to a nice hotel where she'd wait for the next man to pick her up."

"Your client told you all of this?" Standard asked. Grimes nodded. "Do you have proof other than his word? Documents? Dates? Photos? Names? Other witnesses?"

"Proof is for judges and juries, John. It's suspicion that influences boards of directors. That's the prize we're after. The mere threat of a scandal, a whiff of wrongdoing at the highest levels of a company, sends them into a panic. Imagine what would happen if the world learned that the founder and namesake of Scofield Industries was a globe-trotting pedophile. Not only that but the leader of a network of other wealthy pedophiles. If that weren't enough, we could also tell them that we know the true story of how Proctor Scofield died, assuming, of course, that you can fill in that blank."

"The stock would drop like a rock. Orders would be cancelled. Executives would get fired. Totally chaos."

"At least."

"So what Benny picked up from his geek friends about kids getting on Scofield's plane but not getting off was true?"

"If Adams is to be believed."

"So, you're out to destroy Scofield Industries?"

"No. The goal is the same as when you and I first talked. The unions just want to get their foot in the door and they've asked us to help."

"What if the board of directors calls your bluff? Demand proof other than the word of a drug smuggler trying to avoid prison."

"Then we threatened to leak what we have to a reputable news organization. *The New York Times. Wall Street Journal.* Maybe suggest a headline like, "The Secret Life of a Secret Man."

"And if they call your bluff again?"

"Then we follow through on the threat."

"Which you're probably going to do anyway."

"Once we have the proof. If what Scofield was a part of is still going on we can't allow it to continue. The more we look for members of Scofield's little club the more we tighten the screws, and not just on Scofield Industries. There may be other company executives involved."

Standard raised his shot glass. "That's hardball, Harry." They both knocked back their drinks. "But Proctor Scofield is dead. Is anyone going to care?"

"He may be dead, but we believe his network is still alive."

"You could have told me this earlier," Standard said.

"I didn't want to prejudice your testimony. That's a legal term. In other words, I didn't want what I suspected to color what you know."

"Fair enough," Standard said, shaking his head and pouring more tequila for each of them. "Knowing all that, you're going to find the end of my story even more interesting."

40

The Oregon Coast

The next few minutes, Harry, are indelible. The kind of thing that hangs with you forever. Things that keep you up at night, that haunt your dreams. Even after four years it's hard to describe it. A mental scar I guess you'd call it.

It started when Penroy walked into the front room. He didn't see me at first. He just nodded to Roark and Landis then walked to the couch and whispered something to Scofield. He was in mid-sentence when he noticed me.

"Where's Gitchell?' he demanded, looking around. "Mr. Scofield shouldn't be alone with this man. He's a murderer."

It was all Scofield could do to stifle a laugh. He rolled his eyes at me then told Penroy to relax. "The charade is over, Mitch."

"But …" Penroy looked like he was going to start stuttering.

Scofield told him again to calm down then explained how the two of us had been discussing his relationship with Roark and Landis and how events had brought them all together. "A close and loving family," I think he said then looked over his shoulder. "Isn't that right boys?" The two men raised their drinks in mock salute to their mutual fate.

Scofield seemed to be enjoying himself, acting more like a little kid with a box full of toy soldiers than a captain of industry. I couldn't say the same for Penroy. He continued to feign outrage about me being there and the lack of security then demanded to know how much I knew. Scofield winked at me as if we were old friends sharing an inside joke.

"Things sort of fell into place for Mr. Standard when he saw your man Gitchell outside," he said.

It was sort of a light moment, Harry, in an otherwise pretty grim surroundings. It just didn't last long. In fact, things turned serious right away, as in I'm-not-going-to-get-out-of-this-alive serious.

Penroy was no longer the smooth operator I'd chased down in the parking garage of the state capital building. I expected him to start groveling at any moment, maybe get down on one knee to kiss Scofield's ring. He asked what Scofield was going to do with me, pointing out that if I knew everything, he couldn't let me leave.

I looked around the room trying to find answers in the faces of the four men. Penroy and Scofield looked away. The two politicians remained at the bar, showing little interest in what was going on. The silence lingered until Scofield propped his feet on the coffee table again and told Penroy to go find Gitchell. Before he left, Penroy glared at me and we traded insults for a while. He called me a hack. I called him a weasel. Scofield seemed to be enjoying it all before telling Penroy to "shut the fuck up," find Gitchell and get him some coffee.

On his way to the kitchen, Penroy looked at Roark, who put down his drink and went downstairs. He came back a few minutes later with Alfie Gitchell in tow. The old detective's limp told me was still feeling the effects of my knee in his crotch.

"I believe Mr. Standard may have a gun on his person," Scofield said. "Would you be so kind as to find it and remove it?"

Gitchell walked over to the couch, stood looking down at me and pulled back his coat. The gun that I had thrown away earlier was back in his shoulder holster. When he held out his hand, I pulled out the Beretta and gave it to him. Scofield nodded his approval then told Penroy to get the helicopter ready and to get the security team back. He was going to need them. Then he ordered everyone out of the room. When Penroy started to protest, Scofield scowled at him. They were all gone in seconds.

Alone again, Scofield leaned forward so both elbows rested on his knees, the fresh cup of coffee clutched in both hands. It was clear that he had something to tell me that he couldn't say in front of Landis and Roark. Plausible denial, you know.

"I've enjoyed our little conversation this morning," he said, "but I'm sure you realize that you can't leave here alive."

He pointed outside at the helicopter and how it had sufficient fuel to fly twenty miles out to sea and twenty miles back. I would enjoy the trip, he said. At least half of it, anyway. The smile of someone holding all the cards crossed his face.

"So Gitchell is not your only security?" I asked.

"Hardly," he said.

I knew when I decided to confront Scofield on his home ground that I was risking my life. Then, though, it had been little more than an abstract thought. Suddenly, it was all too real. I took a deep breath to force back the panic. The more I thought about bobbing helplessly in the ocean waiting to drown, the more reasons I found to stay alive. Recklessness had its limits, Harry. Even for me.

That's when he told me that I wouldn't be alone: Mitch Penroy would be joining me.

He feigned sadness as he explained that Penroy had outlived his usefulness, that he never liked him that much anyway and the whole scheme to find Krychek's manuscript had turned into a hot mess. What put it over the top, he said, was Penroy's "little cocaine problem." The two of us dying together was "for the sake of efficiency."

I reminded him that would put the body count at six deaths, including Amanda Bishop, which was a lot of bodies to indulge his fantasies about being a kingmaker.

"Leave Amanda out of this," he snapped. "As for the others—regrettable but necessary."

I started searching my brain for a way to get out of this but kept coming up blank. Then I remembered something Benny Orlando told me. It was a high-risk play, but it wasn't like I had anything to lose. "Since I'm on the clock," I said, "why don't you tell me how Amanda really died, and don't give me any bullshit about committing suicide after being raped by your two lapdogs."

That got the reaction I was hoping for. Scofield's face went white, his composure shattered for just a second. I'd hit a nerve. Whatever was going to happen in the next few minutes could well be the difference between getting out of there alive and becoming crab bait.

Scofield started muttering something about not knowing what I was talking about. It was like the question short-circuited his brain. He started running his hand through his hair in a gesture to buy time while the blood returned to his face. Done with his hair, he wrung his hands over and over again like he was trying to wash them.

"She jumped off that overpass," he blurted out, his eyes darting around the room. "You wrote as much in that *Inside Oregon* article."

I started to ad lib: Maybe I was wrong. Maybe she didn't jump off that overpass. Is it possible she was pushed off and that what Roark and Landis did to her had nothing to do with her death?

Scofield ran his tongue over his chapped lips and started cracking his knuckles. He kept looking away, letting his eyes roam around the room over and over again. The tremors in his left hand got worse, the shaking creeping up his arm as if it were ready to take over his whole body. Finally, a confused look on his face. I was wrong, he said. I knew I was wrong. Why was I doing this? Why was I making up stories?

I guess I could have explained about commitments to the dead, about getting even for past wrongs, about good people who die too young for the wrong reasons. Maybe I was just trying to save my own skin. Trying to do all that, however, would be a waste of the one thing I didn't have—time. If there was any good news it was that Scofield looked ready to explode. I laid out my hastily made-up theory: He didn't care what Krychek had found out about Roark and Landis. He cared about what he might find out about him. The more Krychek dug the greater the chance that he'd find something Scofield didn't want found.

When Scofield started to protest, I cut him off. "You concocted this whole charade about protecting Amanda's memory, about making Roark and Landis pay, about living her life through them. All along you pretended the scheme was your way of extracting a pound of flesh for what they did to her. Their families made a deal with the devil, and you're the devil. That's what you want me and everyone else to believe, but there is more to it isn't there? Something darker and more sinister?"

The old man's face went pale and distant. He started babbling about how ordering the death of Jasmine Grant had been a mistake. The same with Krychek. He had no choice until he knew what was in those papers. I wanted none of it. Pressing the old man was my only chance of getting out alive. I looked outside. A man walked across the grass toward the helicopter parked on the concrete pad, opened the aircraft's door, and jumped into the pilot's seat. Behind him were two men with side arms, large men capable of pushing me into the ocean.

Time was running out. I glanced quickly at the clock on the wall behind Scofield. The second hand ticked off what little time I had left. That was when I saw it—the faint shadow of someone standing in the darkness of the hallway to the bedrooms. Someone else was in the house.

I looked at Scofield. He seemed lost in his own thoughts before going back to bleating about how this was all Penroy's idea. After Amanda's death, it was Penroy who came up with the idea of using what they did to control them. He knew them best. Knew their strengths and weaknesses. Knew that Scofield could control them. I'd heard all this before and didn't have time to hear it again. The squeal of the helicopter's engines made me look toward the landing pad just as the rotors started spinning. The faster they spun, the less time I had. If the plan was going to work, it had to start now.

I played my last card. "So, when did you start having sex with Amanda? How long did it take to seduce your own stepdaughter? How old was she? Fourteen? Younger?"

Scofield stared down at the carpet then out the window at the ocean. Tears welled up in his eyes. He started shaking his head back and forth. I demanded he answer the question, hoping it would save my life and trigger some response from whomever was standing in the shadows. "Tell me, damn it. I'm going to die anyway."

"It's not what you think," he said. "She was not like other girls or even other women. When she gave herself to me it was like the devil had taken my hand. I had waited so long for her to grow up. When she did, she was exactly like I wanted her to be. Making love to her for the first time …" His voice trailed off.

I pressed harder. "Was she all crinoline and patent leather? Sachets in her dresser and teddy bears on her bed? Did you tuck her in at night and maybe leave your hand under the covers a little too long? Did you accidentally walk in on her when she was taking a bath? Maybe you went into her room when she was gone. Felt things. Sniffed things."

When Scofield looked away again, I quickly glanced at the shadow in the hallway. The slight movement of one arm, the glint of something shiny and the shifting of weight from one foot to the other.

I kept at it, telling him that what he did was not romance, that he was just a sick old man, who thought seducing his underage stepdaughter made him a loving father rather than a pervert. The same with dressing up his secretaries like Little Bo Peep. Scofield's eyes narrowed.

"Tina told you that?"

"You're not the only one she likes talking to."

Scofield nodded in resignation that no one could be trusted anymore, then asked if I was done. Not even close. There were too many questions about her death. Why did she wait to kill herself? Why not do it right away? Time might have helped heal what happened that night, not made it worse. Why didn't anyone see it coming and do something to help her? Why did she use a typewriter to write one of her suicide notes when she wrote everything else in longhand?

Then I played my last card: "Because she didn't kill herself, that's why. You murdered her."

Scofield looked confused for a second when I mentioned the suicide notes. Then he figured it out. His wife, Margaret. The air went out of him, making his body shrink even more into the oversized bathrobe. I had him on the ropes. I said I knew he used to drive to Eugene to see her. I know that she kept her little costumes in her dorm room. How she told her roommate she was visiting friends for the weekend when she was visiting him. I leaned forward, arms on my knees, getting as close to him as I could. "You're one sick fuck, Proctor."

Outside, the screams of the powerful helicopter engine sent gulls screeching into the skies. The sound beat against the windows like thunder. I saw Penroy, Gitchell and the two security guards standing on the grass yelling at each other over the noise and gesturing toward the house.

I knew now that Scofield was adding Penroy to our little helicopter ride because he knew everything about Amanda. He knew that her death was not a suicide. That made him a threat and I knew how Scofield dealt with threats—real or imagined. He had to kill Penroy.

Scofield was past the point of denying anything I'd said about him, his stepdaughter, or Penroy. What had been a stab in the dark on my part had struck home. The only question left was whether it would get me off the hook. Scofield stood up to look out the window at the screaming helicopter. "It's time to go. Our conversation was interesting and painful. You are smart, too smart perhaps. You knew what was going to happen before you came here, which made me admire you even more."

Admiration was the last thing I was looking for. I let loose with one last barrage, as much for Scofield's benefit as whoever it was standing in the shadows, the person who had heard it all so far and hadn't moved. The person with the gun.

Had Amanda lived she'd be nearly forty, I told him. A grown woman fully capable of understanding what he did to her and why Roark and Landis were where they are. Would she have let things get that far? Would she stand by and watch him bankroll the futures of the two men who raped her? I doubted it. I think he looked twenty–plus years into the future and saw what a threat she could be to his reputation, to the reputation of the company he'd built, and to his ability to do business. He had her eliminated.

"So, who did it?" I asked. "Did you do it yourself or did Penroy do it for you? Is that another reason why he has to die?"

Scofield collapsed on the couch and sank into the cushions, appearing to have aged ten years in the last hour. When he started to speak, I held up my hand and kept going: "You had Krychek and Grant killed because you were afraid Krychek's papers contained proof that you had Amanda killed and that you're a pedophile. You didn't care if people knew that Roark and Landis had raped her, but you couldn't let the true story of how you seduced her first get out."

Scofield rocked back and forth on the couch. His hands slapped wildly on his thighs, tears streaming, face distorted. He was whimpering now, telling me I didn't understand. He would never have murdered her. He would never have hurt her. He loved her in a way no one could possibly understand, in a way his wife could never understand. He wiped tears from his eyes. "Amanda's death was the worst thing that ever happened to me."

The shadow moved one step into the living room. I gave it one more shot. I pointed a finger at Scofield. "You killed her or you had her killed. She had to die or your plans for Roark and Landis would never work. You threw her off that overpass. Now, you're going to kill the two people left alive who know the truth."

Outside on the lawn, Penroy and Gitchell were moving toward the front of the house. It was too late. The fuse was lit. The figure that emerged from the shadows of the hallway was now standing directly behind Scofield. The gun pointed at the back of his head. All I could do was wait for the explosion.

Tina Davenport looked like she wanted to scream but didn't. Instead, she kept saying "You bastard" over and over again. Scofield stood up and turned around long enough to see her and the barrel of the gun just before it went off point blank into his chest. The last look Proctor Scofield gave anybody was a fleeting one of surprise and apology.

41

Zihuatanejo

Harrison Grimes rocked back in his chair so hard Standard thought he was going to fall over backward.

"Jesus Christ, John," he said. "No way did I see that coming." He sat forward, reached for his drink, and drained it. "But why her? She betrayed you, now she's saving your life."

"Hardly," Standard said. "It was Penroy's life she was saving. If Scofield dumped him in the ocean along with me then Tina loses her meal ticket and, presumably, the man she loved. The party girl would suddenly have lost her party."

Grimes let that soak in for a few seconds then looked around for a waiter to order another drink. "What happened next?"

"The first shot killed Scofield instantly. It knocked him back on the coffee table between the couches, his head practically in my lap. Blood splattered across the plate-glass window and quickly seeped out of his chest to pool up around him. I was frozen in place, unsure what Tina would do next. Still pointing the gun at the place where Scofield had been standing, she turned toward me, her face cold and blank. Sleep-mussed hair hung across vacant eyes. I'm not even sure she knew I was there and, if she did, who I was. The hand that held the gun quivered only slightly. Without changing expressions, she pulled the trigger again. The shot shattered one of the five-foot sections of the plate glass windows. Jagged pieces of glass hung for a moment in the casing before falling out onto the deck."

"And gave you a way out."

"Exactly," Standard said. "With the window shattered, the thump of the helicopter rotors and the roar of the engines filled the room. While still staring at me, Tina kept pulling the trigger, firing shot after shot out the broken window until the gun was empty and the hammer clicked uselessly—metal against metal."

"Did she say anything?"

"She acted like she wanted to, but, instead, she glanced at the gun as if she'd never seen it before then dropped it on the floor and stared down at Scofield's body. I felt an urge to say something to her, but doubted she'd hear me. She was beyond my reach."

Standard described looking out through the broken glass and seeing Penroy, Landis and Roark standing on the lawn staring up at the house. Alfie Gitchell stood off to the side with the two guards. While the others looked confused, Gitchell didn't.

"He knew more than any of them about guns and the sounds they make," Standard said. "If anyone knew someone had just died, it was him. When he moved toward the house, the others hesitated, looked at each other then slowly followed him. That was my chance. When they disappeared under the deck, I grabbed a vase from the coffee table and hurled it through what was left of the broken window to clear out the rest of the glass. I turned to take one last look at Tina Davenport. She was still holding the empty gun, watching me as I ducked through the empty window frame. I leapt eight feet to the lawn below just as a panting Gitchell appeared behind me in the living room."

"No one shot at you?"

"No, but I expected it. I ran low, ducking and weaving toward the gate in the stone wall. Sand blasted by the spinning helicopter blades stung my face and hands. The pilot sat at the controls flipping switches, oblivious to what had gone on in the house."

"That would be our client, Nico Adams," Grimes said.

"Must have been."

"So he didn't see or hear a damn thing. He was sitting in the helicopter through it all."

Standard shrugged. "I guess. I don't know what he did later or what he heard. All I wanted was out of there. As I headed for the gate, I looked back long enough to see Penroy standing on the deck next to Gitchell. The glimpse was short, but long enough to recognize the look of two people who'd gone from winner to loser in the time it takes to silence an old man's heart. After that, I was out the gate, back on the asphalt driveway and headed for my car."

"How did you come up with the idea that Scofield had seduced his stepdaughter?"

"I put the pieces together. What Benny told me about kids getting on his plane. How Marcus Towne described Amanda Bishop. How Tina Davenport described Scofield's secretary the same way. The cynical enslavement of Roark and Landis and threats against their families. How matter of fact he was about killing people without even knowing what was in Krychek's manuscript. He was immoral and what do immoral people do?"

"Seduce their underage stepdaughters and kill people," Grimes said, shaking his head, still in amazement. "So, was that it? Was it over?"

"Not quite."

"Gitchell?"

"Yeah. I'd put him out of my mind until I got to the top of the grade and turned around. Here he came, through the gate and up the hill after me. He had my Beretta in one hand the other clutching his chest. I watched for a moment then ran farther up the driveway. Once out of sight around the curve, I stepped into some bushes on the side of the road and waited."

Standard leaned back in his chair to describe how Gitchell eventually trudged around the curve, gasping for air, the Beretta pointed harmlessly at the ground. How, when Gitchell was six feet away, he stepped out of the brush.

"The rest of the story is just sad, Harry," he said. "I told him there was no sense dying for a dead master and to hand over the gun. When he started hacking and coughing, I took the gun out of his hand then placed the muzzle in the middle of his forehead."

"You didn't?"

"No, but I came close. The image of Jasmine Grant, naked and garroted on her own bed, wasn't helping. Neither was being framed for her murder. Instead, I waited until the red circle on his forehead slowly faded to match the purple of the rest of his face. Gitchell fell back on his haunches, too weak to talk, too wrong to argue. My disgust turned to pity. I told him that with Scofield dead, his friends back at the house were going to sell him out. He'll end up with nothing. No money. No self-respect. I remember watching as he went through another coughing fit. How he leaned forward to put both hands on his knees until he caught his breath again then puked onto the asphalt. It was a sad scene. Gitchell was out of options. If the cigarettes didn't kill him there were plenty of others back at Scofield's house who would. He knew it. So did I."

"They would do that?" Grimes looked incredulous.

"Of course they would. Maybe not Roark or Landis, but Penroy certainly could and, if not, there were others who worked for Scofield Industries who would, like those two security guards. So, I waited for

Gitchell to beg for his life. I wasn't disappointed. He asked me to take him with me. He'd tell everything. Blow it all up, including himself."

"Doesn't sound like your kind of offer, but you must have been tempted," Grimes said.

"Gitchell was not on the inside. He wouldn't have much credibility, especially after betraying his own profession. Lawyers such as yourself would make mincemeat out of him. Besides, all I wanted to do was make him suffer a little for what he'd done. I pointed the gun at him again just to see him cringe."

"And?"

"I had no intention of taking him anywhere, but I needed to tie up some loose ends first. Did he kill Mather? Yes, he said. Penroy drove the car, but he went inside, killed Mather, and came out with the manuscript. What about Ivan Krychek and Jasmine Grant? That was Scofield and Penroy. Mather did the wet work on both of them, but they ordered it. He could prove it, but I had to take him with me."

Standard remembered trying to piece together what the next few months would be like if he left with Gitchell. All he could see were reporters, lawyers, depositions, trials, and testimony. In other words, back in the one place he didn't want to be. If there was an upside it would be taking down Penroy. The only person who could do that was Gitchell."

"So?"

"I had what I came for. I put a foot on Gitchell's chest and told him his friends were down there at the house. Then I shoved as hard as I could, sending him rolling backwards down the driveway. I threw the gun into the woods knowing no one would find it because no one would look for it. This place was never going to be a crime scene. There would be no cops or ambulances, only a corporate cover up."

"You know Gitchell has been missing for four years, right?" Grimes asked.

"No, but I can pretty much guess what happened to him. Check with your client. Chances are Gitchell took my seat on the chopper."

Standard and Grimes had one more drink then left to walk down to the waterfront. The city square was filled with vendors selling tamales, *liquados,* and fresh popcorn. A man with a four-foot caiman draped over his shoulder was charging five pesos to take a picture.

"Where's Penroy now?" Standard asked as they stood overlooking the basketball court watching what appeared to be an organized game.

"Hong Kong. Running Scofield Industries' Asian operations from a penthouse atop their corporate headquarters," Grimes said.

"And Tina Davenport?"

"Still together, I guess. She hasn't exactly been on our radar, but she is now, thanks to you."

After that, Grimes didn't say anything for a long time. He seemed to be taking in all he had learned and trying to decide what to do with it. "You know, John," he said, finally. "You could have told me when we first met that Tina Davenport killed Scofield. I would have thanked you and left. Why draw it out?"

Standard expected the question. "Because you didn't level with me at first. I needed to know the real story of why you're here."

"You didn't trust me?"

"Not at first."

"And now?"

"Let's just say that you needed to understand what led up to Scofield's death and how it was more complicated than just someone shooting someone else, regardless of how beautiful or rich they were."

Grimes thought about that for a few moments. "Well, I'm glad you did. It's a pretty good story. Maybe you should write it all down some day. Might make a good book."

"I'll keep that in mind."

Standard was done telling Grimes anything more. The lawyer had what he came for. Now, he could go back to Seattle and use the knowledge that one of the wealthiest men in the world was a pedophile who'd been shot to death by the high-priced hooker girlfriend of his right-hand man. If that knowledge helped him get leverage over Scofield Industries, then more power to him.

42

Zihuatanejo

As luck would have it, Harrison Grimes' plane left the same day Emma Parrish's flight landed. Arturo the taxi driver seemed more than willing to take Standard and Grimes to the airport then hang around long enough to bring him and Emma back to Playa la Ropa.

"I can't thank you enough," Grimes said. They were sitting in the taxi's back seat. "Your story was as intoxicating as the tequila. I've never heard anything quite like it."

"So what now?" Standard asked.

"Not sure. I'll talk to my partners when I get back, but it seems that finding Tina Davenport might be a good place to start, assuming, of course, that you're still determined to stay out of it."

"That's a safe bet," Standard said.

"You know, John, it's been four years since all that happened. Plenty of time for some perspective, especially about Scofield."

"I lack insights into the human condition, Harry. All I know is that Proctor Scofield was corrupted by his own wealth and personal failings. He knew he couldn't be a king, but he could be a kingmaker. In his tormented mind either Roark or Landis would become governor then senator then maybe one day president and he would be pulling the strings. The ultimate puppet master. He created his scheme more than twenty-five years ago, knowing full well that he may not live to see it play out. But he wanted to, badly wanted to. That's why anything that represented a threat had to be dealt with as harshly as possible. Why harshly? Because he knew he would never be held accountable. His wealth and connections would protect him."

"By threat you mean word getting out about his … proclivities."

"That was the one thing he couldn't let happen."

"So in the end it was all about him?"

"Pretty much," Standard said. "My biggest regret is not realizing it earlier."

"I can't help but ask what happened afterwards," Grimes said. "You've never written a word about what you heard and saw, have you?

At least none that we could find. I get the feeling that this is the first time you've told anyone the whole story."

After Scofield's death, Standard had read the Portland papers and went online to read what the weeklies in Newport and Florence had written. It was all the same: The sudden demise of a visionary captain of industry who brought jobs and wealth to a region and the world. He explained all this to Grimes.

"So you went back to scratching out a living," he said.

"More or less. After all that had happened it was hard to go back to knocking out features for airline magazines. Eventually, though, it faded away and I went back to grinding out what passed for entertaining feature writing."

"And the stripper? What happened with her?"

"I finally manned up and walked down the hall to introduce myself. When I asked if she'd like to join me for dinner one night, she joked about whether she needed to dress for the occasion. When I said it was too late for that we both started laughing. We lived together on and off for the next couple of years then sort of drifted apart."

"What happened?"

"That's a story for another day, Harry."

They'd reached the airport. Arturo pulled the taxi up in front of the departure entrance to the terminal. Standard helped Grimes get his bags out of the truck.

"I still don't understand why you didn't sell the story of how Scofield really died," Grimes said. "Why not cash in?"

"I considered it. Even dead, Proctor Scofield was news. It would mean money to hold me over until the sale of the house I'd owned with Christine. After that, there would be no more dingy apartment. No more Vanessa the Undressa. No more Benny Orlando and his calliope music. Maybe there would be enough money to buy back respectability as the man who exposed the Prince of Snakes for what he was. Then fifteen thousand dollars showed up in the mail one day. It was from Margaret Scofield. I thought about tearing it up, but I needed the money."

"Fortuitous, but you still could have told the world what really happened to Scofield."

"I guess I'm not cut out that way," Standard said when they were inside. "The fifteen grand helped, but what really made the difference was that it went against my grain to make myself part of the story. My job had always been to be the benign observer. To witness events rather than be part of them. I thought it best to keep it that way rather than try to make a buck off someone else's misery. I also didn't want to be a meme on the Internet or fodder for conspiracy theories. Besides, I just wanted to be done with the whole thing."

"Noble," Grimes said. "That would make for a good journalist, but a bad lawyer."

They shook hands. Grimes got in the first-class line for the flight to Los Angeles then on to Seattle. Watching him as he headed toward customs, Standard felt his load lighten a little. Thanks to Grimes, the burden of Proctor Scofield was off his back for good … almost. He took out his cellphone, found the text from Fat Tony with the picture of Grimes and the strippers at *Sticky Fingers II* and deleted it.

Standard thought back to the conversation with Jasmine that day over lunch. He told her that maybe fate would provide a chance to repay the debt owed for two dead girls. Fate had held up its end. Standard had held up his. The world was a much better place without Proctor Scofield. Knowing he had saved his own life and avenged the death of Jasmine Grant was all the comfort Standard needed at the time. It was the same today.

~*~

Standard walked the rest of the way down the concourse to meet Emma. Seeing her come out of the gate made him realize how much he'd missed her and how glad he was she was back. Based on the long kiss she gave him, he could see that she felt the same way.

On the way into town from the airport, Emma asked what he'd been up to while she was gone. What she really meant was had he gotten into any trouble that would make living with him more dangerous than it already was.

"I love you," she said, "and you've always made my life interesting, but sometimes I need a break."

Standard assured her that he hadn't done anything more dangerous than endure the rainy season, hit the beach when it was over, and read a lot of books. He did tell her that he'd met an interesting lawyer from Seattle and that they shared stories about cases he had tried and stories Standard had covered.

"That's it," she said. "Doesn't sound like you."

"It's a new me."

Three days later, when Standard told Emma he needed to return to Portland to take care of some business, she didn't argue. She was eager to enjoy the Day of the Dead and get the other house on her property ready for guests who would be arriving in two weeks.

"Go," she said, kissing him on the cheek. "You've been cooped up here for nearly a year." She smiled and kissed him. "Besides, you'd be no help anyway getting the house ready. When are you leaving?"

"I need to make a phone call first," he said. "I'll know more after that."

43

Portland, Oregon

Standard's plane landed at Portland International Airport late on a rainy Monday night. He took an Uber to his apartment building, skipped a chance to drop in on Benny Orlando and went straight upstairs. It was neater and cleaner than when he left, which probably meant Benny had put it on Airbnb and collected double rent.

The next morning he found Benny sitting at his bank of computers, a trio of screens covered in indecipherable code. Calliope music played in the background. Circus posters featuring the bearded lady and the world's strongest man still looked down from the walls. He gave Benny a brief description of the story he'd told Grimes, not that Benny needed it. He was there for most of it. By mid-afternoon, Standard was tired of talking and Benny tired of listening. He gave Benny enough money to cover the rent on his apartment for the next six months, then called Uber again.

The car wound its way out West Burnside then up into the hills overlooking downtown. On a quiet residential street, it pulled through a gap in a massive, neatly pruned wall of laurel, down a circular drive and stopped under an ivy-covered portico. Standard got out, walked up to the massive front door, and rang the bell. The woman who answered was in her forties and dressed like a maid with a black dress and starched white apron.

"You must be Mr. Standard," she said. "We've been expecting you. Please come in."

He followed her through a front room with a massive fireplace and ornate furniture that looked more decorative than functional. They walked through two more rooms, each looking more and more lived in, before the maid showed him into a conservatory. Massive windows overlooked the fog-draped city. Floor-to-ceiling shelves held a few knick-knacks and hundreds of leather-bound books. Margaret Scofield sat in an overstuffed leather chair. She had a shawl around her shoulders and an afghan across her lap. Her eyes were closed. Her chin on her chest.

"Mrs. Scofield," the maid said, putting a hand on the old lady's shoulder. "Your guest is here."

Margaret Scofield slowly opened her eyes. Seeing Standard, she smiled and motioned to the matching chair across from her. She had aged ten years in the four since he'd sat with her in the back of the limousine. Her hair was grayer, her skin paler. Her liver-spotted fingers were long and spidery.

"John," she said. "It's so good to see you again." She pulled at the shawl and fussed with her hair for a few seconds. "You look fit and tan. Mexico must agree with you."

"It does," Standard said.

"And that lady friend of yours. Emily? Is that her name?"

"Emma, Mrs. Scofield. She's fine. Thank you for asking."

"That's nice to hear. I'm glad you're happy now. It wasn't easy, was it, John?"

Standard didn't have to say anything. Both of them knew the answer. Even though he hadn't seen her for four years, they had talked numerous times on the phone since her husband's death. She knew all of his secrets. He knew one of hers.

"Well, thank you for coming, but you really didn't have to. You could have told me everything over the phone."

"I wanted to return these," Standard said, reaching into his pocket, pulling out Amanda Bishop's two suicide notes and handing them to her.

When she held them in her hands for a few seconds, Standard thought she was going to open them, read them again for the thousandth time. Instead, she tucked the notes under the afghan.

"I can't tell you how much I appreciated your calls about that lawyer who found you and your offer to take care of everything," she said. "It sounds like you did, so I guess that means it's all over?"

"I can't guarantee that," he said.

"Tell me about it."

Standard gave her an abbreviated version that included how he told Grimes that it was Tina Davenport who killed her husband.

"Very clever," she said, nodding her approval. "Did he leave satisfied?"

"If by satisfied do you mean did he leave believing that Tina killed your husband then yes."

Margaret Scofield took the two notes out from under the afghan. She held them in her hands, running a finger around the edges of the envelope then put them away again.

While Standard had stayed in touch with Margaret Scofield since her husband's death, they had never talked about that day nor the ones leading up to it. No reason, other than it was too painful for both of them. Watching her now, Standard wondered how much she remembered about that morning. He and Scofield talking in the front room of the beach house. Standard's accusations about Scofield and Amanda. Margret Scofield standing in the shadows listening, holding a gun. Shooting her husband. Watching him die on top of a coffee table, blood leaking out his chest.

Others saw the aftermath of what had happened that morning, but he and Margaret Scofield were the only ones who knew the truth.

"I know you've tried your hardest to protect me and Amanda's memory," she said. "Blaming Proctor's death on Tina Davenport probably went against all you believe in. I can't thank you enough for that and everything else."

"Do you regret it?" Standard asked. "Shooting your husband, I mean."

Standard had a hard time believing that she hadn't asked herself the same questions, still, she waited a long time to answer. "I had known for some time that Proctor had certain … desires. I chose to ignore them, mostly because I couldn't fulfill them and didn't want to. It never crossed my mind that they would extend to my daughter. That morning, standing in the shadows listening to him talk about her that way almost destroyed me. So, do I regret it? Not for a single moment."

Standard knew that some of the things he accused Scofield of might not have been true. It worked at the time. He lived. Proctor Scofield died. And not just him, but everything he represented died with him.

"I accused him of killing Amanda. Do you think he did?"

Margaret Scofield waited long enough to answer that Standard felt she had never thought of the question before or she had and wanted to get the answer just right.

"I blame Proctor for everything. Whether he was directly involved in what happened to Amanda or indirectly, it doesn't matter. He stole her innocence, ravaged her spirit, and killed her soul. I don't know what happened after that. Whatever it was, I blame him for all of it."

There wasn't much to say after that. Silence hung between them until she brightened up a bit, the demons at bay.

"This lawyer, Grimes I think you said his name was. Where is he now?" Margaret asked.

"Probably on his way to Hong Kong to find Tina Davenport."

She smiled to herself. "Did you get the impression that he was a good lawyer? Could he cause problems in the future?"

"I was always suspicious. The story about wanting leverage over Scofield Industries in order to unionize its employees sounded like a lawyer's pipe dream to me. Could be he was just trying to make a few million bucks off the effort. His theory about a global network of pedophiles seemed to be more hearsay than fact. Then again, hearsay was all he needed to put the fear of God in the board of directors."

She thought for a minute then smiled at him, "Do you know the difference between a good lawyer and a bad lawyer, John?"

"No," Standard said, playing along.

"Neither do I," she said with a sly laugh. "Now, I believe cocktail hour has arrived." She reached for a bell on the table beside her chair. "Join me?"

"I'd love to, Mrs. Scofield. Thank you."

EL FIN

Other Books by Tom Towslee

Drug Lord's Daughter
Graves Point
Chasing the Dead
Paradise Girls

Made in the USA
Las Vegas, NV
07 November 2021

33924063R00144